Journey to Felnoria

Bedside Books
An imprint of American Book Publishing
5442 So. 900 East, #146
Salt Lake City, UT 84117-7204
www.american-book.com
Printed in the United States of America on acid-free paper.

Journey to Felnoria

Designed by Dimitar Bochukov, design@american-book.com

Publisher's Note: This is a work of fiction. Names, characters, places, and incidents either are the product of the author's imagination, or are used fictitiously, and any resemblance to actual persons, living or dead, events, or locales is entirely coincidental.

ISBN-13: 978-1-58982-753-0
ISBN-10: 1-58982-753-8

Pertile, Christopher M., Journey to Felnoria

Special Sales

These books are available at special discounts for bulk purchases. Special editions, including personalized covers, excerpts of existing books, and corporate imprints, can be created in large quantities for special needs. For more information e-mail info@american-book.com.

Journey to Felnoria
Christopher M. Pertile

Dedication

I want to dedicate this to everyone at the theatre who had to deal with me while I wrote this.

Preface

Throughout history there have been countless books that have touched the hearts of many, and there are even more books out there that do much more than that. Some people have experienced an emotional attachment to books and have put themselves into the roles of the characters. Others have wished they could live their lives just like the characters in these books. How about you?

Chapter 1

On top of Warville Hill sat an elegant, white Victorian house. This house was the kind of house one drove past wishing to be let in just once to view. The house looked like a tree in a jungle with long green vines climbing every wall. It felt as if one could see to the end of the world when standing beside the house looking at the vast landscape. A warm feeling erupted within anyone who stepped through the front door. However, one day all happiness drained from the house in one fell swoop.

The swollen clouds were pitch black and rain poured relentlessly on that dreaded day. On such a day, the only thing little boys and girls could do was sit at the windowsill and watch the rain fall. The mother and father who lived in this house probably shed as many tears that day as raindrops that fell from the sky. What happened is something that no person should ever have to experience; the two most precious things in their lives disappeared in the blink of an eye.

These two souls, so dear to the weeping mother and father, were the only children they had. For these children, a boy and a girl, rain was not a reason to be isolated inside this wonderful house but an opportunity to create some wonderful game to play together.

What made this brother–sister duo different from most was how they cherished the time they had with one another. The reason for this was related to the house in which they lived. Although filled with beauty and wonder, their residence was also isolated from everything and everyone. This was a good thing; other than being just brother and sister, they happened to be best friends.

On that rainy day, the children had just decided upon the game they were going to play; it was their favorite. The first part of the game consisted of going into their father's library and selecting a book. The best way they had found of doing so was to blindfold one person and have that person randomly pull out a book. Next, that person would remove the blindfold and examine the outside of the book. Once he or she thoroughly examined *only* the outside, that person would speak out loud the title of the book. Then they would describe any illustrations that might be on the cover. With only that information, they would create their own characters and story and spend the rest of the day enacting the many adventures their characters might have experienced in the book.

One may ask how someone can imagine himself or herself inside a story without reading one word of the book other than the title. Their father had once told them at a very early age that a person's imagination is his or her greatest asset. Their father had introduced them to this wonderful game, telling them that he had played the same game with his brother a very long time ago. The only rule the game had was to *never open the book*. That way, the illustrations and title were all the hints the author gave to what actually lay inside, leaving the rest to their imagination.

On this particular rainy day, it was the sister's turn to get blindfolded and select the book. The brother walked to his father's desk, bent down, and opened the last drawer on the right side of the desk. He reached in, moving his father's possessions aside until a long piece of red cloth came into view. He grasped the cloth and pulled it out before carefully closing the drawer. Next, he approached his sister and tied the scarlet cloth over her eyes, waving a hand in front of her to make sure she could not see. Once he was satisfied, he turned her around five times clockwise then three times counterclockwise. There really was no reason to turn each other around, but they always laughed watching the blindfolded person stumble around for a few seconds from the dizziness resulting from the spin. Once all the spinning was complete, the sister began to walk toward one of the bookcases but staggered into her father's desk before she reached her destination. A sharp pain went up her leg from the collision, but she quickly brushed the pain away. Not wishing to further injure herself, she placed her hand down on the desk until she was able to regain her balance. Satisfied that she could walk again, she extended her hands while placing an image of the room into her mind. She turned her body toward the bookcase and started walking toward the array of books.

At that moment everything went wrong, and everything as the siblings knew it changed. The sister's fingers slid over the top of one of the books as she carefully drew it from its place in the bookcase. With her prize in hand, she pulled the blindfold off with her empty hand. She walked back to the desk and returned the blindfold before examining the book. She noticed instantly that this was a book neither of them had seen before. This didn't bother her, though, because Father was always bringing home new books. Noting the cover was blank, she examined each side in hopes of revealing some clue of the contents of the book. Other than the book being as black as the rain-filled clouds and a small crack running down the middle, there were no other external signs of what lay within. Her brother, eager to begin playing the game of imagination, reached out and grabbed the book from her in hopes he could find a hint. Suddenly, there was a deafening crash of thunder and the room went pitch black. A second later, another crack of thunder was accompanied by a bang, but this one occurred within the room.

When the lights returned, the brother and sister looked at each other and noticed neither of them was holding the book. Simultaneously, they looked down. The book had fallen to the floor, open, but upside down. They both reached down and grabbed the book, turning it over together. With this action, there was another crash of thunder and the lights went out once again, followed by another bang, which was not as loud. It seemed like an hour passed before the lights in the room flickered back on.

The door to the library burst open as light illuminating the room revealed the mother and father. With the house in total darkness, they had come upstairs to check on the children. The parents noticed nothing in the room other than a book lying closed in the center of the floor. They shuffled around the room searching for the children, but the two were nowhere to be found. This didn't alarm the mother and father at first because the little ones loved to play hide and seek. The parents believed the pair took the opportunity of the darkness to hide in some cranny upstairs; however, after checking every hiding place they could think of, they began to get frightened. The parents yelled the names of the children but received no response.

They knew the children couldn't have been downstairs because they had been in the living room by the stairs. But they searched the downstairs as well, screaming the children's names relentlessly. After searching every part of the house, the children were still nowhere to be found.

Chapter 2

Many decades later, the same beautiful Victorian house was overgrown with the emerald vines that once climbed its walls so elegantly. Everything else around the house was equally as overgrown; there was a damp musty smell and even the paint had chipped away, leaving most of the building looking dilapidated.

The house had become the basis for legend told by the local townsfolk. Many children have claimed to have seen a woman sobbing from one of the second-story windows. Because of these sightings, children would bike up Warville Hill in hopes of being the next to see the ghostly figure. The children, while waiting around in hopes of seeing the woman, would dare one another to run up to the house and knock on the faded red front door. Many children took up the challenge, but none made it to the door that once cheerfully greeted people.

That door, once the entrance to happiness, had become the entry of fear for anyone who ventured too close. Because of all the attention the house received from the children, the mothers and fathers of the town had raised money to build a massive fence with a huge iron gate that eventually surrounded the house.

Off in the distance, a wispy cloud of dust rose up to the sky, signifying a vehicle traveling up the winding dirt road that led to Warville Hill. The blue car reached the top of the hill and came to a rolling stop at the gate of the protective fence. The door of the car opened with a screeching moan from the hinges. A man in his mid-forties stepped out of the car and took a quick glance at his surroundings before reaching into his right pants pocket to remove a set of keys that one of the locals had informed him would open the gate. Because the fence and gate looked structurally unsound, he cautiously inched his way toward the large iron gate.

Relieved that he had reached the gate unharmed, he fumbled with the set of keys before grasping the lock that held a rusted chain into place. He inserted the key and then closed his eyes in hopes that the lock and chain weren't the only things supporting the gate. He twisted it slowly until he heard a faint popping noise. With the lock disengaged, he opened his eyes and carefully worked the lock out of the loops in the chain. Once the last loop was free, the chain fell down in front of the iron gate, dropping on the man's feet. Instead of cursing from the sudden weight crushing his feet, his eyes shined with relief that the gate had not collapsed onto him and his car. With that out of the way, a more difficult challenge awaited him, as he now needed to move the gate aside. The man planted his feet and pushed with all his might, while at the same time preparing himself to run for his life if need be. Slowly, but surely, he moved the gate aside just enough for his car to pass. With that accomplished, he ran back to his car, happy that the hardest part was over.

As the car drove past the gate, it suddenly veered off the driveway. As the car bounced up and down atop the yard, the man rolled down his window and stuck his head out, making sure not to run over any hidden objects in the overgrown grass. When the car was close enough to the house, the man quickly pulled his head back in and shut off the car. Suddenly, all four of the car doors burst open at the same time and the passengers exited the vehicle.

A female almost the same age as the driver popped out opposite the driver's side door and peered over the car before saying, "Steven, wouldn't it have been much easier if you had driven up the driveway instead of through the front yard?"

The man who had been driving turned to the female's voice. "I intended to do that, Olivia, but when I went to the gate to open it, I noticed there were a few downed trees in the middle of the driveway."

"I guess this was a better route, Steven," replied Olivia as she closed her door.

At that moment, a boy who had been in the back seat directly behind his father poked Steven in the back. His short dark brown hair resembled his father's and his soft blue eyes still held that innocent childish look. He was quite tall for his age and looked like a stretched-out rubber band. He was much stronger than his slender physique implied. To hide his thin frame, his whole wardrobe consisted of baggy clothes that were one size too large for him. He was called many mean names in school because of his size and shape, and since he never defended himself at school, he took most of his frustration out on his sister when the school day ended.

His father turned around to acknowledge the boy's presence and his son inquired, "Dad, how could you call going to this place, or anything we are going to have to do for the next few weeks, relaxation? Have you forgotten the moving trucks are coming tomorrow and it's going to take forever to get everything inside and put where it belongs?"

"Well, Conrad, just like you said, the movers come tomorrow, which means today is for relaxation. Tomorrow is a whole different story," his father replied.

A sweet-looking girl, almost a spitting image of her brother except for her shoulder-length hair much like her mother's, climbed out of the car and turned to her brother. The girl was in love with the color pink, even though most girls at her age had grown out of the love for the color. She made sure at least one article of clothing she was wearing was pink every day. This day she was wearing a shirt with pink stripes running horizontally, and since the shirt was only half pink, she wore pink socks for good measure. Because she looked so much like her brother, she wore makeup and jewelry at all times, sick of everyone telling her how much she looked like her brother.

"Conny, why do you have to be so negative about everything that happens? I bet if you won millions and millions of dollars you would still find something to gripe about," the girl chided.

"Little sis, how can you be so positive about everything that is going on? We just moved thousands of miles from home, have no friends, and as you must have noticed while we were driving up to the house, we are pretty much in the middle of nowhere." Conrad spread out his hands as he accentuated their new surroundings. "That is why I'm so negative, Jasmine."

"Why do you always call me 'little sis'? You know just as well as I do that we're twins and even though you may be a bit taller than I am, it doesn't make you my big brother," defended Jasmine.

If one really wanted to get technical with which sibling was older, Jasmine was actually ten minutes older then Conrad. Steven and Olivia wished never to tell them which one was older because it would just throw more fuel on the fire, knowing the two children never got along. Fighting and yelling were part of the daily routine. When Conrad and

Jasmine were born, the parents decided to divulge the seniority secret when the twins were mature enough to deal with it. Even though the children had just turned fourteen, the parents still didn't wish to divulge that information.

Steven didn't wish to get into the middle of the argument, so he ignored his children's bickering and sauntered to the car's trunk to begin the process of unpacking.

Chapter 3

The door to the house creaked as Steven slowly opened it. With every inch, light seeped in from the outside. Through the open door, each family member cautiously entered the house. The foyer was nothing compared to how it had been in the past. The light from the open doorway was limited and, at first glance, the house seemed to be completely empty. Steven squinted his eyes, peering around until he noticed thick, dark sheets of fabric cloaking every window, which explained why it had been so dark when they first entered the house.

Jasmine wrapped her trembling hands around her father's arm and tugged while she pleaded, "Dad, do we have to stay here tonight? There must be a hotel or something back in town. It's creepy here."

Steven took his eyes off of his new home to look at his daughter and responded, "Jas, it's only for one night, and we have all the supplies we need for twenty-four hours. I think you can tough it out just one night. Please, for me?" Jasmine had a habit of complaining when it came to sleeping in unfamiliar places. Twice a year, the family would take camping trips into the mountains, in the middle of nowhere. She once told her mother she was more scared of camping outdoors than she was of spiders, which she had always claimed was her biggest phobia.

Conrad pretended to cough with the word "wuss" hidden at the end of his coughing spree. Jasmine took the cough for what it really was and swung her right arm back and gave Conrad a strong jab to his left shoulder.

"Now Jas, did you really have to hit your brother?" demanded Olivia.

"But Mom, he called me a wuss," Jasmine cried.

"I never said such a thing," interrupted Conrad, as he rubbed his arm.

"Could the two of you just stop fighting for one second so we can enjoy this?" pleaded Steven.

Steven left everyone's side and walked up to the closest window to brighten the room. He grabbed the side of the nearest black sheet and yanked it down to reveal the outside world while also illuminating the room. He noticed how much light the first window lent to the interior of the house, so he methodically made his way around the room and pulled down the rest of the sheets. Teeny spiders and unidentified bugs scurried into the nearest crevices. With the sun streaming through the dusty air, Steven piled the sheets in one corner of the room. He then spun around and examined his surroundings, pleased at how much better the room looked.

"Nothing a mop and bucket won't fix!" exclaimed Olivia.

"One, two, three—not it!" shouted Conrad.

Olivia turned and shook her head at Conny. "Now, Conny, for being so eager to hand all the work to someone else, I think this room will be yours to clean."

"But Mom—," whined Conrad.

"No buts about it, Conrad James, that's what you get for calling your sister names."

Jasmine glanced at her brother and grinned broadly.

"Well, kids, let's take a look in some of the other rooms and see how much light we can bring in," suggested Steven.

They paraded from room to room, taking down all the sheets they could find, and marveled how the interior of the house brightened with each fallen sheet. Every room they searched was the same as the last; dust covered the old wooden flooring and no furniture was to be found. When the family reached what appeared to have been a living room, a large set of rickety stairs led to the upper level. They all congregated at the stairs, looking up at the unknown.

"Dad, why didn't you have someone hook up the electricity so we would have lights when we arrived?" asked Jasmine.

"I tried, Jas, but tomorrow was the earliest anyone would come," replied Steven. "Let's just check the second floor and then we will be done."

They slowly climbed the stairs, each step creaking more than the last, until the entire family arrived at the top. With a wall meeting them at the top of the stairs across the hallway, the four of them turned their heads to the left and right, seeing a straight hall running in both directions.

"How about we start by heading left?" Steven suggested.

"Sure, honey," replied Olivia.

Eager to be in the front of the search party, Conrad pushed his sister aside and then sneaked between his mother and father. The new leader reached the first door and opened it. Bright light suddenly burst into the hallway, blinding the family for a second. When everyone's eyes adjusted, they noticed a lone window across the room; the black sheet that had once draped the window now lay upon the dust-covered floor. The second thing they noticed when they walked into the room was the ceiling, which sloped downward at a steep angle, stopping only a few feet from the floor at one side of the room. The moment Conrad looked over the room he knew this was his bedroom.

"I call dibs on this room!" exclaimed Conrad.

"All right, Conny, as long as this isn't the largest bedroom in the house and your sister doesn't mind, then it's all yours," explained Olivia. Conrad turned to his sister, curled his bottom lip, and made it tremble, looking as if he were about to cry at any second.

"As long as there's another bedroom this size, he can have this one. I really don't like how the ceiling slants down like that, because it makes me feel like it's going to fall on me," stated Jasmine.

"From this day on, no girls are allowed in this room," announced Conrad.

With the bedroom claimed, Conrad visualized where all of his belongings would be placed in the room, everything from his bed down to what corner his baseball bat would be placed. Pleased, he scurried to the front of the group and led them to the next door. When Conrad entered the next room, he was disgusted by what was before him, but he knew instantly his sister would love the room. Each wall was painted a bright pink color, with ponies etched across the top of the walls. The room being dark, Jasmine walked in and pulled down the sheet from the window so she could get a good look. She was amazed by its beauty. "I wonder if a girl lived in this room," pondered Jasmine.

"I certainly hope so," said Conrad. "I don't see how any boy in his right mind would ever want to live in a room that was painted this disgusting color."

"Now, Conny, try keeping some of those comments to yourself for a change," demanded Olivia.

"I guess I can't really argue much since I got the room I wanted, as long as there is one large enough for you and Dad."

Not at all interested in his sister's room, Conrad ran ahead and found the upstairs bathroom and a few storage closets. The others had just exited Jasmine's new room when he completed the search of the left hall.

"The only thing left over here is a bathroom and storage closets," Conrad explained as he pointed to each door as he named them off.

"Let's search the other half then," Steven commanded as he took the lead from his son. When they reached the first door on the right side of the hall, Steven realized that the door was open a tiny bit. He pushed open the door the rest of the way, revealing a bedroom that was much larger than his and his wife's bedroom in their previous house. "Dibs," said Olivia jokingly.

"Funny, Mom," Conrad remarked with a large smile on his face.

With no furniture and a deep layer of dust, the room still had an elegant feel to it, even in the dark. Two large draped windows graced the eastern wall. Steven removed the sheets and was amazed by the view the windows gave of the surrounding landscape. He could faintly pick out the black and brown rooftops of a few of the houses that lay on the outskirts of town, even though they were miles away. Oak and maple trees dotted the winding streets and dark clouds drifted above.

A large, dusty, crystal chandelier hanging from the ceiling in the center of the room seemed rather misplaced but also just right at the same time. When the light from the windows hit the chandelier, small orbs of light were emitted throughout the room and shimmered on the walls.

Olivia slowly walked around the room. Like Conrad, she also imagined where all her bedroom belongings would be placed. She grinned with satisfaction when she realized there was room for all of her treasures. With her visualization out of the way, she noticed two extra doors in the room. She approached the first door and opened it just a tad, peeking in so she could be the first to see what was inside. "Honey, come here quick," squealed Olivia with a big smile on her face as she swung the door the rest of the way.

"What is it, dear?" asked Steven, as he hurried to Olivia, eager to see why his wife was so excited.

"We have our own bathroom!" exclaimed Olivia as she turned around and looked at Conrad. "Well, Conrad, if you can say that 'no girls are allowed' in your room, then I can say that 'no kids' are allowed in this bathroom," she explained as she stuck out her tongue at Conrad.

"Mom, you can be so childish sometimes," Conrad remarked with a chuckle and a shake of his head.

"I learned it from you!" Olivia shot back.

Excited to see what the other door had in store for her, Olivia left the bathroom and traversed the room, since the other door was directly across from the bathroom. She opened the door just enough for her own eyes again and was equally as happy when she realized what she discovered.

"And look at this, honey. We have a walk-in closet. No more storing my winter clothes in boxes for the summer and summer clothes in the winter. Everything can be hung up all year round."

"Yeah, and maybe I'll be able to get more room for my things, other than the two shirts you allow me to hang now," kidded Steven.

After closing the closet door and making sure she didn't miss a thing, Olivia stared at the ceiling, taking one last look at the beautiful chandelier before moving on to scope out the rest of the house. When everyone was in the hall, they all realized only two more doors were left to check on that side of the hall. Steven approached the closest door and peered in. "Looks like this leads to the attic," observed Steven.

"Let's leave that one for you and Mom," Jasmine quivered, being too scared to go up there.

Steven knew Conrad was going to make some mean comment to his sister so he announced, "Let's go check the last room." He quickly shut the door and made his way to the next door. When the door was open, he could tell right from the start that this room was different. First of all, the door swung open without any creaking and groaning like the rest, and, secondly, it was already lit up like Conrad's room. Also, Steven noticed the room was already furnished. Massive bookcases covered every inch of the walls except for where the two windows and door were located. The rays of light from the two windows shone directly onto an antique wooden desk. The desk sat in the center of the room with a leather chair facing the door. Each bookcase was lined with books about every subject imaginable.

"I wonder why this room still has everything in it," questioned Steven. "When I met the realty agents, they told me the previous owners removed everything from the house when they moved out. Well, let's take a quick look around before we move on." Curious as to what they might find, each of them began looking around. The parents paged through some of the books as the children ransacked the desk. The desk was completely empty except for a tattered red cloth that neither of them wanted to touch because of the cobwebs that surrounded it.

After Conrad completely searched the desk, and with no care to look over the books, he announced, "Looks like we have the searching done with. Let's go do something else."

"If that's what you want, then we can finish emptying the car," stated Steven. That activity was not exactly what Conrad had in mind, but he didn't feel like arguing.

Chapter 4

Later that day, the four family members were busy preparing the "camping trip" within their new house. Steven and Conrad blew up air mattresses for everyone to sleep on while Olivia and Jasmine cleaned layers of dust off the master bedroom floor. Hopefully, no one would be sneezing throughout the night from the dust that blanketed the entire house.

Steven and Olivia made sure all the necessities for the night were unpacked and the air beds were put into place. The family decided to take a trip into town. Their sightseeing thus far had been limited to the small number of roads Steven had been daring enough to explore, not wishing to get lost in an unfamiliar area.

As the family drove through town, they noticed that the quaint buildings had a lot of character. Brick storefronts from the turn of the century ran down the main street, and one lone streetlight flickered yellow at the end of the road. Flowers adorned each store window, giving the customers a welcoming feeling. A barber shop with its candy-cane pole stood at the end of the street.

Olivia and Jasmine spied a clothing shop and convinced Steven they deserved new outfits for the big day ahead. Olivia chose a comfy turquoise sweater and Jasmine laid claim to a hot pink sundress. Stephen paid the clerk and said to his family, "We'd better head back now. It's getting late and I don't want to drive these roads in the dark."

Jasmine gently tapped her fingers against the glass as she daydreamed with her head against the backseat window. She looked up at the sky and noticed voluminous black clouds coming from over the valley, swirling in the direction of their house.

"Daddy, I think we are going to find out tonight if there are any holes in our roof," stated Jasmine as she continued tapping on the window, staring at the rolling clouds.

"Why do you say that, honey?" questioned Steven.

At that moment, everyone else in the car turned in the direction that Jasmine was looking. It was apparent Steven was surprised by what he saw because they all jerked forward when he suddenly hit the brakes.

"Wow, I think you're right, Jas," Steven said in amazement. "We had better hurry up and get home so we don't get caught in a downpour during the drive."

Steven accelerated the car, making it go faster than before Jasmine had sighted the storm clouds. Steven raced up the winding road but made sure to slow down between turns because there was not much traction on the dirt.

They finally reached the house, taking yet another detour through the front yard. The gang jumped out of the car and ran for the front door as fast as they could. When the last of them stepped into the house, the downpour began.

"Now that was a close one, honey," sighed Olivia as she removed her jacket. The rest of the family followed Olivia's lead and took off their coats as well, piling them on the floor next to the door. Anxious to get their new clothes in place, mother and daughter raced up the stairs to the master bedroom and placed their fresh outfits on top of their suitcases. Conrad and Steven, not having anything new, paced around the first floor trying to think of something to do. Since nothing came to mind, they went to the bedroom to join the girls.

Even in the bedroom they found nothing of interest, so Steven decided he would prepare for the night. He dug into his camping supplies and pulled out four flashlights and handed them to Conrad. As Conrad distributed those, Steven rummaged through Olivia's supply case and pulled out a large package of stubby white candles that clearly had seen better days. He ambled around the room and placed them randomly. Steven dug again into his camping gear and produced two battery lanterns that were usually used when hiking at night. He set those on the floor beside him and concluded he was finally complete with his preparations.

Realizing there was a lull in the activities, Steven suggested, "How about we check to see if Jasmine was right about possible holes in the roof?"

"That seems like a good idea," Olivia agreed as she slid her arm around her husband's waist.

"As long as I don't have to check the attic, I'm fine with that," Jasmine said compliantly.

"Fine with me. How about you and Conny checking the other rooms while Steven and I check the attic?" asked Olivia.

"But Mom, why am I stuck with her?" whined Conrad.

"Just go with your sister and when we are finished we can have supper," said Olivia with a note of exasperation.

"Also, make sure to grab one of these lanterns since it's getting dark," added Steven. He snatched a lantern and headed for the attic with Olivia following closely behind. Conrad took the remaining lantern for Jasmine and himself and walked out of the room.

When the parents reached the top of the stairs to the attic, they discovered they needed the extra light source earlier than expected. Even with the lantern, they were having a difficult time seeing. Olivia did not wish to wander off into the darkness, so she followed directly behind her husband as he led her around the attic. Steven searched the attic looking for windows, but there were none. As they made their way around a wooden pillar that stood in the center of the room, Steven noticed something white on the floor. It was a piece of paper. He bent down, picked it up, turned it over and noticed blue ink printing on one side of the aged sheet. He stood up and read out loud.

June 16

I can't believe the suffering we've been through since that horrific afternoon. I don't have the slightest idea why they would have run away. We showed them all the love we could possibly give ... unless they were kidnapped! That would be the worst thing! I don't even know how we could live another day if we found out that someone took them away from us. I don't want to say it, not even write it, but that is the only explanation I can think of. They would never run away, would they? I remember when

"That's all of it I can read," murmured Steven. He held the lantern closer to see if he could make out any of the other words, but they were illegible. Legible words appeared here and there, but were located too far apart to make any sense. It looked as if it had been read many times over from how tattered and torn the page was.

"Oh my, honey, that's horrible," gasped Olivia as she peeked over Steven's shoulder, checking to see if she could read any more of it. Once she proved to herself that the rest was illegible, she reached her arms around Steven and gave him a hug. "I really hope we don't ever have to experience the same thing they did. Do you think this was written by one of the people who lived here before we moved in?"

"I'm not sure, honey," Steven answered as he turned around and wiped a tear from his wife's cheek. "The only thing that anyone told me about this house before we bought it was that the last family lived in here nearly fifty years ago. Other than that, I really don't know. Sorry." At that instant, a loud crash of thunder boomed outside and the house shook.

Jasmine and Conrad started their own search immediately after their parents went up to the attic. After exiting the master bedroom, Jasmine turned toward the library. "Conrad, let's take a look in the library first. A leak in the roof would be disastrous to all those books in there," worried Jasmine.

"Do you really think those books wouldn't already be damaged if there were any holes in the roof? I really doubt any new holes have formed in the roof since we arrived here today," responded Conrad. However, Jasmine was not up for discussion on the matter and headed toward the library.

"I just want to make sure, is that okay?" Jasmine snapped.

"Fine, fine, fine," Conrad surrendered as he dragged his feet in his sister's direction.

When they arrived at the library, Jasmine made her way directly to one of the bookcases and looked up to see if any water marks were present on the ceiling. Not wanting to partake in the search, Conrad went to the desk and placed the lantern on it, lighting the shelving while his sister searched.

"All right, the room doesn't seem to be flooded," Conrad stated. "Can we just check these other rooms quickly? I'm really hungry and we won't get anything to eat if we're messing around with this."

"You're always hungry, Conny," responded Jasmine.

"No, I'm not," defended Conrad.

"Just knock it off!" As Jasmine was saying, "Yest—" Conrad approached his sister.

"You are wrong, Jas," Conrad denied as he raised his hand and pushed Jasmine in the shoulder with a force little harder than teasing. Conrad shoved her at just the wrong moment because Jasmine's foot was right behind the other. Her arms flew backward to brace herself for the fall and she was able to plant her hands on a bookshelf that stopped her from tumbling to the floor. As she slammed the shelves, the bookcase shook and one of the books dislodged, falling upside down and open.

"Now look what you did, Jas," accused Conrad as he pointed at the black book with a zigzag crack running down the middle.

"How can you call this my fault when you're the one who pushed me?" growled Jasmine. They both approached the fallen book at the same time. Almost like a challenge, they both bent down and grabbed for the book at the same time. The siblings put their hands onto the book at the same time and turned it around together. Simultaneously, the thunder crashed violently and the lantern turned off. The last sound that resonated from within the room was the book hitting the floor. Nothing else.

Chapter 5

As pain shot through Conrad's head, he hesitated and slowly opened his eyes. Straining to keep his eyes open, he realized he was not inside the library anymore. As a matter of fact, he was not inside a room at all. Conrad moved his head around carefully and could see only large flowers and tall grass that blocked his view in every direction.

He rolled to his side, planting his right hand onto the ground for support. Pushing off with his right hand, he propped himself off the ground in hopes he could get a better view of his surroundings, but his head started to spin the second he was vertical. Once his dizziness subsided, he looked down and noticed his sister lying in the flowers a few feet away from him.

Conrad made his way to Jasmine. Once he reached her, he gently nudged his sister with his left foot, not wishing to bend down since his head had just stopped spinning and he didn't want a relapse. "Jas, wake up and see this," Conrad whispered. He waited for Jasmine to stir, but when she didn't budge, he nudged her a little harder, this time expecting the worst. "Jasmine, wake up," Conrad insisted, much louder than before.

"Stop kicking me, Conny," mumbled Jasmine as she raised her hand and slapped his leg away.

Relieved, Conrad whispered, "Open your eyes and take a look at this." Jasmine slowly opened her eyes and scanned the unknown territory. Not knowing what was happening, she closed her eyes and started to scream. "Jasmine, you need to be quiet." Conrad fell to his knees, placing his hand over her open mouth to muffle the sound. Conrad placed his mouth next to her ear so she could hear his whisper. "You need to be quiet because I don't know where we are, and I really don't feel safe with you screaming so loud. Do you understand me?" Jasmine opened her eyes and wiped the tears that were now forming in the corners of her eyes. She then nodded her head just enough to signify that she understood.

Conrad reluctantly pulled his fingers away from Jasmine's mouth, but made sure his hand was in the vicinity of her face if another outburst occurred. Once Conrad was satisfied Jasmine wasn't going to scream anymore, he stood up and reached down to grasp her hand. Jasmine stared at the hand for a second before accepting the gesture. She rose to a standing position and gasped in total shock at her new surroundings. Conrad had a feeling Jasmine would have another outburst, so he stayed close to her.

All around them flowers of every sort and color rose from the ground. Red roses, yellow-orange sunflowers, bluebells, and daisies swayed in the breeze. The air smelled like perfume and a soothing buzz of honeybees accompanied the sweet song of a bluebird. In the distance, thick groves of trees loomed in every direction. Since the ground they now stood on was actually a little hill, they could see the tops of the first rows of trees. Small flocks of finches flew above the trees, some trying to find perching spots within the branches. As one group of birds landed in the trees, a new set would spring up, trying to find a new nesting position. Butterflies flitted from flower to flower in hopes of nectar. Both the birds and insects seemed unbothered by the new intruders to their land. Under different circumstances, Conrad and Jasmine probably would have thought this was the most beautiful place in the world. But this was no ordinary day.

"Conny, where are we?" inquired Jasmine as she stood with her mouth agape.

"I honestly haven't the slightest idea. The last thing I remember, we were in the library and I knocked you into the bookcase. We both picked up that book, and then," Conrad extended his right hand in a presenting sort of manner, "we were here."

With his hand already raised, Conrad reached to the back of his head. "My head hurts horribly. If you weren't here with me, I would think I was knocked out and dreaming right now. I guess I could still be dreaming, but I really doubt it because I've never had a dream that felt this real. How about you, Jas? Do you have a headache?"

"Yeah, I feel just like you said. Almost like somebody hit me in the head with a bat and knocked me out," responded Jasmine as she reached to the back of her head with both of her hands. She ran her hands through her hair in search of any lumps, but none were present.

Conrad watched as his sister examined the rest of her body for bumps and bruises. Just to be on the safe side, he started his own search. Conrad was bent over rolling up his left pant leg in search of injuries when a faint low-pitched drumming noise resonated from within the trees. "Do you hear that noise?" asked Jasmine as she crept closer to her brother. Conrad quickly rolled down his pant leg and raised himself onto his tiptoes in search of the new sound, unaware of his sister closing in on him.

"Yeah, I hear it," Conrad replied as he finally realized where the noise was coming from. He turned and pointed in that direction. "I'm pretty sure it's coming from over there." Jasmine was now in arm's reach of her brother, so she grabbed onto the hand that wasn't pointing in the direction of the sound.

"What do you think you're doing?" asked Conrad.

"I'm scared; I just wanted to hold onto your hand."

"You have another hand, hold onto that," Conrad snorted as he pulled his hand away from his sister. Jasmine was upset by her brother's reaction, but quickly forgot about it since the drumming grew louder.

As time passed, the drumming grew to the point that Jasmine's ears started to ring. She placed her hands up to her ears trying to make the noise lessen. Remembering what her mother taught her during a thunderstorm, Jasmine began to hum, trying to drown out the drumming noise. When she found that didn't work, she just gave up and put her hands over her eyes to cover the tears that were about to fall.

As Conrad looked in the direction of the incessant drumming, a large flock of red-winged blackbirds flew out of the trees and frantically searched for a new perching site while emitting angry chirping noises to whatever disturbed them. Conrad turned his head to see if his sister noticed the birds as well. Seeing that she had her eyes covered, he asked, "What's the matter?"

"Nothing is the matter with me," she sniffled. "I just had something in my eyes."

"Well, something is happening over there," Conrad remarked as he pointed in the direction from which the birds flew.

Jasmine looked in the direction of Conrad's pointing, noticing birds frantically flying around in circles. As they watched the birds circling around, someone burst out of the trees. "Who is that?" Jasmine asked curiously.

"I'm not sure, but we'll find out soon enough," replied Conrad as he realized the person was running somewhat in their direction.

When the being came close enough to see, Jasmine realized it was a man, but not like one she had ever seen before. The person almost appeared to be running above the grass with how swiftly he traversed the landscape. He looked taller than an average man and it almost looked like someone had yanked his head and stretched it out just a bit. When she noticed how long his face was, she also noticed the long pointy ears that stuck out from the side of his head. He was dressed in the purest white clothing she had ever laid eyes on. Two gleaming swords hung from his waist, one at each hip, both flapping from side to side as he ran.

He ran through the flowers, with no concern about crushing any, and repeatedly looked over his shoulder without missing a stride, despite the rugged terrain. Jasmine couldn't believe the man hadn't noticed them, since he wasn't running directly toward them. She wanted to yell and motion to him to come over. Fortunately, after turning around one more time to check whatever was chasing him, he veered in the direction of Jasmine and Conrad.

"You need to run, little ones," the man yelled when he was within earshot of them. They heard what he said, but stood motionless, not knowing whether or not to obey this newcomer. He started to slow down as he neared them, but instead of stopping, he sidestepped so he would run right between them. The second that the man ran between them, he quickly reached down and grabbed both of their hands.

Having no choice, Jasmine and Conrad's feet struggled to try to keep up with the strange man. Conrad attempted yanking his hand away when he was able to get his footing, but for some reason, his gut instinct told him to run with the man. As Conrad kept pace with the stranger, he looked over to his sister and noticed she was also struggling between running with or away from this new person. They ran for a few hundred yards before the ground began to slope downward. As the base of the trees were disappearing out of sight, Jasmine looked back, hoping to see whatever was causing this man to run for his life. Suddenly, a large group of horrific green creatures stormed out from beneath the trees.

"Humans!" a deep voice shouted as the trees were lost from view.

Chapter 6

People experience ups and downs throughout their lifetimes, and places have those ups and downs as well. When people have their down moments, friends and family are usually nearby to help them get through bad times. The problem with places having downs is they have a much harder time finding anyone to help them get through the troubled times. Because of this, sometimes the land needs to search elsewhere for help and this is why the children were destined to arrive at this place.

Jasmine and Conrad were not aware of this yet, but when they appeared in this new land, others were watching the very location of their arrival. The land was called Felnoria and it contained different sorts of people, just like any other place. What made this land unique was that there were also different sorts of intelligent creatures with both friendly and harmful intentions. At the time Conrad and Jasmine arrived, the evil sort ruled most of the land.

On the southernmost border of Felnoria, a cascading mountain range named the Thundering Mountains stretched as far as the eye could see. The tallest mountain was so overwhelmingly high that the top of it was never visible because it stretched so far into the clouds. Even on a clear day, clouds seemed to linger around that area. The Thundering Mountains were the home of an assortment of treacherous creatures that lived within the mountain where they had built a vast network of tunnels like veins in a human body. These creatures that lived inside the mountain were all considered to be the most dangerous in all of Felnoria and were slowly expanding their reign across the land. If anyone journeyed near the Thundering Mountains, he or she would never return to tell the tale. No towns were ever built within the shadows for fear of destruction. Even those built a safe distance away felt the wrath of the diabolic creatures. On the other side of the Thundering Mountains, there was an untamed region stretching toward the horizon where other strange creatures roamed and humans had never set foot.

Goblins were the most abundant race inside the mountains. These goblins were about the size of humans, but other than size, they had no humanlike features. Their wrinkly skin was a dark green color with mottled black dots covering parts of their bodies, similar to toads. The heads of goblins were overly proportioned for their bodies. Goblins always looked like they had trouble keeping their heads on their shoulders as they walked. Their eyes had catlike pupils surrounded by bright yellow irises, their teeth were razor sharp, and the smell that wafted from their mouths was putrid.

Nevertheless, the goblins were enslaved by the less-abundant creatures who dominated them. The creatures that ruled the Thundering Mountains with the power of fear were a race known as trolls. These gargantuan creatures were much larger than an average man; their height was nearly seven feet and they were as wide as two men standing abreast. Their dry skin was a very ugly pale green color, but their heads were the most disturbing part of their bodies. The tops of their heads were almost completely bald, with a few wispy hairs straggling around. Their faces wrinkled up to the point where the skin folds overlapped each other, making it look like a festering green ooze was running over them constantly. Sticking out of the midst of the ooze was a large nose, looking almost like a cucumber, but curling down at the end.

Deep inside the Thundering Mountains, a troll sat atop a throne carved from rock in the center of a poorly lit cave. Huge scars ran across the troll's chest and only a tattered loincloth covered his body. On top of the throne, skulls of many species were aligned; each skull facing in the same direction as the troll. In the back of the room, a statue of a great troll stood overlooking the rest of the chamber. A wooden table stood alongside the eastern wall with various meats laid out at all times for the troll. Since trolls had lived in caves for generations, their ability to see in the dark had become as good as human sight during the day, so few torches were lit in the chamber. This chamber, in particular, used to be the throne room of a great dwarven lord, before it was forcefully taken, but no signs of its previous usage existed any longer. Many decades had passed since peace had been celebrated within those stone walls.

The mighty troll's crooked, clawed fingers tapped impatiently on the arm of the throne, emitting a small thump that echoed throughout the chamber with every consecutive tap. Another troll, dressed in a large robe, which was not the normal attire for trolls, entered the throne room, mumbling to himself as he made his way up to the throne. When he approached the seated troll, he bowed down, his nose brushing the rocky ground in the process.

"I'm sorry, Master Uzgal, for asking you to see you." The troll shivered.

"What is the meaning of this, Sage Morlok? I am supposed to summon you, not the other way around. I should have your head for that," raged Uzgal as he formed a fist and slammed it onto the arm of his throne. The impact caused tiny bits of the armrest to crumble to the floor. Morlok stood up, quite frightened for his life at that moment.

"I...I'm sorry, Master, but I wouldn't have done it if I hadn't a good reason. While sleeping, I had a premonition of two humans coming from afar to rid this land of all the hatred you have so successfully created. I saw them appear in a field of flowers with trees surrounding them in every direction, kind of like the place from the other time."

"Why do you feel you need to tell me about every bad dream you have? You constantly tell me bad things are going to happen, but they never occur. I don't even know why you have the title 'Sage.' I doubt one correct premonition in fifty years is really a good enough reason to bestow you with such a grand title!" shouted Uzgal.

"You are probably correct, sir, but if you remember, the one I did get right had to do with the two humans who came here and helped Zolar defeat your father and his army," defended Morlok as he stepped back a few paces from his master. When Morlok stepped back, Uzgal leaped out of his throne and approached Morlok, unhappy with the mention of his father. Morlok slumped down, waiting to be punished for his comment about Uzgal's father.

All the trolls feared Uzgal because of the wrath he bestowed upon his enemies, and it showed in Morlok's eyes. Uzgal stood a foot taller than any other living troll and he used that to his advantage when need be. Uzgal believed that threatening death and causing death with his own hands were the correct ways to rule a land. "If they fear me, they will listen, but if they don't flinch when I approach them, something's definitely wrong," his father told him at a young age, and Uzgal took it as his motto.

"Unless you can give me proof right now, I'm just going to take this as another one of your bogus visions," growled Uzgal as he clenched his fist to hit Morlok, only to decide against it at the last second.

"But, Master, how am I supposed to give you proof if it was just a dream—I me...mean—premonition?" Morlok stammered as he corrected himself. After hearing that, Uzgal didn't feel like holding back any longer. Uzgal lifted his left foot off the ground and thrust it into Morlok's chest, causing him to fall to the rocky floor. Uzgal watched as Morlok curled into a fetal position gasping for air.

"So you said yourself that it was just a dream," stated Uzgal.

"I didn't mean to say dream, Master," Morlok pleaded, once he could breathe again. "Please forgive me, I...I'm just distraught and the wrong words spilled out of my mouth." Morlok braced himself for another kick. When no punishment came, he continued, "I swear, this premonition is real this time!"

"How about I give you time to think it over, then you can tell me for certain if it was a stupid dream or a true premonition," said Uzgal.

Confused as to why Uzgal was giving him another chance and knowing something was up, he cautiously made his way upright from the ground, expecting to be knocked down again any instant.

"Thank you, Master!"

Morlok started to turn away to leave the room before Uzgal could change his mind when Uzgal shouted, "Guards!" Suddenly two large trolls encased in armor and carrying spears stormed into the room. "Escort Morlok down into the dungeon, and make sure he's in a nice dark cell of his own so he has time to think peacefully."

"But...but, Master, what have I done to you to be treated in this manner?" asked a startled Morlok.

"You hand me problems I have no time to deal with. I've spent too much time and effort on these things that you called 'premonitions' in the past, and I'm sick of it!" As Uzgal said that, he considered hitting Morlok one last time. Instead, he strode back to his throne.

When the guards were within arm's reach, Morlok thought about running. Instead, he just slumped down and held out his clawed hands so he could be escorted out of the chamber knowing there was no way he could escape. Each guard grabbed one of Morlok's arms, forcing him to turn toward the exit of the room. Refusing to be mobile, he went limp, requiring the guards to drag him out. All hope of living seeped from his body as he crossed the threshold to a narrow dank hallway leading to the dungeon.

Uzgal climbed back onto his throne, pleased with his authoritarian decision. "Morlok has been a pain for many years, and I'm happy I will not have to deal with the likes of him ever again," Uzgal said to himself.

Chapter 7

In the northern region of Felnoria, there was a castle unlike any ever built. It was completely assembled of white stone and had square-topped towers rising at each corner of the stronghold. Multiple gables and balconies jutted out, framing the richly colored drapery in front of the elongated rectangular windows. The stones were old and weathered, built from ancient deposits deep in the Soaring Cliffs, and blended into the landscape. They appeared sturdy enough to hold off a horde of rampaging trolls. The white stone shone brilliantly in the sunlight, a welcome sight to weary travelers and village folk alike.

An enormous courtyard sprawled at the front of the structure, with wide marble steps in the center leading up a rise to the castle. At the bottom of the stairs a road ran straight through the courtyard, exiting out of the castle walls and leading into the nearby village. If one of the enemy races ever attacked this castle, an enormous wrought iron gate blocked entry to all but the most loyal allies. The gate was designed in such a way that a single person could close off the castle from any intruders.

Houses circled the castle except around the northern wing, which sprawled atop a high cliff that overlooked the ocean below. The king and queen and their most loyal advisers resided in the northern part of the castle. The peasants of the surrounding village lived near the castle for two reasons. First, it gave them protection from all the horrible beasts that lurked in the land, and second, the two people who ruled over them were thought to be the heroes of Felnoria. Because of this, the peasants didn't live in fear of their rulers and they obeyed them with open hearts.

This castle and the houses that surrounded it were known as Yarlanzia, the capital of the human race in the land of Felnoria. If any neighboring town had a problem with the menacing people or creatures of the land, they would always come to Yarlanzia for aid. To support the needs of so many, thousands of troops were stationed in Yarlanzia at all times and more were ready for a time of need.

For the past fifty years, everything had been peaceful, but in the last few years, things had changed for the worse. The trolls' reign over Felnoria had stretched into parts that once were protected by Yarlanzia. Small villages that once existed in peace were now just charred remains of buildings. The king and queen of Yarlanzia tried their hardest to keep peace among the people of the neighboring villages, but thoughts of destruction and death clouding everyone's minds made it difficult. In the past, they had signed treaties with both the elves of Fos Faydian and the dwarves of Zolar to help each other in time of need. But events long ago had changed many things. Now, only the dwarves would help if called upon and only with strong persuasion.

The king and queen met with a diplomat from each of the elven towns to maintain peace and to mend old wounds between the two races, but elves had a hard time forgiving. Neither the elves nor the dwarves had ever lived with humans; they thought highly of their own race and preferred to live with their own kind. The rulers believed that the elves still met with the humans only to keep an eye on them. This way, the elves would know if Yarlanzia was up to anything foolish.

Inside the royal chamber of the castle, a discussion was taking place about the condition of Felnoria. A pair of thrones sat in the middle of the room with two steps leading up to them. The thrones were a beautiful shade of dark mahogany and contrasted nicely with the carved white pillars that lined the walls, more for decoration than support. On each wall, various tapestries depicting royal themes hung to the floor. The primary tapestry behind the thrones was woven with a scene of a sunlit meadow full of flowers, giving the room a homey feel. Small pedestals were also placed around the room with vases of posies upon them, each giving off a sweet fragrance. The room was designed with these features to give the guests a safe and secure feel while they spoke with the king and queen. Even with the extraordinary size of the room, one never felt overwhelmed by the size.

"How are we supposed to defend all of the villages with the number of soldiers we have?" asked a soldier named Kadon, who was holding a helmet in one hand and the hilt of his sword in the other. This man had shoulder-length, curly, black hair with a full beard growing upon his face. He had handsome features and dark eyes that shone with intelligence. The armor he wore concealed muscles that were honed to battle for many hours without rest as a result of years of training under the king and queen's command. They had treated him well and he would sacrifice his life for them in an instant.

"Perhaps we should go from village to village trying to recruit more soldiers," suggested the king, who was sitting on the throne, stroking his beard. Alongside him sat a stunning woman dressed in a blue satin, floor-length gown with a multitude of gems stitched on the bodice. A crown sat atop mostly white hair with faint pieces of light brown that cascaded halfway down her back and flowed with the contour of her body. Even in her older age, her face had a look of someone much younger, but her pale blue eyes said otherwise.

"That sounds like a splendid idea, Ralph," responded the queen as she turned her head toward the king.

"There might be a slight chance the elves will come to us in a time of need, but it seems they have given up hope on us humans for the time being," noted King Ralph as he lost interest in stroking his beard, placing his hand back onto the throne's arm. Not responding, Queen Synthia looked over to her brother and noticed from his eyes that he was in another place.

Ralph thought back to when they had first arrived in Felnoria. So many things had happened in so little a time. Before they had even known where they were, they had been forced to travel across the land. With not even time to sit down and collect their thoughts, many heroic feats were thrust upon them. When everything finally calmed down, the rein of Yarlanzia was given to them. Even with the entire land their responsibility, everything had seemed less complicated when they started their reign. Early on, they had many people and circumstances who helped them heal Yarlanzia and even Felnoria. But now that they were much older, most of their advisers had passed on, and it was all up to them.

Age had treated the king well, and he was still well equipped to defend himself if need be. This was accomplished by hours of training he demanded of his body each and every day. Unlike his sister, his facial features were showing age. A long white beard flowed to his chest and silver hair feathered around his crown. The crown hid the large bald spot that was forming at the top of his head, so the king made sure to wear his royal headgear at all times. His face was lined and there were creases around his eyes. His attire consisted of a red velvet cape full enough to completely wrap around him from head to toe. Beneath the cape he wore a crisp white shirt with ruby buttons and red velvet pants that hung loosely over his jeweled shoes. His posture wasn't as elegant as his sister's, and it was common to see him slouching while sitting on the throne. Finally, his eyes seemed to flicker to life and he looked at his sister. "Synthia, when's the last time you heard from either High Elf Mylinia or the Dwarf Lord Bontarest?"

"Honestly, I can't remember, but I'll check with my chambermaids to see if they recorded our last visit with either race."

"Captain Kadon, select two sets of ten reliable men from within your ranks and have them on standby to depart immediately. They must go from town to town in search of new recruits. We will have one unit scour the eastern part of Felnoria, while the other takes the western," commanded Ralph. "We have not had new recruits in a year, and it is imperative that we conduct a search now."

"Yes, Your Highness," replied Kadon. Kadon bowed slowly, once to Ralph, again to Synthia, then pivoted and marched out of the room.

Once Kadon left the throne room, Synthia arose and stepped down from her royal chair. With everything on her mind, she began to pace around the room.

"We really need to do something about those trolls," stated Synthia as she started pacing faster. "Just last week, Verlin was burnt to the ground because of those horrible creatures. That town isn't even *near* the Thundering Mountains."

"If we can band enough new recruits, we can dispatch some to each town. Perhaps that way the towns will have a better chance of defending themselves," Ralph explained as he rose from his throne and approached his sister.

Ralph gently took his sister's arm to lead her back to the throne when a man clad in a worn brown robe burst into the room followed by four guards. Wanting to explain the situation, one of the guards ran ahead of the robed man. "I'm sorry, Your Highnesses! He demanded to see you right away and he wouldn't wait for permission to see you." Before the guard could continue, the man in the brown robe swerved around the guard and approached the king and queen.

He bent down onto one knee. "I have good news for you," the robed man informed them as he rose.

"The guards could have killed you for what you did. Couldn't this have waited until you were granted permission to see us?" queried Ralph.

"Forgive me, Your Highness, but this couldn't wait. We have just received information that two strangers were sighted crossing the same field Your Highnesses traversed when you first came here."

"You are dismissed," Ralph commanded with a dismissive gesture to the guards. "Resume your posts outside the entry." Ralph noticed his sister readying herself to pace around again so he quickly reached out to hold her in place. Synthia struggled at first to be released from her brother's grasp, but gave up when she realized he was glancing at her with concern.

Once Ralph and Synthia were satisfied that the guards were out of earshot, they continued the conversation. "Are you certain?" questioned Synthia.

"Yes, my queen. We have kept watch over the flower patch within the Trilaz Woods through our pool of sight ever since we built it."

The pool of sight was located inside the castle in the sages' chambers. These people had magical powers of foresight and were responsible for building and watching over the pool of sight. With the king's help, the sages had fashioned a small, circular body of water in one of their rooms as the king and queen had commanded. Once it was in place, the king taught them how to reproduce an image of any nearby land into the pool. One particular sage questioned the king about how he had learned this magical process. The only response he would give was that he had learned it before he arrived in Yarlanzia. Once the pool of sight was complete, the sages realized it took great magic to transport an image into the water. The sages surmised the king and queen must have brought such magic with them from their origin. Because of that, the flower patch where the king and queen were discovered permanently shone through the pool of sight. It was important to monitor it constantly, so a sage was kept on duty around the clock hoping to see if someone else came to their land.

"We have a p...p...problem though," stuttered the man, so frightened to tell them the rest. "They were spotted with a large group of trolls chasing them." Ralph lost hold of Synthia and she fell to her knees.

"Are the two safe?" Ralph questioned as he knelt down to help her back up.

"From what one of the sages told me, an elf came to their rescue. The sage watching the pool lost sight of them when they entered the Trilaz Woods." Synthia stood up with some effort from her brother, still in shock by the realization that someone else had finally come to Felnoria and probably wouldn't make it through the day.

"Please, keep us informed if anything new comes about on this subject. You were right to have brought this to our attention. You are dismissed."

"As you wish, Your Highnesses." The man bowed, pivoted, and exited.

Once the king and queen were alone, Ralph helped his sister to her throne and he returned to his own. Comfortably seated, Ralph turned to his sister, placing his hand on hers.

"We must find them as soon as possible, Synthia. We can't have those trolls capturing or killing them. They might be crucial in regaining the land we lost from the trolls."

Chapter 8

Conrad and Jasmine ran alongside the pointy-eared man to the best of their ability. As they tried keeping pace with him, the drumming seemed to stop, leading them to believe that whoever or whatever was behind them had ceased pursuit. They almost ran into a large crop of rocks that loomed at least ten feet above the field of flowers. With no time to stop, the odd man veered to the left, pulling them with him. Conrad anticipated the turn, but Jasmine didn't and lost her footing. She fell face down. With no concern if she was harmed in the fall, the stranger stopped only to yank her back onto her feet and resume running.

Once the trio rounded the rocks, the landscape before them transformed instantly. Knee-high flowers changed to hundred-foot trees that overwhelmed Jasmine and Conrad. Huge bushes grew so thickly at the base of the trees that their progress was brought to halt.

"What are those things chasing after us?" panted Jasmine as she let go of the man's hand and quickly searched her body for injuries. She found a bleeding scrape on her knee but disregarded it for a larger gash on her cheek. Ripping a piece off his shirt, Conrad reached over and swiped the blood away.

"Now is not the time to waste your breath on chatter," the man remarked as he released Conrad's hand and stepped ahead of them to search for a path through the bushes. Once he found what he was seeking, he returned to them. Jasmine was brushing off her clothes from the fall when the man took her hand again. He reached out and grabbed Conrad's as well. "I am sorry you fell," the man said sincerely while looking at Jasmine.

Before Jasmine could respond, she was tugged forward toward the forest. Conrad and Jasmine struggled to keep up with him, stumbling over obstacles that were concealed by the flowers.

Upon their entering the forest, the drumming began again, growing louder than before. Jasmine's ears hurt more than ever. The man led them between two bushes that made it difficult to run while latching onto each other. The man released their hands, knowing free movement would make it easier to weave in and out of the thick vegetation. "You need to follow me if you wish to live," warned the man. "Follow close behind me and whatever you do, do not look back."

He expertly maneuvered through the trees and bushes in order to find the easiest route through the forest so they wouldn't have to struggle. Conrad and Jasmine were not as adept at navigating the wild as their guide. It seemed like every bush they brushed against had large thorny tips that ripped their flesh. The deeper they progressed into the forest, the more the ground level changed. Bushes and plants were sparse due to the lack of sunlight. The ground was carpeted with dead leaves that smelled like perpetual autumn with a tinge of decay. Long streams of light filtered through the towering trees, looking like spotlights piercing the canopy above. It was cooler in the forest and it was almost totally silent.

Adapting to the change of surroundings, the man began to run again, but at a much slower pace than when they were racing through the flowers. The more they ran, the softer the drumming pounded in their ears. After what seemed like hours of flight, the drumming was just a faint beat to them. The party continued running until the man stopped so the two young people could catch their breath. Jasmine and Conrad collapsed and sprawled in the dead leaves as their stomachs heaved.

"We still are not safe, but we are getting closer to a place where they will not be able to reach us," he informed them.

"Can you tell me now what those green monsters were?" Jasmine asked between the heaving of air through her lungs.

"You saw them?" questioned Conrad in shock, as he turned his head to look at his sister.

"Those are what are known as trolls. They are the fiercest of creatures that live in Felnoria."

"What's Felnoria?" both asked simultaneously.

The man raised an eyebrow at Jasmine and Conrad and gave them an odd look. "How can you not know what Felnoria is? It's the land where you live."

"Well, you see, we just got here a little while ago," answered Jasmine as she clumsily tried to stand up.

"How can that be? We are nowhere near the ocean for arrival by ship, and humans do not have wings so you could not have flown here," exclaimed the man.

"We really don't know ourselves," explained Conrad as he followed his sister's lead and rose from the forest floor. "One second we were in a library and the next we were here."

"Were you in the library in Yarlanzia?" the man asked. "I know there are many magical books there. Maybe one teleported you here."

"No," responded Jasmine, as she brushed herself clean of the dead leaves that clung to her clothes. "And neither of us has ever heard of Yarlanzia."

After hearing that, the man decided that it was pointless to cross-examine them any further at this time. He knew it was going to take much longer than the time they had to obtain the information he wanted.

"We will speak more about this later. For now, we need to keep going unless you wish to be the trolls' supper tonight."

"One last thing before we go," interrupted Jasmine. "You look like a human, but then again you don't. Some of your features are similar to my brother's and mine, but then things like your pointy ears are much different than ours."

"I am what you would call an elf," he stated.

"Elf! I've read about them in fairy tales, but I've never thought they existed," Jasmine exclaimed as she approached the elf, taking an even better look at him. "If you don't mind my asking, what is your name?"

When Jasmine asked his name, the elf bowed down elegantly and introduced himself. "My name is Lestron Forvalo D'lan."

Desiring to be as proper as Lestron, Jasmine curtsied in front of him and said, "My name is Jasmine Felsworth, and this is my brother, Conrad Felsworth."

"I am pleased to have made your acquaintance, Jasmine and Conrad, but now is not the time for any more useless chatter. We must hurry along," Lestron said as he turned and continued his journey through the forest, checking to make sure the two humans were following behind him.

The children paused as they encountered things far stranger than any they had observed before in a forest, but Lestron didn't give them time to study the oddities. At one point, they both noticed at least twenty chipmunks congregating near a tree stump.

As they were walking past the chipmunks, they heard them talking! Jasmine and Conrad were initially startled by hearing animals converse, but curiosity took over and the siblings were fascinated by the chipmunk conversation.

"We must all band together and fight back against the rats of this forest," proclaimed a large chipmunk as he stood atop the tree stump, addressing his fellow chipmunks. "They are hoarding all of the acorns for themselves. If this keeps up, we will not have enough food to feed our children through the winter."

"But the rats are so much bigger and stronger than we are. How do you think we could possibly win?" inquired one of the smaller chipmunks in the back of the group.

"We have greater numbers than they do. What we need to do is scare them away, not fight them," the large chipmunk shouted.

"But how?" several asked in unison.

They were eager to hear more about their dilemma, but Lestron wasn't slowing down, and the twins didn't wish to be lost alone in the forest because of curiosity. Once out of the chipmunks' sight, they looked at each other and shook their heads at the same time.

"This place is messed up," Conrad muttered as he looked back to try to catch one last glimpse of the chipmunks but failed.

Chapter 9

After hours of walking and running, Conrad detected a faint sound of rushing water in the distance. The closer they came to the source, the louder the noise grew. Jasmine noticed that bushes started appearing again, causing them to walk slowly in hopes of not getting scratched by the thorns. Not wishing to make the same mistake twice, Conrad and Jasmine watched how Lestron made his way around the bushes without getting scratched. As they watched, he seemed to weave around the bushes, moving his body in just the right position not to be injured. If branches brushed any part of his body, they seemed to flow with the natural direction of the plant so no harm was done.

They tried to mimic his moves by pivoting their bodies from side to side and tucking their arms close to their body. The process worked, decreasing their pain greatly in comparison to when they entered the forest. As they made their way past a huge berry bush, a great river appeared before them.

The wide river stretched out to their right and left, twisting and turning before disappearing behind brush and trees. In the distance, small animals congregated near the river to drink the clear water. As they watched, they wondered if every animal in this strange land could talk like the chipmunks.

Wanting to get to a safer place, Lestron walked to the edge of the river with Jasmine and Conrad close behind. Lestron bent down and ran his hand through the water, testing the temperature and current. Satisfied the temperature was warm enough but not pleased with the water flow, he straightened up.

"We are almost there," Lestron informed them as he wiped his hand on his pants.

"Almost where?" asked Jasmine.

"You will find out soon enough," stated Lestron. "First, we need to get across this river. Then it will only be a little farther. Up ahead, the water should be shallow enough to walk across. Just wait here for a second and I will be right back."

Lestron ran back into the forest, returning momentarily with a long branch in his hand that was about the size of a walking stick. Beginning where the children stood, he waded upriver, poking the stick into the water every so often. The children followed behind him, not knowing exactly what Lestron was doing. He kept going until a few rocks popped out of the surface of the water in the middle of the river. He poked his stick into the water yet again to make sure the river bottom was safe for walking. Satisfied with his initial examination, he bent over and placed his hand in the water to test the strength of the current. "This is the spot! The water is shallow enough and the current does not seem too fast," Lestron stated as he stood up.

For extra support while crossing, Lestron placed the stick firmly into the sand below the water while he stretched out his other hand. "Take my hand, Jasmine, and you, Conrad, take Jasmine's. It will be much safer if we hold onto each other. That way, if someone falls in, one of us can pull the other back up. Whatever you do, do not let go of each other, no matter what." Jasmine reached out and grasped Lestron's hand while she offered her other hand to Conrad.

Shivers ran up Jasmine's spine as she made her first step into the ice-cold water. By the time she made her second step into the water, goose bumps covered her entire body. Conrad was next to enter the water and had the same reaction as his sister. The deeper and farther into the river they traveled, the riverbed slowly changed from firm sand to smooth rocks. The slippery, slimy stones caused Jasmine to struggle to keep her footing. When Jasmine looked at Lestron, wading surefooted, it seemed he didn't even notice that the rocks were slippery.

At the center of the river, the water was above waist level and a strong current was tugging at their legs, making the trek across the river much more difficult. They struggled to maintain their balance while still pressing onward. At one point, Conrad was lifting his foot to take a step when something solid collided with the leg that was supporting him. The sudden impact caused him to lose his balance. Because of the slimy rocks, he slipped and fell backward into the water. Luckily he didn't lose his grip on his sister's hand. Conrad tried planting his foot back onto the rock but the slime was just too slippery underneath.

"Hold onto him, Jasmine! Whatever you do, do not let him go!" shouted Lestron as he pivoted his body to face Conrad.

"I can't hold on much longer. He's too heavy for me," Jasmine hollered in return as she struggled to maintain a hold on her brother. The more she pulled, the more she lost her grip, both on her brother's hand and her own feet. "I'm slipping, Lestron!" shouted Jasmine as she struggled to stay upright.

Needing both hands, Lestron threw the stick and stretched out to Conrad. The second Lestron reached out to grab Conrad, Jasmine slipped on the rocks and fell in. Since Lestron was stretching out to grab Conrad when Jasmine fell into the water, the tug on his arm was too great and he lost his balance and fell in as well. All three were taken down the river, with the current pulling them faster and faster while the water was getting deeper and deeper. Jasmine, not the best of swimmers, began to flail her arms in hopes of staying afloat. As she struggled, her whole body submerged under the surface. A few seconds later, she reappeared. She managed to get the water out of her stomach, but panicked and swung her hands out viciously. Lestron was quick to react and regained his grip, but Conrad was out of reach.

Once Conrad lost his sister's hand, he was pulled into a heavier current than the other two encountered. He was relieved to see Jasmine holding onto Lestron. As he watched them, he felt his body moving farther away. He tried swimming in their direction, but with every stroke of his arms their distance grew instead of lessened. He continued until exhaustion overcame him and his muscles strained from keeping him afloat.

His luck didn't get any better as his body was carried toward a huge boulder in the center of the river. He mustered just enough strength to swim again to get out of the current that was hurling him right toward the rock. The last thing he heard was his sister screaming from a distance before everything went dark and blinding pain shot through his head.

Chapter 10

When Conrad awoke, the first thing he noticed was that instead of floating in the water he was lying face down on a solid surface. He also noticed he was still drenched from head to foot, so he must not have been out of the water for long. He started to move his head around to check where he was when a sudden pain shot through his head. The excruciating pain coursing through his head jolted his memory of the events before he blacked out. He tried to focus on those events instead of the throbbing going on inside of his brain. When the pain finally subsided, he heard a crackling noise beside him but didn't wish to turn his head again in fear of the pain returning.

"Don't move, Conny, you bashed your head on the rock," soothed Jasmine.

Conrad reached up, even though it caused him pain, and put his hand to the back of his head. He felt around until his fingers brushed against a large lump and a warm liquid ran down to his palm. Startled, Conrad pulled his hand away from his head to confirm his suspicions. When he held his fingers in front of his eyes, his assumption was confirmed.

"I'm bleeding," exclaimed Conrad as he swung his arm to the ground and wiped the blood away on the grass beside him.

"Yes, I know. Jasmine and I were just going to go into the forest to find some balsap herbs so I could make an ointment for you," responded Lestron.

"What are balsap herbs?" asked Conrad.

"They are a small, red plant that grows only in these woods. When ground up, they form a gummy substance that can be placed on cuts. It promotes the healing time of the cut and also the swelling subsides greatly," explained Lestron. "Just stay where you are, and Jasmine and I will go collect the herbs for you. I have built a fire nearby, to discourage enemies from bothering you."

Conrad gingerly looked aside and noticed a small fire burning beside him, finally realizing what the crackling noise was. Risking the pain, he carefully slid his body closer to the fire as knives of pain poked repeatedly into his skull.

Lestron watched as Conrad inched his way to the fire. He could tell that Conrad was struggling to move, but couldn't do anything to help him until he found the balsap herbs. Satisfied that Conrad wasn't going to move anymore, he beckoned Jasmine to follow him.

They made their way into the forest and searched for what they needed. As they searched the forest floor, Lestron pointed out various types of mushrooms that were growing near tree trunks. He described to her what each of the mushrooms was used for in an attempt to keep her occupied. Jasmine realized quickly that most mushrooms were poisonous, but there were a select few that were beneficial.

Lestron was walking ahead when Jasmine noticed him stop suddenly. Thinking that the trolls had found them, she started to turn, readying herself to run away. Lestron turned around and noticed that Jasmine was flustered. "Are there trolls around here?" whispered Jasmine.

"No, come here, and I will show you a sight to behold," Lestron whispered back as he beckoned to her. Jasmine hesitantly made her way toward Lestron, cautious where she stepped. When she reached him, he pointed in the direction he was looking. Jasmine's mouth hung open as two beautiful animals grazed with no worries in the world. They looked like white horses, but right between their eyes a long pearl-colored horn stuck out.

"Are those unicorns?" asked Jasmine.

"Yes, they are. We elves believe they are the most majestic animals in all of Felnoria. It is said that if one dies, the rest lose a year off their lives."

"How long do they live?" questioned Jasmine.

"Hundreds of years, but even if one year of their life is taken away, it is a tragedy. We also believe they are the gods of the forest. They protect everything that is good in this forest and every other like it." As Lestron and Jasmine talked about the creatures, the unicorns continued grazing, knowing no harm would come from the two watching them.

"They are the most beautiful animals I've ever seen," Jasmine said in amazement as she slowly crept toward them.

Lestron noticed her curiosity and offered a gentle hint. "If you get permission from them, you might be able to pet one if you would like." Hearing that, Jasmine stopped, her face gleaming with happiness.

"How do I ask for permission?" asked Jasmine. In reply, Lestron kneeled down and stretched both his arms out as wide as he could.

"What you want to do is approach the unicorn and then bend down and stretch your arms out like I am doing now. Next, you want to look into the unicorn's eyes without blinking. If the unicorn approaches you and touches your hand with its nose, you are given permission to pet it."

"But why must I not blink?" inquired Jasmine as she tried copying Lestron's technique.

"When a unicorn looks into your eyes, they are looking into your soul to see if you are a good person or not," explained Lestron. "Blinking causes them to break their link to your soul, which could cause mixed readings."

"They can look into your soul?" Jasmine inquired, confused.

"They can, but do not worry. You will not even know they are doing it. So, would you still like to try?"

"I certainly would," replied Jasmine as she excitedly made her way toward the unicorns. Once she was a few feet away from them, she went onto her knees and spread her arms as Lestron had shown her. One of the unicorns approached her and looked down into her eyes. The breath from the unicorn's nostrils blew a few strands of her hair as she strained to keep her eyes open. The unicorn continued to look into her eyes, but the harder she thought about it, the harder it was for her to keep them open. As her eyes were closing, a voice came into her mind.

"You are of strong will, little one," spoke a voice within her head. "I have met many of your kind and you struggled to keep your eyes open harder than any I have ever met." Jasmine took a quick glance at Lestron to see if he gave any indication he heard the voice as well. "We unicorns can communicate telepathically, little one. He cannot hear me unless I wish him to hear."

Jasmine had this brilliant idea that if she tried talking to herself in her mind, the unicorn could hear her. She thought of just speaking out loud, but decided that if the unicorn talked to her through her mind it would only be courteous to do the same in return. "Can you hear me?" Jasmine thought to herself.

"Yes, I can. I am very pleased that you tried talking through your mind and not through your mouth like most do at first. You are much smarter than I thought."

"I was wondering if it would be all right if I petted you."

"Yes, you may, little one." The unicorn moved its head and brushed its nose over her left hand to give her the proper gesture. Upon getting the permission she yearned for, Jasmine rose from the forest floor and stepped to the side of the unicorn. She raised her right arm, running her hand through its mane. Though the mane looked coarse at first glance, it felt smooth and soft like rabbit's fur.

"Thank you for letting me do this," Jasmine mentally said to the unicorn while a smile shone on her face. She continued petting the unicorn until it stepped back, causing her arm to fall to her side. Taking that as a sign, Jasmine turned to leave when an idea popped into her head. She turned back toward the unicorn and asked mentally, "Also, would you by chance know where I could find some balsap herbs? My brother is hurt and Lestron needs to make an ointment out of it."

The unicorn described to her telepathically where she could find the herbs, and also sent a picture in her mind of the place, for good measure. "I hope to meet your brother sometime, but I must leave you now." The unicorn turned away from Jasmine and started galloping away, the other unicorn following closely behind.

Jasmine watched the two unicorns jump over a bush that was nearly as tall as she, then disappearing out of sight. She sat there staring into the distance, absorbing everything that had just occurred. As she stood there pondering, she felt pressure on her shoulder. She looked over and noticed Lestron's hand was there. "It seems that you were given permission," congratulated Lestron as he patted her shoulder.

"The unicorn talked to me!" Jasmine exclaimed with a large smile on her face. "It told me where we could find the herbs that we are looking for." When Lestron heard this news, a smile formed on his face, larger than that of Jasmine's.

"You are smart, Jasmine. Because of you, we will not be searching for hours looking for the herbs. If I had thought of that, I would have spoken to the unicorn myself." Pleased, Lestron patted her shoulder once again, recognizing a job well done. "You have surprised me, Jasmine, and I hope that you surprise me more as we travel together." Jasmine was elated by his kind words.

"Let us linger no longer," urged Lestron, "for we must find these herbs so we can stop the bleeding on your brother's head. Lead the way."

It didn't take long before the image the unicorn had sent her manifested itself on the forest floor. Jasmine pointed out the small patch of red plants and watched as Lestron picked enough herbs to produce the ointment they needed. With the herbs in hand, the two of them made their way back to Conrad.

On the return trip, Jasmine explained to Lestron everything she said to the unicorn. Lestron walked alongside Jasmine letting her describe everything without asking her any questions, surprised that the unicorn had talked to a human. When she reached the end of her story, Jasmine asked, "Do you mind if I run ahead and tell my brother what I did?"

"Yes, you may," replied Lestron. With Lestron's approval, she left his side and scurried off to gloat to her brother.

When Jasmine reached the fire, she realized that Conrad was fast asleep. Instead of waking him, which she knew was something he would have done to her, she turned around and waited for Lestron to emerge from the forest. The second he appeared, Jasmine raised one of her fingers to her mouth, signaling Lestron to be quiet. She then pointed down to her brother, showing Lestron that Conrad was sleeping. Lestron inched his way toward Jasmine and whispered, "With a blow to the head he shouldn't be sleeping," commented Lestron, "but you two have a long journey ahead of you so I will keep an eye on him while he gets some rest. How about you take a little nap as well. This ointment will take a few hours to prepare and it looks like you could use some rest."

Jasmine nodded her head in acknowledgment and crept toward her brother. She lay down beside him, curling into a ball before falling asleep.

Chapter 11

After a few hours of rest, Jasmine awoke. She stared at the sky and noticed that daylight was slowly fading away over the horizon. She lay on the forest floor, groaning as she stretched her arms and legs from the uncomfortable sleep. As she arose, pain resonated from every muscle in her body. The running from earlier that day was finally taking its toll. "If I feel like this now, I don't want to know how I'll feel tomorrow morning," Jasmine muttered to herself.

She tried to relieve some of the pain by shaking her arms and legs to loosen the muscles. With that not working, she lifted her upper body off the ground and started massaging her legs. With the pain nearly gone, she stopped rubbing, looked around, and realized that neither Conrad nor Lestron was there. Jasmine felt warmth radiating from the fire by her side and noticed logs had recently been placed to fuel the blaze. Knowing the guys must be close by, she turned in every direction in hopes of seeing one of them.

Once Jasmine realized neither was nearby, she left her resting place suspecting that Lestron had taken Conrad to see the unicorn. Jasmine ran into the forest until she reached the site where the unicorns had grazed earlier. She discovered they were not there either, so she traced her steps in the opposite direction. Jasmine's heart beat faster as she searched the forest for the missing travelers. The fire had just come into her view when she heard splashing noises coming from upriver. Following the noise, she made her way around a bend in the river where Lestron and Conrad were standing in the water a short distance from each other.

"What are you doing," panted Jasmine as she closed in on them, "and why do you have that stick in your hand?"

"Lestron is teaching me how to fish with a spear," Conrad responded calmly as he held out his new tool for his sister to see. The spear was a little bit longer than Conrad was tall and was simply a branch sharpened at the end. "It's a lot easier than it looks."

"Why didn't you guys wake me up when you left camp?" questioned Jasmine as she stooped to pick up a large stone from the ground.

"We thought you might need the rest," explained Conrad.

"That's no excuse to leave me alone," Jasmine retorted as she hurled the rock in Conrad's direction. The rock landed beside him, causing water to fly into the air, which soaked her target and Lestron at the same time. Lestron, not wishing to be a part of the squabble, or to get splashed again, departed upriver with his spear.

"Why did you do that?"

"Because you left me," shouted Jasmine as she reached down for another rock and prepared to hurl it.

"You left me alone earlier when you went out to get the herbs for my head," defended Conrad as he braced himself for another splash. Jasmine, realizing he had a point, threw the rock to the ground where it collided with another rock and split in half.

Reassured Jasmine wasn't going to throw any more rocks at him, he returned to his fishing. Conrad patiently stood ever so still until a black shadow came into view. Seeing his opportunity, Conrad coiled as far as he could with the spear in his right hand, as Lestron had taught. Conrad's eyes darted around, keeping pace with the black swerving shadow until it was right before him. He hesitated for one last second while holding his breath to steady his hands. Finally, he thrust down his spear as hard as he could until it pierced the sandy bottom. He withdrew the spear, revealing a fish on the end of it. "I caught one! I caught one!" squealed Conrad with glee. Jasmine sat ashore, astonished at how quickly her brother had produced a fish from the river.

Hearing Conrad's excited shrieks, Lestron made his way back to Conrad, grabbing the end of the spear that Conrad grasped. He pulled the wiggling fish off of the end of the spear and examined Conrad's catch. Pleased, Lestron stated, "We should now have enough to feed the three of us." Conrad, taking what Lestron said as a sign of a job well done, waded through the water until he was ashore. Lestron followed closely behind him.

Once ashore, Lestron placed his spear near the riverbank and walked over to a large flat rock where five other fish lay. Conrad did not need his spear any longer so he placed it next to Lestron's. Jasmine, noticing the other fish, approached Lestron. She recoiled when she saw him drawing one of his swords, and she figured it was best not to watch him kill the fish.

"I'll be back at the fire while you clean the fish," Jasmine interjected with a repulsed expression on her face.

Jasmine sat patiently near the fire as she focused on the bend in the river and waited for Lestron and Conrad to return. Her brother appeared before Lestron. Both of them held out their hands with freshly cut fish meat in each of them. Lestron placed the slippery pink meat onto a large green leaf while Conrad piled his alongside the first stack of fish.

"Jasmine, when we were in the woods together, I noticed a few raspberry bushes," noted Lestron as he pointed in the direction of the discovery as a reminder. "How about picking a few so we have a treat to eat with the fish?"

"Sure!" Jasmine said excitedly, eager to contribute to the meal. "Hey Conny, you want to help me with the berries?"

"Nope, I'm going to stick around Lestron. Maybe I'll learn some more if I watch him carefully." Conrad responded as he bent down, handing the first fish fillet to Lestron so it could be cooked over the fire.

Not wanting to ask a second time, she withdrew from the fire, perturbed by her brother's response. She walked with her face down, and her feet dragged the entire way until she entered the trees. She looked back one last time, hoping her brother was watching, but was even more upset when she noticed Conrad's back turned toward her. Convinced her little show wasn't even observed, she returned to the task at hand.

She remembered where she passed a few berry bushes on her way to find Lestron and Conrad, and she headed in that direction. She was relieved when it didn't take long to find the raspberry bush, because she was getting hungry. When she reached the bushes, she placed a few of the lush red berries into her mouth to make her hunger subside.

Her hands were not large enough to carry all the berries, so she grasped the bottom of her shirt and pulled it away from her midriff. With a homemade basket formed, she picked quickly to fill it up. When satisfied that not one more berry could be placed in her shirt, she returned to camp. A wonderful aroma of cooked fish wafted in the air and made Jasmine's mouth water.

Conrad placed the fish side-by-side upon four large leaves. There was one for each person, and the remaining one was for anyone hungry enough for seconds. Jasmine noticed an empty leaf near the others, and fell to her knees over it and dumped the berries from her shirt. The berries tumbled, with most landing on their intended destination. Jasmine was so famished she forgot her manners when she reached over and grabbed one of the leaves of fish with one hand while grabbing a handful of berries with the other. She plopped herself by the fire and immediately began to eat. The two men followed her lead and took a leaf of fish and berries before joining Jasmine by the fire. They kept to themselves as they feasted and saved conversation for later.

"That was a fantastic meal," said Jasmine as she patted her stomach. "I've never tasted fish this good. I don't think even Mom makes it this good." As Jasmine stretched, she noticed Lestron piling branches and logs a few feet from the fire.

"Why are you placing our spare wood so far from the fire?" questioned Jasmine.

"I'm making another fire," responded Lestron as he started placing the branches in a teepee formation.

"Why do we need two fires?" asked Jasmine.

"It is getting late so we must spend the night here," explained Lestron as Conrad appeared from the trees with a clump of dried grass in his arms. "I also want to make sure you and Conrad watched how I make the fire, because you might need this skill in the future."

Conrad knelt by the teepee of wood and tucked the dried grass in the open spaces. "I will keep watch throughout the night," explained Lestron. "I am not setting this spare fire just for training. It is always wise to have two fires. They deter intruders and wild beasts. Hopefully, two fires will make it seem like there are more camping out then we really have."

"Uh, Conrad, did you tell Lestron that I'm not a fan of camping out?" asked Jasmine with a grimace.

"You bet, I told him you were a wuss, but we are pretty far from home, so you'll have to deal with it," snapped Conrad. She reluctantly accepted the truth of what he said and occupied her time by watching Lestron start the fire.

Once Lestron was satisfied with the arrangement of branches and grass, he poured two rocks out of a leather pouch that lay beside him. They appeared to be two ordinary rocks like those found on any beach.

He continuously struck the rocks together next to the dried grass until tiny sparks began to fly. After what seemed like a lifetime to Jasmine, the grass caught on fire and smoke finally started to fill the air. Lestron quickly dropped the two stones into the pouch when the smoke appeared. He then placed his face close to the source of the smoke and carefully blew small puffs until a small flicker of light ignited inside the fire teepee. All three watched quietly as the faint spark transformed into a flame.

"Tomorrow we are going to have to leave here and resume our trek to our destination. I do not wish to stay around any longer than necessary in case the trolls are still chasing us," stated Lestron.

"Are you ready yet to tell us where we are headed?" asked Jasmine.

"You will learn in due time," replied Lestron. "We were very close when we were crossing the river, but we washed off course. We have a lot of backtracking to do. We also have a decision to make, which we will discuss tomorrow morning. Now that the fire is lit, I believe you two should go to sleep. We have a long trip tomorrow and I want you both well rested. I will wake you when the sun rises."

Conrad and Jasmine ambled to the first fire, and curled up on the hard ground, where they had rested earlier. Neither of them made it more than five minutes before they were in dreamland. As they slept, Lestron kept watch near the second fire until the first rays of light shone over the tree tops.

Chapter 12

At daylight, Lestron approached Jasmine and Conrad in order to wake them and was startled when Jasmine suddenly began to thrash around in her sleep. Her movements became wilder as he got closer. They escalated to the point where she began to scream at the top of her lungs. Concerned, he ran up to her, dropped to his knees, and began to shake her. "Wake up, Jasmine!" Lestron shouted, but with no success.

"What's the matter?" Conrad moaned as Jasmine's screaming finally woke him up.

"I am not sure. I was just coming over to wake you two when she started screaming in her sleep."

"Not to worry. She does this all the time when we're on camping trips," explained Conrad, wincing at the soreness from sleeping on the ground. He put his sore muscles on the back burner and made his way to Jasmine. He bent down and gently shook Jasmine while softly saying her name.

Jasmine's eyes shot open and her head moved back and forth as she tried to get her bearings. When she realized where she was, it was apparent her dream was real. She lifted her right hand to her head and wiped the sweat from her brow. She jumped up from the ground, not caring what Lestron and Conrad were thinking about her at that moment. She ran behind the closest tree, wrapped her arms around the trunk, and began sobbing.

"Should we do something?" inquired a concerned Lestron.

"No, she just needs to be by herself for a while," responded Conrad with little concern on his face; he had dealt with these circumstances in the past.

Letting her be, Lestron and Conrad occupied themselves with extinguishing the two fires. They had no way to carry water to the fire, so they threw handfuls of sand onto the embers until both fires were snuffed out. As the last embers died, Jasmine appeared from behind the tree. Her cheeks were flushed and her eyes were swollen from crying.

"I'm sorry," said Jasmine. She wiped away the last of the tears that lingered on her face.

"There is no need to apologize. You have been through a lot in the last twenty-four hours," consoled Lestron. Jasmine, craving a little comfort, sidled up to Conrad with her arm touching his. She wished her mother were there to comfort her, but that wasn't an option at the moment. Conrad sensed what she was thinking and placed an arm around her waist.

Once Lestron noticed Jasmine had calmed herself, he positioned himself so he was facing both of them. "We need to choose which of two paths to take. We were lucky enough to come ashore on the other side of the river, so we will not have to cross again. We can either go back upriver following the water," Lestron explained as he pointed in the direction of the river, "or we can go through the forest," pointing to the trees in a completely different direction.

"What's the difference between following the water and going through the forest?" questioned Conrad.

"Going upriver may result in running into the trolls that have been following us, if they are still on our trail. I am assuming they lost our tracks once we were washed away, but then again, they might have thought we went into the water to try to lose them. There's a possibility they could still be tracking us. If we run into them again, I do not know what the outcome will be. No offense, but I can run much faster than either of you and I can barely outdistance them when alone. Our second option is the forest, but it is equally dangerous. The route we will need to take leads us to where a nest of giant wood spiders once existed."

"I'm not scared of spiders," interrupted Conrad as he stood tall.

"Well, I sure am," shivered Jasmine. "You know I'm deathly afraid of spiders, Conny."

"We can take care of a few measly spiders," Conrad said proudly.

"These are not the normal spiders you are thinking about, Conrad. These spiders are larger than the bears that live in this forest. They hunt and kill anybody who intrudes upon their domain."

Jasmine cringed when she heard how large the spiders were and clung to her brother's arm.

Conrad took it in stride, thinking to himself, "Everything else is messed up here, why not the spiders, too?"

"So why don't we go upriver and take our chances?" implored Jasmine with no desire to tangle with spiders, much less giant ones.

"The reason I presented both routes is because we know it is likely the trolls are somewhere upriver," Lestron explained while both of them nodded their understanding. "Even though there may be spiders in the forest, I mentioned that option because I have not heard much about them in years; they may have moved on." Jasmine pushed herself away from Conrad and shook her head in disagreement, still not wanting to risk a meeting with the eight-legged predators.

"I truly believe the forest is a safer route, because it's less likely we will encounter trolls. We will have a better chance of making it alive. We may just have a delightful walk through the forest if we do not follow the river," encouraged Lestron, sounding confident about the forest journey until he added, "but, then again, I could be wrong."

"I vote walking back upriver," elected Jasmine as she raised her right arm.

"Well, I'm with Lestron, I say we take the forest," argued Conrad.

"But what if we run into the giant spiders?" Jasmine trembled.

"What if we run into the trolls?" countered Conrad. "Lestron said he believes the forest is safer and I believe him. Plus, Lestron can protect us from pesky spiders," Conrad defended as Lestron nodded his head in agreement.

"Fine, but if we see those spiders, you need to promise me we will turn around and head back the other way," Jasmine compromised as she looked from one to the other. "You must *swear* that we will turn around."

"I swear," both agreed in unison.

Chapter 13

The route was established, but another issue had to be addressed. Lestron knew the importance of all three of them being armed during the journey. He turned away from them without saying anything and headed upriver. "Where you going?" asked Conrad.

"Just wait here and I will be right back," Lestron called without looking back. Lestron rounded the bend in the river and disappeared from their view. Once he reached where they fished the day before, he found the two spears that were still on the riverbank. He picked them up and looked them over quickly to make sure they were appropriate for the idea he had. Satisfied, he turned back toward the camp with both spears in hand.

When they saw Lestron rounding the bend, they ran to meet him halfway. He hoisted the spears in the air, showing them why he had left so suddenly. Lestron handed one of the spears to each of them. "Make sure to hold onto these at all times. There is a good chance you will need to use them."

"But you said we could run away if we see the giant spiders," stated Jasmine as she fumbled awkwardly with the makeshift spear. Conrad, however, swung his weapon around, getting the feel of spearing motion.

"The spears are just a precaution, in case something unforeseeable goes wrong," explained Lestron. "Any other questions?" He stared at the two waiting for either to speak. When no response came he continued, "Are we ready to go then?"

"Yup," Conrad eagerly said as he thrust his spear into the air. Jasmine just nodded her head unenthusiastically, unhappy knowing that she was outvoted.

Lestron led the way with Conrad just behind and Jasmine dragging her feet as she followed. They were not far into the forest when Jasmine remembered she had never told Conrad about the unicorn she had met the day before. Hoping to make her brother jealous, Jasmine stopped dragging her feet and ran to her brother. Jasmine started rattling away about the unicorn she met the day before.

Not believing a word out of her mouth, he asked, "Lestron, she's lying, right?"

"She is telling the truth, Conrad. If we had not met the unicorns, we still might be looking for the balsap herbs." Once Lestron confirmed the story, Conrad was more intent upon hearing the remainder of the story. Jasmine was reluctant to resume her story since her brother hadn't believed her at first, but his apparent jealously spurred her to continue.

As she was finishing her story, both paid no attention to their surroundings. Lestron suddenly drew both his swords, startling them. Conrad and Jasmine followed suit and grabbed their spears in anticipation of danger. Lestron scanned all directions and positioned in a defensive stance and whispered, "Shhh." Jasmine heard rustling noises coming from the bushes to her right. Lestron glimpsed the bushes moving. On instinct, Lestron dashed back to Jasmine and Conrad to protect them. However, before he could reach them, a chipmunk darted from the undergrowth. Lestron stopped suddenly and let out a sigh of relief and sheathed his sword.

In a matter of moments, dozens of chipmunks emerged from the bushes following the lead chipmunk. They were marching single file. Jasmine and Conrad were amazed at what they were witnessing. When the last of the chipmunks were out of the bushes, the head chipmunk shouted a sing-song chant. "I don't know what you've been told," and the marchers hollered, "Rat meat's better by the load. March on. March. One two three four."

Jasmine couldn't control her curiosity about where they were going. She rushed over to the commander chipmunk. "Where are you headed?" questioned Jasmine. The lead chipmunk stopped and stood on his hind legs, using his fuzzy tail to keep his balance.

"Company, halt!" shouted the chipmunk as the little army ceased marching, some running into each other before coming to a complete stop. "We are going to meet our brethren in the Worling Clearing, young miss."

"Where is the Worling Clearing?" asked Jasmine.

"In the eastern part of the Trilaz Woods. All chipmunks in the woods are uniting to ward off the rats that have plagued our land. They have doomed us to starvation if we don't do something."

"Is there anything I can do to help you?" asked Jasmine with a concerned look on her face.

"No, this is our fight. We must muster all the strength and courage we can to deal with those rats ourselves. I'm sorry, young miss, but you have taken too much of our valuable time. We must be on our way."

"Good luck," Jasmine said encouragingly. The head chipmunk jumped back up on his hind legs.

"Company, march!"

Jasmine smiled while waving good-bye to the chipmunks as they marched by. She continued watching until the last of them rounded a tree and disappeared out of sight. The last thing she heard before turning back toward her brother was a faint "Rat meat's better by the load." With a grin still on her face, she turned around and skipped back to her sibling.

"What was that all about?" questioned Conrad.

"A group of the chipmunks is marching to Worling Clearing to fight some rats, I think. I would assume it has something to do with the group we saw yesterday."

Conrad shook his head, noting, "This place is strange. Every time I think I've seen and heard everything, something else weird happens. This surely is not like home, Jas."

Chapter 14

Conrad noticed the trees were gradually becoming sparse the farther they ran into the forest. The wider spaces between trees made it easier for Conrad and Jasmine to run alongside each other. Lestron was running ahead of the pair when he stopped suddenly. He turned to wait for them. When they caught up with him, he gave them a minute to catch their breath. Both Conrad and Jasmine were hunched over, breathing heavily from the continuous running. They realized neither of them was in shape for the demands Lestron placed on them. It didn't help that their bodies still ached from the rigorous trek the previous day. When Lestron was satisfied he would have their undivided attention, he began to talk.

"We are nearing where the spiders could be lurking, so we need to be much more wary from this point on. If we do get attacked by any of them without a chance to escape, make sure to aim your spears at their underbellies. When a spider attacks, it will raise its front legs, leaving itself vulnerable for a second. There will be a small purple circle near its stomach. Think of it as a bulls-eye." Jasmine and Conrad nodded their heads in understanding, but Jasmine began shaking from the realization that giant spiders could be around any bend.

Lestron turned around after informing them about the spiders and began to creep slowly through the woods. Conrad followed closely behind Lestron while Jasmine kept mere inches from Conrad. She trembled with each step and jumped at every thud, rustle, or snap from within the woods. Lestron constantly searched for any clues of spiders. He checked each tree they passed for spider webs or carcasses that might have been hanging from the tree branches.

Conrad helped the best he could by also searching the trees. Jasmine, on the other hand, was too scared to do anything but follow her brother's lead. Every once in awhile, Jasmine swore she heard scuffling in the distance, but when she looked around there wasn't anything there.

At one point, the ground started to feel soft under their feet in certain places, like walking on moss. A minute after they stepped off the mossy ground, Jasmine claimed she heard the same scuffling noise again. She looked back to find the source of the noise, when she was suddenly halted by her body hitting something solid. When her head spun forward, she found she hit her brother.

"Why did you—" is all she uttered before her mouth dropped, too paralyzed to say another word.

Right in the middle of their path, was the largest, ugliest brown spider imaginable about ten feet from the group, staring at them from what seemed like a million different eyes. Each of its eight fuzzy legs bent at an angle and rose to a height taller than any of them. Poisonous saliva ran from its mouth where razor sharp pinchers protruded on each side. The pinchers snapped open and closed repeatedly, making a horrific clicking noise each time. Barely visible from the front, a stinger about the size of one of Lestron's swords protruded from the back end of the spider.

"Now would be the time to retreat," urged Lestron in a soft voice as he and Conrad turned to Jasmine. Jasmine stood in total shock, as if frozen. She could not take her eyes off the spider and did not respond to Lestron. He shook her by the shoulders in an attempt to bring her to her senses. "We have to leave, Jasmine!" Jasmine stared with a blank look on her face, as she offered a slight nod indicating she heard him. Lestron glanced past Jasmine and realized escape wouldn't be an option any longer after he saw what was behind.

Three identical holes had been formed in the mossy ground. In front of the holes, three huge spiders blocked the only escape route. "Do as I tell you!" Lestron ordered as he pulled out his swords. "Do you understand me?" Lestron growled through clenched teeth as he planned a strategy.

"Yes," Conrad acknowledged as he gripped his spear harder.

"I'm scared," trembling Jasmine whined. Tears ran down her face. "I don't want to die!"

"Jasmine, just stay behind me and do what I say," Lestron stressed. "Make sure not to drop your spear and don't hesitate to use it." Jasmine focused and moved directly behind Lestron, who announced, "We are going to attack that lone spider first. If we can take it down quickly, we will not be boxed in."

Lestron turned and faced the menacing spider. Conrad slipped to Lestron's side, pointing his spear at the spider while Jasmine eased around in order to get behind her brother. She shot a fast glance behind her to make sure the other three spiders remained where they were. All three arachnids were where they had been and appeared to be anticipating the trapped prey's next move. Lestron cried out, "Follow my lead!" as he charged the spider, with swords aimed straight forward. Conrad and Jasmine were close behind.

The second before Lestron advanced on the spider, the big hairy thing lowered its back legs, similar to a cat readying itself to pounce on its prey. The spider lunged at Lestron, but the clever elf anticipated the attack and sidestepped at the last possible moment. He thrust a sword to his side as he ran past the spider, slicing off all four legs on the spider's left side. With no support on its left, the spider's body toppled onto its side, exposing its soft abdomen to Conrad. Conrad took advantage of the opportunity and plunged his spear directly into the center of the purple circle on its underbelly. Yellowish liquid sprayed out of the wound and the spider's legs quivered before it died.

Conrad was amazed at his prowess and abandoned his spear as he gloated. He did not drop his guard for long once he remembered there were three more enemies to face. His spear slowly disappeared as the corpse began to roll back onto its abdomen. With great effort, he jerked his spear and yanked it out before the spider's carcass could envelope it. The whole thing happened so quickly. The fight was over before Jasmine could respond.

With the first enemy dispatched, all three quickly spun around to face the remaining three spiders. The spiders weren't waiting around any longer. In fact, they were poised to attack after witnessing one of their own perish. They wanted revenge. Not having much of a choice, the party stood side-by-side, bracing themselves for the attack. Lestron was in the center with his swords ready while Conrad proudly extended his spear with confidence gained from having downed one already. Jasmine timidly extended her spear, but still had no desire to fight.

Lestron braced himself as the spider in front of him positioned for attack as the first spider had. This time, however, Lestron decided sidestepping was out of the question. He fell onto his back when the spider lunged at him. As the spider passed over him, he raised his swords, inflicting two large slashes across the spider's underbelly. The spider flew over Lestron and landed ten feet from him. The spider's legs shuddered trying to get back up, while letting out an ear-piercing squeal. With no fight left in it, the spider collapsed, never to rise again. Two lines of yellow blood ran from the spider's body and stopped where Lestron lay, covered in the fluid.

Conrad had a much harder time with his second opponent. Each time he thrust his spear at the creature's body, the spider parried using one of its eight legs. He continued jabbing until he finally came to the realization that he needed a different strategy. He gripped the end of the spear and heaved it at the spider's mouth. The spear missed the target, grazing the side of the spider's face. As he started pulling back the spear, the spider's pinchers clamped together, catching the spear before Conrad could react. The point of the spear snapped like a twig while the other end was snatched from Conrad's grip.

Jasmine was having an even more difficult time than Conrad fending off her spider. Having no prior experience with a spear, she thrust her spear without aiming for anything in particular. The thrusting technique wasn't effective, so she opted for a more familiar position. She now held the spear like a bat and swung it against the spider's leg, not thinking at the moment that it had seven more legs to keep it upright.

Lestron lifted himself off the ground and saw Jasmine and Conrad fighting the two remaining spiders. Both were struggling to keep their spiders at bay, but when he saw that Conrad had lost his spear he knew who needed help first. With the spider busy with Conrad, Lestron ambushed the spider and dove to the ground as a leg passed over him. At the opportune time, he jumped to his feet and centered himself behind the spider. He raised one of his swords and hacked the spider's stinger from its body, causing the spider to let out a horrible screeching noise that was deafening. The attack was enough to cause the spider to lose interest in Conrad.

Before the spider could face its new adversary, Lestron leaped onto the backside of the spider. The spider felt Lestron's landing and bucked like a bronco. Not wishing to be flung off, he crouched down and held onto small clumps of hair on the spider's back. As Lestron rode the spider, he raised his left sword up into the air as he got a feel for the bucking pattern. Lestron thrust the sword downward and plunged it into the spider's back. On impact he knew he hit something vital. The spider fell instantly to the ground, lifeless.

While Lestron was slaying his foe, Jasmine stepped back to dodge an oncoming leg from her challenger. While retreating, she lost her footing because she stepped into a hollow. The sudden change in height caused her to lose her balance and fall backwards. Her whole body landed in the hole. The spider seized the opportunity and jumped into the air to crush her. With split-second thinking, she raised her spear into the air. Before the spider landed, it impaled itself upon the raised point. Jasmine screamed as the spider's body slid down the spear and covered her body with gooey ooze.

Lestron and Conrad witnessed Jasmine's fall into the nearby hollow. They rushed to come to her aid, but could only watch as the spider landed on top of her. Together, with shoulders lowered, they charged at the spider's body and hit it dead on. The impact was great enough to roll the spider, revealing a goo-covered Jasmine. Lestron dove to his knees and placed his ear next to her mouth in an attempt to hear her breathing. As Lestron was bent over her, Conrad observed blood covering the bottom half of her left leg.

"Sh...sh...she's bleeding," stuttered Conrad as he pointed to her leg.

Lestron detected shallow breathing and exclaimed, "She's alive!" He then turned his attention to a gash from which blood was flowing. Lestron momentarily took his eyes off the cut and looked over to the dead spider that lay next to them. Blood trickled down the tip of the spider's stinger.

"We need to get her to the elf village as soon as we can!" exclaimed Lestron as he examined her leg more thoroughly. At last, Conrad realized where they had been headed the entire time and he willingly agreed to the plan. "The poison these spiders' inflict can kill her in a few hours if she does not receive the right kind of treatment."

Lestron grabbed onto the top of his shirt, and ripped off the sleeve. He made a makeshift tourniquet and tied it around Jasmine's leg. He knew her bleeding was not the problem, but he wanted to slow the poison from traveling inside her. Unable to do more for her in the forest, he lifted her into his arms. "We must hurry, for time is not our friend," Lestron remarked as he started to run. Conrad was in shock that his sister might die. He ran alongside Lestron, overwhelmed by what had transpired in a matter of minutes. Nevertheless, he forced himself to keep up with Lestron.

Chapter 15

Deep inside the Thundering Mountains, a group of trolls was returning from the Trilaz Woods. Thick brown-leather chest armor and bracers covered all but one of the trolls, and scars from previous battles were proudly displayed on all of them. Their eyes reflected disappointment because they had been unsuccessful in fulfilling their orders. Uzgal had sent them to capture an elf who was a diplomat for the elf community. The troll scouts had spotted their subject but had lost track of the elf near a river. They knew Uzgal wasn't going to be happy with them, and each of them prayed that the punishment wouldn't be too severe.

Inside the strategy room, Uzgal stood at a large wooden table. The table was placed in the center of a large cave, so all of Uzgal's advisors and generals could circle around it. The cave itself was designed so no moisture could find its way through the cracks in the wall and ruin any of the important documents that were aligned on shelves throughout the room. A map that depicted the entirety of Felnoria was spread on the table. Uzgal's advisor had small stone figures placed on strategic locations across the map. Names of human villages that were now controlled by the trolls lay under each figurine. Next to Uzgal was his strategic advisor, contemplating the map for their next conquest.

"I believe taking Yiorling would be best for us," commented the strategic advisor as he reached across the table and grabbed a statuette from the side of the map and placed it where "Yiorling" was written. "That way, we would have all of the southern regions of Felnoria and could easily make our way to Yarlanzia without disturbing the elves or dwarves."

"Yes, but I wish to rid this world not only of humans but of dwarves and elves as well. I want all the land in Felnoria to be mine," grumbled

Uzgal as he circled the table, examining the map for more places to conquer. "But I see your point in taking Yiorling next. The only problem is that Yiorling is the second-largest human city in Felnoria. It would be a great test for us, but taking it would definitely cripple human civilization for a long time."

Uzgal reached down with his right hand to where he kept a dagger strapped to his leg at all times. He yanked it out of its sheath and flipped it around in his hand. He then raised the dagger and thrust it into the map, splitting the wood underneath. On one side of the dagger, the map read "Yar" and on the other, "Ianzia."

"Find out how many goblins and trolls we have available to begin this invasion. Also, go down to the forges and get them working overtime to stockpile more weapons," Uzgal demanded as a sneer grew on his face with the happy thought of slaying more humans.

"Yes, Master," obeyed the advisor as he bowed down. Knowing he wasn't needed anymore, he left Uzgal to daydream about human massacres.

Satisfied with the meeting, Uzgal readied himself to leave when one of his guards entered the room. "Master, Second in Command Quilzar is here to see you."

"Send him in," Uzgal responded.

Quilzar entered the room with a large sword strapped to his back. The sword's hilt stuck out over his head and the tip of the sword almost dragged on the ground. Usually only giants would carry such a weapon, but Quilzar was no ordinary troll. He could easily lift five times more than any other of his kind. A fellow troll once said about the sword, "If you ever see his sword pointed at you, that will be the last thing you will ever see."

He never wore chest armor because he believed it restrained his movement in battle. Thus, dozens of scars crisscrossed his chest. Other than his sword, a tattered, blood-stained loincloth was the only covering on his enormous body.

Quilzar scanned the room before approaching Uzgal, instinctively checking for any possible dangers before proceeding. Once before Uzgal, he bowed down until his nose touched the ground. "Forgive me, sir, but we were not able to capture the elf."

"How could that be? You had a simple task of catching one stupid elf and you couldn't even do that!" shouted Uzgal as he approached a tray of meat. He grabbed a raw slab of meat from the tray and stuffed it into his oversized mouth.

"We almost had him, sir. We were on his tail until we entered a field and two human children were there waiting for him."

Shocked by hearing the word "human," Uzgal spit out the meat and approached Quilzar. "Where exactly did this occur?"

"We were in the Trilaz Woods when it happened. We came to a clearing and saw the elf running with the two humans next to him."

"Morlok recently had a premonition that two humans had just arrived in Felnoria to rid the land of everything we had accomplished over the last ten years," explained Uzgal. "Can you describe to me what the humans looked like so I can check if Morlok's premonition was correct?"

"Other than one was male and the other female, and they are not full grown, none of us got a good enough look at them to describe more. I am sorry, Master. The female spotted us, but she was too far away for us to notice anything specific." Uzgal shook his head, not pleased by what he was hearing. "And Master, I humbly ask how one can believe anything Morlok says. Every premonition ends up the same. We spend much time and effort on wild goose chases with no success because his visions are never real."

"You are correct in that matter, but considering your sighting coincides with his premonition, I really can't brush off this one. I'm already getting a head count on our available soldiers, and the forgers have just been informed to make more weapons. I will discuss this matter with Morlok if he hasn't yet rotted away in his cell."

"What are we attacking now, Master?" questioned Quilzar.

Uzgal felt the strategies would be easier to conceptualize if Quilzar saw the plans on the map. He led his second in command to the table.

"We are going to attack Yiorling and lay it to ruins," explained Uzgal as he pointed at the newly placed stone figure. "That way, Yarlanzia will not have reinforcements when we attack them. We must crush Yiorling and find those humans before they reach Yarlanzia," Uzgal snarled as he perused the map.

"I need you to gather up twenty of your strongest men to accompany you to the Trilaz Woods," explained Uzgal. He then pulled the dagger out of the map, leaving a slit in its place. He used the dagger as a pointer and placed the tip where "The Trilaz Woods" was written. "You are to capture the children and take them to Yiorling where I will be waiting for you," Uzgal commanded as he moved the dagger across the map and stopped next to the slit. "We will have it destroyed by the time you arrive."

Chapter 16

Inside the throne room of Yarlanzia, Ralph and Synthia were seated as they patiently listened to a villager's problem.

"How am I supposed to keep my sheep alive if wolves keep coming down from the Soaring Cliffs and killing them?" queried a villager in tattered clothes. In addition to the worn garb, he looked and smelled like he hadn't bathed in weeks. "I thought the dwarves were supposed to keep the packs controlled so they wouldn't kill our animals."

"The dwarves may have problems of their own at the moment," replied Ralph. Ralph sat quietly pondering what would satisfy the villager before continuing. "We will replace half of your lost livestock and send a group of soldiers to the Soaring Cliffs to thin the packs ourselves."

It was obvious to Ralph and Synthia the villager wished to protest receiving only half of what he lost, but they knew he wouldn't openly complain. Once the villager reconsidered the proposition, he got on one knee and said, "Thank you, Your Highness."

Nearby, a guard stood watch over the proceedings with a hand near his weapon, in case anything went amiss. The guard saw the villager drop to one knee, and realized the shepherd was pleased by the king's gift. The guard stepped forward and escorted the villager out of the room. The guard returned and announced, "There is only one more person waiting to have an audience with Your Highnesses."

"Very well, please present the petitioner," consented Ralph. "Could you then inform Captain Kadon that I wish to speak with him?"

"Yes, Your Highness," the guard replied, before exiting the room. Ralph and Synthia discussed the issues of the day as they waited for their last guest to enter the room. Both of them seemed eager for the day to end. Out of all of the duties they performed for Yarlanzia, this always seemed the most challenging. Once each week, villagers from all around Felnoria could request an audience with the king and queen. These villagers consistently arrived with tales of despair and loss. The royals then had to right the wrongs in the villagers' lives. Some issues were simple, such as replacing dead livestock or lowering taxes; but on rare occasions, the villagers demanded things that were far beyond the king and queen's realm. Some believed the royalty possessed magical powers, and they wanted them to bring back dead loved ones or to magically erect a new village after their previous one was burnt down. These villagers could not believe the king and queen were unable to comply with their request. On these instances, the guard who kept watch over the proceedings usually had to forcefully remove the enraged villager out of the throne room. Synthia was always hurt when this happened, but she also understood that they could not please everyone.

As Ralph and Synthia discussed what do to about the wolves, the last petitioner—one of Synthia's chambermaids—entered the room. She approached the king and queen, bent on one knee, and greeted them. Returned to standing position, she reached into her draped garb and pulled out a worn book.

"I have done what you requested and found the last time we were visited by either elf or dwarf." She flipped through the pages until she found the page for which she was looking. "By our records, an elf by the name of Lestron was the last to visit. You may recall he serves as a diplomat between us and the elves." Scanning for more information, the chambermaid ran her finger down the lines in the book until she stopped suddenly. "It also says here that it was around a month ago when he last visited."

Hearing that, both Synthia and Ralph tried thinking back a month. They strained to remember any elf they might have seen. They had many responsibilities, so it wasn't shocking to either of them that they didn't remember. "I don't recall seeing any elf recently," remarked Synthia as she looked at Ralph. "How about you, Ralph?"

Ralph popped out of his trance once he heard his name and answered, "I don't have any recollection of any elves either."

"If memory serves me, that was when Your Highnesses were in Yiorling evaluating their defenses," stated the chambermaid as she leafed through the pages for proof of her speculation.

"Do we know anything else about Lestron?" asked Synthia.

"Other than his residence in Fos Faydian, that is all that is recorded."

"Fos Faydian is located in the Trilaz Woods," pondered Ralph.

"That is correct," responded the chambermaid as she closed the book.

"I would like you to search through that book of yours and see if Lestron's name pops up anywhere else, and notify us if you locate any more information on Fos Faydian," directed Synthia.

"I shall, Your Highness." The chambermaid bowed in response to the request.

"That will be all." Synthia dismissed her as the guard returned to the room to escort her out.

"Captain Kadon is here to see you," announced the guard before walking the chambermaid out of the room.

"Please send him in," responded Ralph.

Kadon knelt on one knee once he was in front of the steps leading to the thrones, then rose. "You beckoned me, Your Highnesses?"

"Synthia and I have discussed what we should do about these children." Ralph glanced at his sister and then at Kadon. "We wish for you to form two more parties."

"Why two, sire?" Kadon said confusingly.

"I wish for one led by you to march to the Trilaz Woods to locate the children. We believe they might be in Fos Faydian because we have received information that an elf helped them when they first arrived."

"But elf villages are hidden from the outside world. It is common knowledge that humans are not allowed in their villages," confirmed Kadon.

"Yes, but they may also be wandering the forest or heading this way at this very moment. I would like you to take ten of your best men with you. When you find the children, escort them directly here."

"For the second party, it has come to our attention recently that the dwarves are not taking care of the wolves in the Soaring Cliffs. I would like you to assign five of your finest hunters for this mission. Have them meet with me prior to their dispatch."

"Is there anything else?"

"Yes, I wish to lead that group of hunters," explained Ralph. Synthia shot a surprised look at Ralph.

"We never discussed this!" snapped Synthia. "You are not as young as you used to be. Why do you wish to go along with them?"

Ralph faced Synthia while clasping her hand to calm her. "While we are in the cliffs, I can meet with the dwarves to find out why they haven't been dealing with the wolves," Ralph explained.

"But can't you send someone else?" pleaded Synthia.

"No, I haven't been hunting in a long time, and I also want to see if the dwarves will help with our predicament with the trolls. You know as well as I do that the dwarves usually don't like dealing with humans, and that you and I are exceptions." Synthia knew she wasn't going to be able to win the discussion, so she pulled her hand away from her brother's, still displeased by his decision.

Kadon stood in silence as his king and queen quibbled over the situation. When Synthia quieted, Kadon continued. "I will send the men to you as soon as possible. When do you plan for us to leave?"

Ralph turned away from his sister's sad eyes and looked down at Kadon, "We will leave in a few days when all the preparations are complete. Prepare two extra horses to take along for the children to ride when you find them."

"Is there anything else you wish?" Kadon implored as he looked back and forth between the two rulers.

"That will be all, Kadon. I will come to you personally when it is time to leave. Spend some quality time with your family and I will meet you at your home."

Kadon bowed and arose with a large smile on his face, pleased by his king's request. As he walked out of the throne room, he envisioned the things he would do with his family over the next few precious days.

Chapter 17

Jasmine opened her eyes, but all she could see was black. She raised her hands to her eyes and rubbed them in hopes that it would cure the blindness. When she pulled her hands away, everything was just as dark as before. She squinted her eyes, but no matter how hard she tried, she couldn't see anything. She spun around in circles, trying to find any glimpse of light, but in every direction all she saw was nothingness.

"What's going on? Am I dreaming?" Jasmine asked herself, as panic was setting in. "Where am I?" she screamed. "Why can't I see anything?" Jasmine continued screaming until her throat was raw and her voice cracked. Exhausted from screaming, she extended both of her arms, feeling for any object that might be near. She flailed her arms but encountered only open space all around her. She pivoted her body in hopes of finding anything. Then, she took a step forward, and still found nothing. She dared a few more steps, each as unsuccessful as the last in finding anything to hold onto. The more daring she became, the more she felt like she was standing in a complete void.

Suddenly, soft scuffling noises surrounded Jasmine. The sounds seemed to be getting closer and louder. Jasmine turned each way in hopes her vision would return and she could see what was approaching. "What's going on!" shrieked Jasmine. As she screamed, all the rustling noises ceased except for one immediately behind her. Her body trembled and she was too terrified to turn around.

"You will be my supper tonight, human," a voice rasped behind her. Jasmine jumped and spun around quickly and still only saw darkness.

"Who are you," the trembling girl demanded. "Oh, why can't I see you?"

"You see only nothingness because your mind is lost from the rest of your body," the voice responded.

Jasmine moved her hands over her body, and found she could still feel everything. "But my body is here. I don't understand what you mean!"

"Your body is present, but in the conscious world, your mind has been separated from it. You will be lost in limbo until your mind finds its body or you die in the conscious world," the voice responded, followed by a horrific laugh.

"You're not making sense."

"But I am, human. I poisoned you before you killed me and now your body wants to die, but your mind is resisting" Not understanding how a spider, let alone a dead one, was speaking to her, she crouched down and put her arms around her legs and rocked herself back and forth. Her shaking became uncontrollable.

"You are lying," Jasmine denied as she started crying.

"What reason do I have to lie to you?"

"This is just a dream. That's all it is!" shouted Jasmine.

"This is no dream, but I must tell you I have a confession to make."

"Wha...what?" she stuttered.

"I am here to drive you mad."

"What would posses you to do that?" questioned Jasmine. The response was accompanied by a wild, sinister laugh.

"Because, human, the more insane you are, the harder it is for your mind to reunite with your body. There are only two ways for your mind to find its way back. One is for you to find it through all of this blackness, which I doubt will happen, and the second I do not wish to tell you."

"But I can't see anything."

"That's what makes this so fun," the spider's voice crackled with laughter. "How about you run along now so I can chase down my food. Having you just stand here without putting up even the slightest fight bores me to death."

"P...Please, what's the second way. How do you expect me to run, I can't even see my hands when I put them in front of my face. Just tell me, please!"

"Enough of this stupid nonsense." Suddenly, what sounded like breaking bones but actually was the spider cracking its jaw, resonated from behind Jasmine. The sudden horrific sound made Jasmine's hair stand up on the back of her neck. She let out the largest screech that her dry throat would allow before running for her life.

With her mind racing, she couldn't think clearly. Her body bounced off unseen objects almost like a pinball making its way around a table. Many times her legs were tripped up by debris on the ground. She would tumble to the ground, but quickly stood back up and started running again. If Jasmine slowed down for more than a few seconds, the spider would crack its jaw again, reminding her that she wasn't safe here.

Jasmine ran on for what felt like a lifetime. Her legs were exhausted, her body was banged up and bruised, and her lungs burned from all the heavy breathing. All she wanted was to be back home with Mom, Dad, and Conrad. Everything that Conrad had done to her over her lifetime was nothing compared to what pain and suffering she was feeling at the moment.

Suddenly, another object tripped her and she tumbled to the ground. This time her arms couldn't do what they had done so many times in the past. The weight of her body was just too much and she collapsed back to the ground before her legs could support her.

With not much left in her, Jasmine curled into a ball and started weeping out of control. She didn't have any fight left, and she waited for the inevitable. She waited for the attack, but it never came.

Confused and frustrated, her mind couldn't handle it any longer. She cracked under all the stress and started flailing her body uncontrollably. Small objects flew in every direction as her limbs hit them. As her hands thrust around, she grabbed onto something and threw it in no particular location.

"Make another noise so I can hit you," shouted Jasmine. Not waiting for a sound to come, she continued grabbing anything she could get her hands on and throwing it all into the darkness.

"This is more entertaining than I ever expected from a little, fragile girl like you," teased the spider.

Jasmine threw in the direction of the voice but the spider had already circled around her before the object could hit its target. "This is so much fun," the voice said from behind her.

"Light things up and how about we make this a fair fight," demanded Jasmine. "Or are you a chicken? What fun is playing with your food if you don't even give it a fair chance to defend itself? Is it because you think I will kill you, again?" Out of all this nonsense, Jasmine somehow caught herself chuckling at her last statement.

"You don't frighten me, Little One. This place doesn't create light," explained the spider. "Only someone alive can shine light in this world and I doubt there is anyone alive that cares enough about you."

Jasmine thought about it for a second and realized that the spider was probably right. The only person who knew what world she was even in was Conrad. If the spider was telling the truth, she really doubted he cared enough about her to shine even the faintest of lights.

"Fine, get this over with so I can die already," shouted Jasmine. "If you aren't going to make this a fair fight, and I have no chance of winning, then stop playing with your food like a cat does with a mouse."

"I'm not done playing with you, my little mousy," chuckled the spider.

"What do you want from me then?"

"Well, I noticed there was another human with you when you killed me," explained the spider.

"So, what's the point?"

"I've been thinking. I want to tell you the second way to get out of here."

"You make absolutely no sense. One second you want to mess around with me for what seems like eternity and now you want to tell me an option of how to get out of here." Jasmine knew there was going to be some loophole in this that would benefit the spider, but what did she have to lose?

"I think I might have more fun if I tell you," the spider said as it cracked its jaw closed a few times.

"Well then, tell me already."

"You must call on someone you dearly love while they sleep. If they love you as much as you love them, they will come to your aid. Next, they will have to defeat me, which will instantly release you from this void. But if they fail, they will be trapped here with you. And that is where it benefits me. I'll have two playthings just in case I accidentally kill one of you."

Just as she thought, the second way benefited the spider. But the spider didn't know that her brother didn't care for her as much as the spider was hoping for. If deep down her brother did care, she had no intention of having him suffer with her in this limbo. Not wanting to be helpless any longer on the ground, she called on the last of her strength. Her arms wobbled and burned but held long enough for her to get to her feet. Drowning out the pain, she ran for her life. As Jasmine ran, she screamed for someone to rescue her, "Oh Conrad, Lestron, where are you?"

Laughing, the voice asked, "How are you holding up?"

The last thing she wanted to do was converse with that thing. She continued trying to get away and bumped into unseen obstacles again in her attempt.

"Why are you ignoring me, human? Am I getting on your nerves?" the voice snickered.

Above the voice's irritating laughter, Jasmine thought she heard someone call her name. First, she thought it was a figment of her imagination, but she heard it again. She fought to ignore the sick laughter in an effort to maintain her sanity. She strained to hear over the menacing voice so near to her. She came to a complete halt and swung her body around, blind and frantic. She heard her name called again and realized the voice was her brother's. The dead spider's maniacal laughter continued and Jasmine began to run again, to distance herself from it. If only she could see her brother.

Just as she thought of seeing Conrad again, a faint white light was visible to her. The light seemed far away at first.

"Jasmine! Jasmine!" screamed Conrad.

As he screamed her name, Jasmine realized his voice was coming from the same direction as the light. As she tried to stumble toward the light, a warm sensation flowed through her body. All the pain she was feeling suddenly disappeared and her stumbling transformed to running.

"No! No! No!" chanted the evil voice.

Dreading being alone in the dark with a dead spider's soul for eternity, she ran directly into the light.

Chapter 18

High amid the tree branches was a tiny wooden house constructed with utmost precision. Magic infused in the wood gave the house unusual qualities. When wind blew through the trees, the house would sway with the branches, but the occupants of the house had no sensation of moving back and forth. Also, even though the house was not far above the forest floor, it was invisible to the naked eye. This wasn't the only home of its sort; dozens of identical houses formed a small village throughout the treetops. The abodes were connected by suspension bridges that spanned the trees and enabled the residents to visit each other with safe passage.

One of these houses sheltered the first humans to be in that place in decades. Most of the villagers were not pleased about this, but under the circumstances they didn't have a choice.

Jasmine opened her eyes gradually because the light stung her eyes. Everything was blurry, but eventually, her eyes focused on her brother who stood over her with a sincere look of concern. She was slow to arouse because she wanted to linger in the lusciously soft sheets atop the bed where she lay. She did a double take at her brother, who wasn't wearing the same clothes as before. Instead, he was dressed entirely in white clothing that appeared to be as soft and comfortable as the sheets that covered her. Jasmine lifted her sheets and was shocked to see that she, also, wasn't wearing the same clothing as the days before. Her apparel was similar to her brother's. The major difference was that instead of pants, she wore a simple white dress.

Jasmine repositioned the sheets and scanned her surroundings. Everything in the room was quite plain. There was a bed alongside hers, which she believed was where Conrad slept. A wooden chair stood beside a door and that was the extent of the furniture. A lone window was the only view to the outside world and from where she lay, and the only thing she could see were leafy tree branches and a patch of bright blue sky.

She planted her hands by her sides and slowly pushed herself up so her back was against the wall, keeping her lower half under the sheets. That simple task of pushing herself up caused her to become winded, which surprised her greatly.

"How long have I been out?" Jasmine asked herself. As she turned her head to ask Conrad, a small red carnation fell from somewhere and landed on her lap. She looked to see if there was something above and saw nothing. She then raised her hand and touched a flower stuck in her hair above her ear. She grabbed the fallen flower and placed it over her other ear just for fun.

"Where am I?" she asked.

"You are in Fos Faydian," replied Conrad.

"What's Fos Fay...dee...an," Jasmine asked as she struggled to pronounce the words.

Conrad chuckled a little and replied, "Remember when Lestron kept saying we were heading somewhere but never telling us where?"

"Uh huh," responded Jasmine as she looked through the window.

"Well, Fos Faydian is an elf village," responded Conrad. "When you were poisoned by the spider, Lestron rushed you here."

The second she heard the word "spider" come out of Conrad's mouth, Jasmine shrunk against the pillow. She really had been fighting for her life inside her mind.

"Are you all right?"

"While I was unconscious, I had this horrible dream. Well, I thought it was a dream, but now after what you told me, I really don't think it was."

"You're not making any sense." Conrad shook his head.

"Where's Lestron?"

"He left a while ago, but said he would come back soon." Conrad figured Jasmine might be less distressed if Lestron was near. He turned toward the door to search for the elf and asked, "Would you like me to go get him?"

"No, I want you to stay here with me, but when he comes back I'll tell you both what happened because I don't want to tell that story twice. Where was I stung?" Jasmine changed the subject as she searched her arms for any clues.

"When the spider jumped on you, you killed it with your spear but its stinger impaled your leg," Conrad explained.

Jasmine lifted the sheets with one hand, higher this time. She then pulled her dress up to her calf and saw white gauze wrapped around her left leg.

She touched her leg with a finger and then touched it again. "There's no feeling in my leg! Conrad, I can't feel my finger touching my shin." Afraid of the outcome but doing it anyway, she ran her fingernail down her leg in hopes she would feel it. She didn't. "Why can't I feel or move my leg?"

"It's the effect of the poison. Don't worry, sis. Lestron said you will regain movement and sensation over time," consoled Conrad. "He was afraid at first that you might not make it. It took us much longer than he expected to get you here. By the time we got to Fos Faydian, Lestron said the venom had taken its toll on you. He then said that he had never met anyone who lived as long as you had without proper treatment. Even the clerics had their doubts about your surviving."

"What are clerics?" asked Jasmine.

"Apparently they're what we would call doctors at home," explained Conrad.

"How long have I been here?"

"Five days."

Hearing how long she had been unconscious from the poison, she shook her head and lay back down, overwhelmed by what happened. "I can't believe I've been gone for that long. Was it *really* that bad?"

"When we first pushed the spider off you, we thought you were dead. I noticed that your leg was bleeding and Lestron saw blood on the spider's stinger. He then bandaged you the best he could, picked you up, and carried you to the village.

"When we got to the village, the elves wouldn't let us in. Apparently we are the first humans to set foot here in ages; however, when Lestron explained to them what happened, they brought us to this house and sent for a group of clerics. They brought in bottles of weird-colored liquids. Some of the stuff was for you to drink and others to be put directly onto your leg. They worked on you day and night until last night. That was when they ran out of ideas and left you to fate."

"I'm sorry I put you through so much," Jasmine apologized as tears ran down her cheeks.

"It wasn't your fault," Conrad said consolingly and placed his right hand onto her shoulder. "Look at it this way, you survived and the spider didn't."

Jasmine wiped her tears and then turned away from Conrad. "If you don't mind, Conrad, I'm getting tired and want to go back to sleep. My mind is having a hard time coping with all of this."

"I'll sit here while you nap, and I'll also tell Lestron you want to talk with us later," Conrad reassured her as he sat on the edge of his bed.

"Thank...you..." was the last thing Jasmine said before slipping into a deep sleep.

Chapter 19

Small blue birds fluttered around the tree branches outside the window of the house where Jasmine slept. Leaves and flower petals fell from above the house like rain falling from the sky. At times, only a few fell while at other times, when a large gust blew, they could almost block the light from coming in the room. During one gust in particular, two birds perched themselves on the windowsill near Jasmine's bed until the wind died down. The birds, anxious to be on their way, began to sing.

The beautiful melody woke Jasmine from her sleep. She smiled to herself because of how peaceful it made her feel. Suddenly, Lestron's voice came from across the room, scaring the two birds. Jasmine watched as the two birds fluttered off then turned toward Lestron's voice.

Jasmine propped herself against the wall again, not as exhausted this time from the menial task. She spotted Conrad sitting in the chair, looking up at Lestron, who was standing. Lestron's back was to her.

"What are you guys talking about?" queried Jasmine.

Surprised to hear Jasmine's voice, Lestron stopped the conversation and quickly turned away from Conrad to face Jasmine. "The elves want you two out of here!" answered Lestron.

"What do you mean?" asked Jasmine.

"They said that you have been here long enough," Lestron explained as he approached her. "They are letting you stay for only a few more days and then you must leave." Conrad rose from the chair and stood alongside Lestron.

Doing a quick examination, Lestron placed his hand on Jasmine's forehead. She did not feel as hot as she had the last few times he checked. "At least the fever has gone down a bit," Lestron stated as he withdrew his hand. Still concerned about her high temperature, he reached into a nearby bucket of water and removed a small white cloth. He wrung out the water and placed the cloth on Jasmine's forehead. "This should help a little."

"What are you going to do about the elves kicking us out of town?" Jasmine questioned as she held the rag to her forehead.

"There is nothing I can do. You should consider yourselves lucky they allowed you two to stay here this long."

"Where do we go?"

"I have decided to escort you to Yarlanzia. That is the human capital where they should be able to care for you."

"Where is this Yarlanzia?" asked Jasmine.

"It is at the northern tip of Felnoria, a hike that will take many days to reach. Conrad has described to me how you two arrived here. I do not understand it myself, but magic perplexes even the brightest person. Maybe someone there can help you get back to where you belong."

"Do you think it will be safe there?"

"I have met the king and queen a few times in the past and I believe they are trustworthy people."

Conrad stood in silence as the other two conversed until he remembered the request his sister made earlier. "I told Lestron that you wanted to speak with us when you woke up," Conrad interrupted as he left Lestron's side and sat on his bed facing Lestron and his sister.

Hearing her brother mention that, everything from the dream flooded her memory. A tormented face looked at Lestron before she began to explain. "I had this weird dream when I was under. Well, I don't know if it was a dream or not because it felt so real."

Jasmine explained everything she could remember about her experience in the endless darkness in great detail. Lestron and Conrad quietly listened to the story that she spun. Both were surprised by the events that unfolded and how, by hearing her brother's voice, she returned to consciousness. When she reached the part about her running into the white light and waking, Lestron shook his head with a smile on his face.

"You have surprised me again, Jasmine."

Hearing Lestron's response made her return the smile. She rolled onto her side and reached out with both of her arms and gave Lestron a hug. Lestron was surprised by the hug, since elves never embrace another person that way. However, not wanting to be rude, he placed his arms over her shoulders and returned the gesture. When she pulled away from Lestron, her face was red and tears were running down her cheeks. She turned and reached to Conrad in hopes that he would get off the bed and meet her halfway to embrace.

"You know we don't hug," Conrad reminded her, while giving no signs of reaching to her.

Jasmine was disappointed by her brother's response, but didn't wish to force him into doing something he didn't want to do. Instead, she leaned back against the wall and wiped the tears from her face.

"Since we need to head out in a few days, I think it is best if you get out of bed and try out those legs of yours," suggested Lestron.

"I tried moving my left leg before I fell asleep earlier, but I could barely budge it, and there was no feeling."

"Yes, one of the poison's effects is mild paralysis that will slowly pass over time. You will have a long road ahead of you before you will be able to walk normally."

"Any idea how long?"

"From what the clerics have told me, I would say it might take around a month."

"A month!" shouted Jasmine, shocked by the length of time.

"I am sorry, Jasmine, but losing full use of your leg is minor compared to what could have happened. A few of my brethren have been inflicted with the poison over the years, and it usually takes that long for the paralysis to subside." Not wishing to go into detail, Lestron quickly changed the subject. "Let me help you out of bed and see how bad it really is."

Jasmine pulled the sheets away and swung her legs to the edge of the bed, having to use her right leg to move the left. She planted her hands on the bed and pushed herself up, making sure all of her weight was on her right leg. For a second, it looked like it might work, but then she tried shifting some of her body weight off her right leg onto her left. The moment she transferred her weight, her left leg gave out and she began to fall to the floor. Acting quickly, Lestron lunged and caught her before she hit. He slowly lifted her up while encouraging Jasmine to steady herself on her right leg.

"I will get a cane for you and you should be mobile enough to travel. But right now, I will support you while you walk around the room," Lestron offered.

Accepting the offer, Jasmine swung her left arm around Lestron's shoulder so she could use his body for support. "We will take it slowly," Lestron explained as he took a step forward. Jasmine stepped gingerly and ended up hopping on her good leg to move forward. The left leg was of no help. Conrad jumped off his bed and followed right behind them with his arms extended, just in case anything happened. Jasmine limped around the room twice before beads of perspiration dripped down her face and she panted for breath.

"I think you have done enough for now," Lestron noted as he helped her to her bed. Lestron placed his hands around her waist, and helped her sit down. He then lifted her feet onto the bed while Jasmine swung her body to follow her legs. With Jasmine safely in place, Conrad sat at the end of his bed.

"How much longer do I need to keep the bandages on my leg?" inquired Jasmine. Before responding, Lestron covered her with the soft white sheet.

"When you wake up tomorrow, I will have a cleric come to check your leg. He will know better than I how long the bandages must stay. He may also have some suggestions about how to improve your walking. For now, I think you should sleep."

Jasmine was exhausted so she pulled the sheet to her nose, rolled over, and fell asleep.

"So what are the plans for tomorrow?" whispered Conrad once he was satisfied Jasmine was asleep.

"We will meet with High Elf Mylinia if your sister is up for it."

"Who is this Mylinia person?"

"You should always address her as 'High Elf,' and she is the ruler of the elves in Fos Faydian."

"I will remember that, but if Jas could barely walk around the room today, how is she going to walk around the village tomorrow?"

"The clerics should have some type of potion to help her regain her strength," explained Lestron. Conrad wanted to ask about this potion, but he knew he would just get some mumble-jumble he wouldn't understand, so he kept quiet. "For now, she needs her rest, so I'll see you in the morning." Lestron crept away from sleeping Jasmine and quietly walked to the door.

"Wait up," Conrad whispered as he arose from his bed to exit the room with Lestron. "It's still early and I'd like to see some more of the village."

Chapter 20

Deep under the Thundering Mountains wound a maze of caves. Water droplets dripped, dripped, dripped from the ceiling and formed small pools on the cave floor. The water slowly seeped into cracks in the rock. This water cycle was so constant that the pools never overflowed. Small rooms with only one entrance were cut into the cave walls. Each was separated by heavy wooden doors. The cubicles were damp, and the walls were slippery. Large slugs, the size of a fist, slowly crawled across the floor and walls, leaving small trails of ooze behind.

In one of these chambers, Morlok was curled into a ball with no hope of ever being released. Since he arrived no food was brought down to him. His body was thinner, and his face was slightly sunken. The robe that he always wore was tattered and torn so much his green body showed through in many places.

He detected the faint sound of a door opening. Morlok heard a few words being exchanged between a newcomer and the two guards on watch in the so-called prison. The conversation was not clear enough for him to understand. Once the talking ceased, he heard footsteps coming closer to him until they stopped outside his cell. Keys rattled and the lock clattered as its bolt was turned. The door hinges creaked as the door opened, allowing light to filter into his cell.

With no hope left in the world, Morlok didn't have the will to turn his head toward the opening. The only thought left in his mind was hope that the executioner was coming to do his job. The footsteps entered and finally ceased right behind him. Suddenly, a burst of pain shot into his back as something hard struck him. The impact made Morlok coil into a tighter ball.

"Morlok, get up and face your master," came Uzgal's voice as he stepped back after having kicked the prisoner. Morlok, not having enough strength to stand, uncurled himself and twisted his body around just enough to look into Uzgal's face. The slight movement caused a burst of coughing, which caused Morlok to shudder. His body lurched forward with each cough and he tasted blood.

Uzgal was shocked at how wretched Morlok looked, but made certain not to make his reaction visible. "It looks like you were right about the children, Morlok, or should I say, *Sage* Morlok," Uzgal admitted, tight-lipped, as he stared down at the pathetic looking troll. "We are going to attack Yiorling in a few days and I am dispatching Quilzar to round up the children. Have you had any more premonitions?"

"I'm starving and so weak; I have no energy or will to think any more." Morlok groaned between violent coughs. Disgusted, Uzgal turned away from Morlok and looked at the two guards standing at the cell entrance.

"Take the prisoner to his former room and feed him. Make sure someone looks after him," commanded Uzgal.

"Yes, Master!" both guards chimed in unison. Uzgal stepped aside as the guards reached down, each grabbing onto one of Morlok's arms. They lifted him from the ground until his feet grazed the rocky floor. Akin to when Morlok was dragged down to the cell, his feet hung to the ground, letting the guards do all the work. The only difference was that this time he actually had no strength to walk. Uzgal watched in silence as the guards hauled Morlok out of the cell and immediately left to prepare for the battle on Yiorling.

The guards were disgruntled at having to carry Morlok to his room. They kicked open the door and dragged him to his bed. They shoved him on the bed and he flopped around like a rag doll. With their duty done, they exited with a hard slam of the heavy door. A slow-moving troll servant arrived a few minutes later with a wooden plate of chicken and dry bread. The troll guard tossed the plate at Morlok, causing most of the food to fall on the floor. He also left the room with a slam of the door.

The next morning Morlok lay fitfully asleep atop the bed. One of his coughing spells started suddenly and his body jerked spasmodically as he hacked. He woke himself with his cough. When he opened his eyes, he was surprised to see a troll standing next to the bed, looking down at him. This troll almost had a kind look to him, unlike the ones he had encountered previously. Whoever it was held a worn brown bag in both of his hands.

"That cough sounds horrible," stated the troll. "I have been ordered by Master Uzgal to examine you and do what is necessary to keep you alive." Morlok silently stared at the healer as he placed the bag on the bed. Morlok's stomach growled. Ignoring the troll, he slipped to the floor and crawled around frantically to claim the scattered morsels that had flown off the plate earlier. He stuffed his face, barely taking time to breathe. When each piece of chicken was eaten down to the bone, he nonchalantly tossed the bone aside and crawled to the next piece.

The troll stared on in silence as Morlok devoured the chicken and bread. When everything was consumed, he watched as Morlok crawled back to his bed and smacked his lips and burped loudly. Satisfied Morlok was going to give him the time he needed, the troll reached into his brown bag and retrieved a vial of bright green liquid. "If you drink this once a day, for three days, that cough should be gone."

Morlok snatched the vial from the troll's gnarled hand. He yanked out the cork and tossed it aside to join the scattered bones. Morlok raised the vial to his mouth and drank half the bottle in one gulp. Warmth coursed throughout his body. He placed the remainder of the vial next to the empty food plate and released a long sigh. With his stomach full and medicine in his body, Morlok rolled over and went to sleep, never saying one word to the troll.

When Morlok awoke, Uzgal was standing beside him. "Have you had any premonitions yet?" barked Uzgal. Still not ready to talk, Morlok just shook his head no. Morlok ignored Uzgal and reached over and grabbed a leg of venison from the refilled plate. After eating, he grabbed the vial of remaining liquid and placed it to his mouth. He finished off the drink and threw the vial to the floor. The vial exploded into countless pieces upon impact. Again, his stomach full and his body warm from the medicine, Morlok rolled to his side and returned to sleep.

Uzgal was irate that Morlok would behave this way in the presence of his master. Uzgal's first inclination was to punish him for his insubordination. He reconsidered, knowing Morlok would be of no use to him sick. It would not be wise to make Morlok suffer anytime soon. Instead, he stormed out of the room mumbling to himself.

Morlok was sound. His mind saw the two children again. This time they were in some sort of elf village. A girl, the same one from the previous premonition, lay asleep in a bed. The male human who had come with her sat on a bed near her, watching her sleep. An elf was also in the room, looking down at the girl. The elf's and boy's mouths were moving as if in conversation, indiscernible to Morlok.

Morlok awoke wide-eyed and looked left and right for any sign of anyone in his room. He was furious that no one was there when he finally wanted to speak. He yelled out in hope that a guard was posted outside of his door. Sure enough, a troll holding a spear burst in and glared at the screamer.

"Tell Master Uzgal that I have information for him," demanded Morlok of the guard.

The guard was not pleased at being told what to do by a peon like Morlok, but Uzgal had ordered him to report any changes. The guard stormed out, slamming the door behind him as had every other troll. The door flung open a short time later. This time, Uzgal entered. "What nerve you have to summon me, Morlok, when I am the one in charge!" snapped Uzgal.

"Sorry, I just had another premonition, Master. I just assumed you would want to hear it immediately," explained Morlok. He felt another coughing spell coming so he quickly reached to the floor and was happy to discover two new vials waiting for him. He grabbed one of them, uncorked it, and downed half of the bottle's contents before placing it down.

"Enough already. What did you see?" demanded Uzgal impatiently.

With a new dose of the medicine in his body and the coughing sensation gone, Morlok told everything right down to the last detail. When Morlok finished his story, Uzgal stood silently, pondering the sequence of events over the past week.

"From what you have envisioned and what Quilzar saw, I would have to conclude that neither of you is lying. We are departing soon for Yiorling and you will come along. Be ready at all times. Quilzar is leaving for the Trilaz Woods today and will then meet us in Yiorling." Uzgal turned away and walked out of the room without allowing Morlok time to respond. Again, the door slammed.

Chapter 21

Just outside of Yarlanzia there was a large farmhouse surrounded by many acres of prime farmland. Its walls were masterfully made from stone carried by hand from the Soaring Cliffs. The acreage was dedicated to crops and livestock tended by the occupants of the house. There were five small wooden cabins near the main building.

The house had been a gift from the king and queen to the previous owners in appreciation for commendable acts. Those owners had passed away and the estate was inherited by their only child. The child, now an adult, had a loving wife and three children. Because their family was so small and their land was so large, they hired many local peasants to take care of the crops and livestock. This family was wealthy, so if any of their employees needed lodging, they were always welcome to stay in one of the cabins without charge.

Inside the main house, the husband and wife were having a discussion about expanding the number of cabins on their land to accommodate the influx of peasants migrating to Yarlanzia for work and lodging. Their discussion was interrupted by knocking on the door. Before opening the door, the husband peeked through the front window to see who was there. He was stunned when he caught sight of the unexpected visitor. He quickly opened the door, dropped to one knee, and bowed his head.

"Your Highness, is it really time to go already?" Kadon asked as he stood up and motioned for the king to enter.

"Unfortunately, it is. I was hoping you could have a little more time with your family, but all the preparations were completed faster than expected," stated Ralph as he entered the house, quickly scanning the interior. The first thing Ralph noticed was a woman approximately Kadon's age, sorting through some papers in the center of the room. Each page contained ideas on how to help the new peasants arriving in Yarlanzia. She was dressed in a flowing, soft pink dress that accented her bright blonde hair that cascaded to her knees. Her beauty would make most men speechless.

"Before I leave, I would like to introduce you to my loving wife, Julia," said Kadon as he turned and motioned Julia to come forward. Julia joined Ralph and properly curtsied as Kadon had taught her years earlier.

"It is a pleasure to meet you, Your Highness," Julia said as she rose, smiling the entire time.

"The pleasure is all mine, Julia," the king responded as he reached out and took Julia's hand, placing it up to his lips to kiss it gently. "I see you have kept Kadon's father's house in great condition," he added, returning Julia's hand.

"Thank you, but I don't do it all by myself. Kadon helps out when he can and the children do chores as well. We also have many people who help us with the farming and tending livestock."

"Synthia and I continually devise new ways to help eliminate poverty in Yarlanzia. We have some good ideas, but none good enough to have an impact on everyone in need." Ralph knew talking about something and doing it were two completely different things, but you always needed to start somewhere. Not wanting to get into a deep conversation about the matter, he changed the subject. "I hate doing this to you, but we really must get going. I will wait outside, Kadon. Come out when you are ready." Not wanting to intrude upon Kadon's farewells, Ralph nodded to him and Julia and left the house, closing the door behind him.

They watched as Ralph walked out of the house and turned to each other once the door was closed. "I wish you didn't have to go," Julia sniffled.

"I should be back within a week," Kadon reassured her as he reached out to hold her. She stepped into his open arms feeling the comfort of his embrace. They didn't move until Kadon pulled away. "I'll say good-bye to the children and then I'll be right back."

Kadon left his wife's side and walked to one of the back rooms, glancing back at his adoring wife. He hesitantly opened the door of the playroom, knowing what was going to happen once he told his children he had to leave again. As expected, the children burst into tears when he told them he was going away. He didn't want to leave Julia with three crying children so he stayed with them until they were composed. He left them to play again, taking one last look before closing their door.

With his farewells completed, Kadon needed to get outfitted for the journey. He walked down the hall and entered his bedroom, where he reached down and grabbed a large black bag from the corner of the bedroom. He hoisted it onto the bed, having trouble the last few inches because of the enormous weight. He grabbed the bottom of the bag and held it upside down until all of the contents lay on the bed. He tossed the empty bag to its corner and stared at all the armor he needed to strap on. He slowly put on the armor one section at a time, tugging at each part to make sure it was secure before moving to the next. Each piece of silver-plated armor was custom made for him, so every joint of armor contoured with his body. Even after years of use, it shone as brightly as the day King Ralph had presented it to him.

He knelt down and stretched until his stomach almost touched the floor. He reached underneath his bed with his armored right arm to extract a sword that shone as brightly as his armor. The sword blade was made from the same metal as his armor. The hilt was plated in gold with a large ruby inlaid at its base. He awkwardly arose with his sword and sheathed it at his side before leaving the bedroom.

Kadon faced Julia, whose eyes were now red and puffy from sobbing. He held her close, and she felt his warmth despite his cold armor. "I will return soon, I promise." Kadon was feeling emotion well up within him and pulled away from his wife's arms, not wanting to prolong the inevitable. He held back his emotions as he walked to the door. As he opened it, he gave her a loving smile and was gone.

Kadon's eyes squinted in the bright sunlight, which seemed blinding in comparison to the dimly lit house. When his eyes adjusted, he noticed Ralph astride a magnificent horse with another standing next to it. Assuming the horse was intended for him, he easily mounted the horse, despite the weight of his armor.

"All set?" Ralph asked.

Kadon nodded his head.

Ralph grasped the reins and turned his horse toward the castle. Ralph gently put pressure between his legs to signify to the horse that he was ready to go. The horse trotted forward. Kadon, taking his king's lead, turned his horse and rode alongside him.

"Are the men waiting for us at the castle?"

"Yes, they are. Actually there are more than just our men waiting for us," responded Ralph.

"What do you mean?" asked Kadon.

"You will find out in due time," Ralph smiled.

Kadon tried to get Ralph to tell him, but with no success. The only thing Ralph would talk about was the preparation for the journey. When they reached the castle, the answer to his question was apparent. Along the main road to the castle, thousands of people stood watching the king and Kadon arrive. It was as if they were the main attraction in a parade. The throng of people cheered and blared horns as the two rode to the castle steps.

Thirty-five men suited for battle sat patiently on horseback in front of the castle steps. At the top of the steps, Queen Synthia gazed over the crowd. Once the king and captain reached the steps, they dismounted and passed their reins to a soldier before climbing the stairs, stopping in front of Synthia.

Kadon bowed at the waist and stood to her left. Ralph took his position on the right side of his sister and raised his hand to silence the crowd.

"Today, we journey across Felnoria on a mission to change our destiny." The crowd cheered, then quieted when the king raised his hand again. "I have formed four parties, all equally important," Ralph announced.

"One party will be dispatched to the western villages and one to the eastern to enlist more soldiers to support us in our time of need. Our third party, which I will lead personally, will head to the Soaring Cliffs to ask the dwarves for assistance. The fourth will be lead by Captain Kadon. He is to travel to the Trilaz Woods, where the queen and I believe there are two humans who might be of great help to us." The crowd muttered in confusion at the revelation that there were humans in the Trilaz Woods, since only elves lived in the woods. The king raised his arm yet again to silence the crowd.

"For now, wish us all luck that we will all come home with new hope of returning Felnoria to its rightful condition." The crowd went into a great commotion and cheered in hope of restoring Felnoria to its former glory.

Knowing that was the end of the speech, Kadon turned to kiss Synthia's hand. Ralph repeated the gesture to his sister before turning to face the crowd. Wanting to get the journey underway, Ralph and Kadon descended the stairs and mounted their horses. The crowd tossed flowers at them as they cantered down the road with the thirty-five soldiers behind. The crowd's actions gave them hope.

Everyone rode in silence until the townspeople were just specks in the distance. Ralph stopped his horse and turned toward his men. First acknowledging the two parties whose job it was to find more recruits, he began, "I wish for you all to return within two weeks. Have safe travels and bring every able-bodied man you possibly can." With that said, the first two parties galloped away, one to the east and one to the west.

Ralph then moved his horse alongside Kadon. "I know I don't have to tell you how important your job is," Ralph said.

"No you don't, Your Highness," Kadon replied shaking his head.

"If you find those children, make sure to safeguard them as you would protect one of your own."

"I will protect them with my life," pledged Kadon as he placed his right arm to his heart.

Pleased by Kadon's response, he ordered Kadon's party on their way. Ralph watched as his best soldier and men rode southwest toward the Trilaz Woods. When they disappeared over the horizon, Ralph turned his horse toward the Soaring Cliffs and broke into a gallop with five hunters following close behind him.

Chapter 22

The next morning, Jasmine got herself in a seated position at the edge of her bed. The simple task wore her body out and she stopped to catch her breath. She looked over and noticed a wooden cane propped against the wall.

"I wonder where everyone is," she said to herself. Feeling rather warm, Jasmine tossed the covers off herself. With her whole body uncovered, she tried wiggling her left leg, but it was as unresponsive as it had been the day before. She looked at the cane and then back at her leg.

Deciding to give using the cane a shot, she swung her body around until her legs hung over the side of the bed. One leg gently stepped to the floor and the other flopped ungracefully with a thump. Jasmine hesitantly grasped the cane and firmly planted it on the floor for support. She pushed herself up with all her strength. Just like before, she initially placed all her weight onto her right leg, but this time she slowly transferred some of the weight to her left hand, which held the cane. Satisfied, she took a step forward with her right leg then her cane. Her left leg dragged behind like deadwood. Wishing to see the outside world, she slowly limped to the window.

When Jasmine reached the window, she was shocked at the realization that she had been recovering all this time high above the ground. She leaned forward, sticking her head out of the window, and noticed the house was built among thick tree branches. She was amazed.

"There are so many weird things about this place. I'm not going to let a tree house bother me," Jasmine remarked out loud as she chuckled a bit.

She watched as elves went about their daily activities, unaware that they were being watched. She continued watching until her arm and leg began to ache from propping herself against the window sill. Before she was completely drained of energy, she turned around and began her attempt to return to bed when the door swung open.

"Ahh, I see you are using the cane I set out for you," smiled Lestron who was standing with another elf behind him.

"Yes, thank you very much for getting it for me," responded Jasmine as she eyed the new elf while trying to concentrate on reaching the bed. She sat down slowly and asked of Lestron, "And who's this?" She cocked her head in the direction of the unfamiliar elf.

"This is Cleric Kareese. I brought him to assist with your rehabilitation to get you walking again."

"It's a pleasure to meet you, Jasmine," Kareese greeted with a slight bow. "Unlike most of my fellow elves in this village, I am happy to see a new face." Kareese walked over to Jasmine and looked down at her leg. "If you would put your leg up onto the bed we can begin our work."

"I can get my right leg up, but I will need help with the left one," stated Jasmine as she stretched over and placed her cane alongside the bed. Kareese bent down and lifted her leg up onto the bed as Jasmine swung her body to follow her legs. After she propped her back against the wall, Kareese placed his hand on her forehead.

"I see the fever has broken," stated Kareese. He then looked at the bandage, which was slightly noticeable from below her dress.

Kareese transferred his backpack to the bed and placed it beside her injured leg. He reached into the bag, quite similar to an old-fashioned doctor's bag, and removed a small knife and a clean cloth bandage. He set aside the bandage and then carefully slid the knife under the gauze wrapped around her leg. He slowly pushed up on the blade and cut through the bandage like butter until the bandage fell away.

Lestron was anxious to see how the wound was progressing so he stepped closer to examine it. He was surprised at what he saw. The portion of her leg where the stinger pierced was completely healed over. Not even a trace of a scar was present. "It does not look like I am going to need to put that other bandage on," commented Kareese as he returned the knife and fresh bandage to his bag.

Jasmine, curious to see her leg, glanced down and was amazed to see it looking perfectly normal. "If my leg looks as good as new, why am I having such trouble walking?" asked Jasmine.

"The puncture may have healed, but the poison still runs through your veins," explained Kareese. "I have seen many cases similar to yours. All of them had muscle weakness around the vicinity of the wound for at least a month, but I think Lestron mentioned this to you already."

"Sure, he said it would take a month, but it doesn't make sense to me when my leg looks normal."

"Well, I brought something along to help you with that predicament of yours." Kareese reached into his bag and extracted a vial of blue liquid. "This potion should do the trick."

"What kind of potion is that?"

"It will make your legs stronger. Well, not just legs. We cannot make potions that specific. Your whole body will be much stronger than it is now. But to be on the safe side, I would keep the cane around because the potion wears off quite quickly," explained Kareese as he handed the potion to Jasmine.

"How much stronger, exactly?" questioned Jasmine as she accepted the potion.

"Let us just say you would have no trouble beating up your brother if he got out of line." Kareese smiled as Lestron laughed.

"Where is Conrad, anyway?" Jasmine asked as she finally realized he wasn't near.

"I told him to wait outside until the examination was completed," Kareese informed her, still chuckling.

He reached back into his pack for three more potions and a thick piece of wood. Kareese placed the three bottles alongside her bed and then handed Jasmine the wooden slab. "Go ahead, try to break it," he dared.

"Why?" asked Jasmine as she gripped the board.

"Just to show you how well the potion works."

Thinking it best to use her leg as support while trying to break it, Jasmine managed to turn and hang her legs over the edge of the bed. She placed the board on the thigh of her good leg and pushed down with all her might with a hand on each end. She continued pushing, but the only thing that felt as if it were breaking was her leg from all the pressure she was putting on it. Realizing there was no way she would break it, she stopped and pulled the board away from her leg.

"Okay, now take a sip of the potion, only a sip, and then try again."

Jasmine placed the board alongside her, carefully uncorked the bottle, and placed it to her lips. The smell of the liquid hit her before she could take a drink. To her, it smelled like Conrad's gym bag left in the sun for two days. However, Jasmine was determined to get better so she closed her eyes and sipped the foul fluid. The taste was as revolting as the smell and it took some courage just to swallow.

"Yuck, that was disgusting! To top it off, I don't feel any different!" Jasmine gagged and huffed.

"Try breaking the board now," Kareese suggested as he took the potion from her.

She reached for the board again and, immediately after she held it up, she knew something was different. The board felt as light as a feather. For some reason, she felt she didn't need to place it over her leg to break it. She gripped with both hands again and stretched her arms straight out. The second she pushed with one of her hands and pulled with the other, there was a loud cracking noise and the board split in two. Splinters flew in every direction. Jasmine quickly turned her head to protect her eyes. When she realized what she had just done, her mouth dropped open and she threw the two pieces to the floor in shock.

She looked over to Kareese and Lestron with her mouth still agape and they both just nodded their heads. Taking that as a sign, she planted her hands onto the bed and lifted herself, making sure to place all her weight onto her right leg. Taking a risk, she slowly placed more and more weight onto her left leg until she supported her whole body with just her bad leg.

The second all of her body weight was on her left leg, she knew she could walk again. Jasmine smiled with relief. She knew it was risky, but she jumped up and down with joy. She ran over to Kareese with her arms open wide. Kareese was surprised by the big hug she delivered, but he did not discourage it. She then pulled away and went over to Lestron and did the same. This time Lestron accepted the gesture without hesitation.

"I know you are excited you can walk again, but please take it easy. When I said earlier that it wears off quickly, I meant it. The last thing you should know is that the potion usually lasts about four hours in a grown elf, and I am not sure how long it will last in you. Since you are smaller than an average-sized elf, it should be a little longer. So make sure to keep at least one vial with you at all times and keep that cane with you just in case."

"I will, but it's going to be gruesome drinking that concoction. But, thank you anyway, because if it weren't for you, I'd be stuck in that bed for a month." Jasmine bowed her head to Kareese and walked out the door. The only thing on her mind at that moment was showing her brother she could walk again.

Chapter 23

Outside, Conrad stood watching five or six yellow butterflies fluttering from flower to flower. Every once in a while a gust of wind would blow, causing the butterflies to lose their course, but eventually they found their way to the next petals. While in his daze, a blossom tumbled in the wind from the tree branches above him. The flower, which resembled an apple blossom, eventually alighted next to Conrad's feet. He bent down to pick it up. As he was placing it into his hand, the door next to him opened suddenly.

Jasmine stood at the door without help from anyone. She looked through the tree branches, amazed that she was walking around above the forest floor. She stepped out into the sunlight and gazed in awe until she noticed her brother holding a flower.

"Is that for me?" asked Jasmine as she pointed to the flower.

Feeling generous at the moment Conrad replied, "Why yes, it is. I picked it earlier and thought you would like it." As he spoke, similar blossoms cascaded with another gust of wind, exposing the little white lie.

Jasmine smiled and shook her head saying, "I guess the wind spoke the truth." Not knowing what to say, Conrad stretched his arm out and offered her the flower, anyway.

"It's the thought that counts."

"I guess!" Jasmine responded by accepting the gift from him.

Lestron exited the house at that moment, sparing Conrad any more humiliation. "I think you forgot something," Lestron stated as he presented the cane that Jasmine was supposed to keep with her at all times. She sheepishly took it from Lestron, knowing she was already disregarding doctor's orders.

"Oops," was all Jasmine could say. Lestron stepped aside so Kareese could leave the house as well.

"And do not forget these either," Kareese reminded as he presented Jasmine with the four bottles of potion. With an awkward grin on her face, she took one bottle at a time and placed them into pockets sewn into her dress.

"What's that stuff?" asked Conrad as he pointed to her pockets.

"You want to see?"

"Sure!"

"Okay, put out your hands." Conrad reached out with both hands, palm side up, expecting Jasmine to place one of the potions in his hand. "No, with your palms facing me," Jasmine requested. Conrad obliged as Jasmine raised her hands in the same manner and interlocked her fingers with his. Conrad finally realized what she was doing.

Back home, Conrad would do this with Jasmine all the time. Whenever Conrad wanted to prove his male superiority, he would grab her hands and place his fingers between hers. He would then squeeze his fingers together, causing shooting pain in her fingers, until she would cry "Uncle."

Wanting to be first, Conrad started pressing his fingers together as hard as he could. Pain shot through his fingers. "Uncle," Conrad yelled as he pulled his hands away. "What did they do to you in there?" Conrad rubbed his throbbing fingers.

"That's for me to know and you to find out," Jasmine taunted as she stuck out her tongue.

"That is enough, you two. High Elf Mylinia wishes to speak with us," Lestron reminded them as he looked at Jasmine. "She told me that when you were up and about she wished to meet you."

"I must get back to my work as well," Kareese remarked as he slipped between Jasmine and Lestron. "I hope to see you two again before you leave." Kareese then walked to a house a few trees down.

"Lestron, could you, by chance, show me around a little before we go there?" asked Jasmine. "I have a feeling High Elf Mylinia is going to want us to leave the village once we have met her. I know we are not welcome here."

"If that is what you wish."

Lestron guided Jasmine and Conrad, allowing Jasmine to stop every so often to take in the sights. Very few elves passed them as they toured the village. The elves that they did pass turned their heads away when the siblings approached them.

Jasmine asked Lestron, "Why are the elves behaving that way?

"An incident with two humans many years ago destroyed this village. Because of that, many elves dislike humans too much to make eye contact. Looking eye to eye is a sign of respect in our culture," Lestron responded. "How about I take you to my favorite spot in the village? There usually aren't any elves there." Jasmine and Conrad were happy to get away from the elves so they nodded their heads in approval.

They strolled through the village until they came to a single bridge leading to a tree quite far from any of the houses. As they were crossing the bridge, Jasmine noticed a small group of elves up ahead. "Are they going to allow us to pass?" asked Jasmine as she pointed in their direction.

"One of my good friends should be working the lift, so we should be safe," responded Lestron. Once they reached the other end of the bridge, Lestron was relieved to see his buddy among the elves. Lestron introduced his friend to them before they stepped onto a large square platform made of logs. The platform was suspended in a sling made of rope that ran over a huge tree branch. The end of the rope that was nearest to Lestron's friend was tied to the tree trunk. When the rope was untied the elves stood in a tug-of-war formation, with the rope passing through their gloved hands. Lestron nodded to his friend, indicating they were ready to be lowered to the forest floor. The crew of elves carefully let the rope slide through their hands. Jasmine and Conrad were jolted at first by the sudden decent but quickly regained their balance. They cringed as the lift creaked from the weight and the rope screeched as it slid across the worn tree branch.

When the makeshift elevator finally thumped on the forest floor, they both jumped off, relieved to be safely off the homemade lift. Lestron held back a laugh at their reactions.

"The place I want to show you is not too far from here. Follow me." Lestron led them through tall, thick grass. In some places the grass was as high as Jasmine's shoulders, making passage difficult. Before long, a faint rumbling noise could be heard in the distance.

"What's that noise?" Jasmine inquired as she moved closer to Lestron.

"You will know in due time." They followed closely behind the elf and the rumbling grew louder with each step. Suddenly, Lestron disappeared through a thick clump of grass as if he fell into a hole.

"Where did he go?" questioned a confused Jasmine as she stopped dead in her tracks. Before Conrad could respond, Lestron's voice sounded from ahead.

"Just keep walking forward. There is a steep slope up ahead, so be careful."

They cautiously advanced until one of Jasmine's feet didn't hit the ground as she expected it to. Her body got ahead of her feet and her arms swung about. Her momentum was too great for her body to regain balance and she began to barrel full speed down the slope. Thankfully, Lestron was near at bottom and caught her before she tumbled.

Conrad proceeded cautiously after seeing his sister's awkward decent. "Wow!" was the only word that came out of his mouth as he met Jasmine and Lestron at the base of the slope.

"This place is beautiful," Jasmine whispered, awestruck. At one end of the small clearing in the woods, a waterfall cascaded into a circular pool of water. On the opposite side, the water appeared to be falling off the end of the earth. In actuality, it was another waterfall dropping into another body of water hundreds of feet down below. Flowers bloomed profusely around the pool, and birds sang from the treetops. The babbling water, chirping birds, and sweet-scented air created a sense of peace. The clearing was a special place.

"Here you go," Conrad smirked as he held out a bright yellow rose for Jasmine. "I picked this one for you."

"Thanks, Conny. I hope it wasn't too much of an effort to get this beautiful flower for me," remarked Jasmine as she carefully took the flower from her brother with a shake of the head.

"It was nothing," responded Conrad with a smirk.

"Allow me to show you something," Lestron suggested as he beckoned them to follow him. Lestron walked toward the waterfall that cascaded into the pool. The air was cooler there and fine droplets sprayed their faces. To the left of the waterfall, Lestron changed course and led them to a cave in a stone edifice a few hundred feet away. "Follow me," Lestron motioned as he stepped into the cave and disappeared from their sight. They followed with curiosity until they rounded a bend in the cave where water gushed down the rocks before them.

"This is directly under the waterfall," shouted Lestron so they could hear him over the water's roar. "This is my favorite spot in Fos Faydian."

"It's absolutely wonderful," Jasmine yelled back.

Jasmine stood on a flat rock allowing the water to spray her. She stood there with her eyes closed, enjoying the moment. Conrad, however, was more assertive. He held his right arm straight out and slowly moved it toward the water torrent. When his hand hit the water, his arm was thrust down violently. He wasn't injured, but he learned a lesson not to do that again.

Jasmine wanted to enjoy the water in a more sensible way. "Lestron, would it be all right if we went swimming for a little while?" Jasmine asked.

"I do not see the harm in it. I will show you where I usually swim," Lestron offered.

Lestron led them to a small recessed bay outside the cave. The water was calm there and it was crystal clear.

"I will stay here and watch while you two have fun in the water," Lestron chuckled as he sat down on the sand. Remembering the potions, Jasmine reached into her pocket and pulled them out so they wouldn't be lost in the water. She handed Lestron the medicine and her cane for safekeeping. Jasmine cast Conrad a challenging glance and the two turned in the direction of the water.

"One...two...three," Conrad shouted, and started running on "three," a split second before Jasmine took off. Conrad reached the water first, winning the race by a hair. With the water up to his waist, Conrad raised his arms and dove into the water, disappearing from sight.

A little while later, Lestron looked up at the sun and then at Jasmine. "Jasmine, come here for a second," shouted Lestron. Jasmine popped out of the water and approached Lestron.

"Take a drink of your potion and then you can go back in the water." Jasmine took a bottle from him, uncorked it, and sipped it more bravely despite the disgusting taste. "Done. May I go back now?" asked Jasmine. Lestron nodded approval and she skipped back to the water.

A few hours later, Lestron announced, "I believe it's time to meet High Elf Mylinia." Jasmine and Conrad shook themselves off and let the sun do the rest of the drying.

"Yeah, I suppose so," said Jasmine. Jasmine really wanted to meet High Elf Mylinia, but then again, she knew what might happen once they finished speaking with her.

"Just follow me, and when we reach the cliff I will help you up, Jasmine," Lestron stated while handing her the potion and cane. They backtracked until they arrived at the lift. Neither of the two humans wanted to ride on the lift again but they didn't have much of a choice. Lestron rang a small bell that was attached to the platform rope once all three of them were safely aboard.

Shortly after the bell rang, the lift began rising, and they were jostled again. This time, Conrad and Jasmine huddled together during their ascent. When they reached the top, both quickly jumped off while Lestron thanked his friend for helping them to go to the forest floor. "Let us now go see High Elf Mylinia," said Lestron as he headed toward town. Jasmine and Conrad followed closely behind until Lestron stopped in the center of Fos Faydian.

Chapter 24

Before the trio stood a structure that was much larger than the rest of the elf houses. Each corner of the house was supported by a separate tree. Another tree, growing right through the center of the house, provided additional support.

The biggest difference between an elf village and any other community in Felnoria was that posted guards were not necessary to provide security. Since they lived in the trees and the only way up was the lift, they were safe from intruders. If, by some chance, someone or something attempted to enter, the trees that supported the houses were laced with magic that prevented anyone from climbing them. It would be like climbing a tree covered in oil.

"This place is huge," an awestruck Jasmine said as she scanned the outside of the house.

"Yes, the High Elf's house took many of us a long time to build," Lestron responded as they walked closer to the house. "Magic holds up this building. It would take me forever to tell you all the spells our mages put on this structure. You will understand when you see it.

"When you meet High Elf Mylinia, the first thing you must do is bow." Lestron demonstrated by bowing down to Conrad, keeping his face looking forward and staring into Conrad's eyes. "When you bow, you must remember to never break eye contact."

"Is that because she is looking into your soul, like the unicorn?" asked Jasmine.

"No, we just believe it is impolite not to look at a High Elf when being introduced. Also, always let High Elf Mylinia finish speaking before speaking yourself." Before entering, Lestron added, "You two should be fine. Shall we go in?"

Conrad and Jasmine exchanged nervous glances and then looked at Lestron, "We're ready," they both conceded.

Lestron opened the door, revealing the inside of the house. When all three were in the house, they noticed instantly what Lestron was talking about. Even though the house was huge from the outside, it was even bigger inside. Just by entering the first room they could tell that this house was at least twice as big internally as it appeared to be externally.

"I see you have noticed the illusion," Lestron said, seeing their amazement.

"How do they do that?" asked Jasmine."

"Magic," was all Lestron said. The room, despite its size, was completely empty except for ten identical wooden doors that lined the opposite wall.

"Why so many doors?" asked Conrad.

"Each door leads to another set of ten doors and then again one more time. All of our history is stored in this house and it takes a lot of room to hold it. We had a library in the past that held much of our history, but that was lost to us in a fire many years ago." Not wanting to go into detail, Lestron changed the subject. "Humans are not permitted in those rooms, so I will lead you directly to High Elf Mylinia."

Lestron walked to the third door from the right and opened it, revealing a room identical to the one in which they now stood. Conrad and Jasmine followed Lestron through the maze of doors until he stopped at an entry identical to the others. "This is it," Lestron announced as he turned the knob and entered. Conrad and Jasmine followed.

The first thing they felt upon entering was a sudden burst of warmth inside their bodies. They had the feeling that as long as they were in this room, nothing bad would ever happen to them. The walls were covered with white silk. Elven words were carefully embroidered into the material. To an outsider, the elven words would look like various wavy lines and shapes, but to an elf, they were the magical words that protected the village. This house was placed in the center of the village to allow the magic woven into the silk to radiate for miles in every direction.

A jeweled chandelier hung from the center of the ceiling, casting colorful reflections around the room. On one side of the room, five tree branches rose through the floor and bent in chair-like configurations. There was a larger branch shaped the same way at the end of the room.

On that chair sat the most beautiful woman Jasmine and Conrad had ever seen. The woman's hair, nearly the color of the sun and equally radiant, cascaded over her left shoulder and fell into her lap. She was dressed entirely in white, similar to Jasmine and Conrad. Atop her head sat a crown of multicolored flowers.

Lestron approached the woman first and kept eye contact as he bowed. He stepped aside so the other two could follow his lead. The children stepped up to where Lestron was and bowed down simultaneously like Lestron taught them.

"I bring to you Miss Jasmine and Master Conrad Felsworth," Lestron announced. "They have journeyed from afar to be here with you, High Elf Mylinia."

"I am pleased that you are recovering, Miss Jasmine. I once had a brother who went through the same spider ordeal as you. But, sadly, he was not as fortunate as you have been," Mylinia said with a forlorn look on her face.

"I am so sorry to hear that, High Elf Mylinia," Jasmine said consolingly as she fought the urge to take a step toward her.

High Elf Mylinia looked like she was in another place for an instant but then she said, "Thank you for your condolences. He was a good elf who helped make this village what it is today. Most of the magic in this house was created by him."

Following Lestron's advice, Conrad patiently waited until he was certain Mylinia finished speaking, Conrad said, "I wish to thank you for letting us stay here as long as you have, High Elf Mylinia."

"If you do not mind, I wish to tell you a story about two other humans, just like yourselves, which may explain things for you."

"I love stories," Jasmine commented as she quickly sat on the floor, placing her cane across her lap. Whenever Jasmine was told stories back home, her entire family would sit on the floor in a circle and listen as Mom and Dad read stories. Conrad was not as fond of story time because he preferred more action-type activities; nevertheless, he always participated.

Mylinia motioned to Conrad to sit down next to his sister. Conrad did as suggested and stared at Jasmine without enthusiasm on his face. Lestron, not wishing to sit on the floor, sat on one of the chair-like branches.

"The story begins nearly fifty years ago, when I was not yet High Elf.

My brother and I were in the forest foraging for berries when we stumbled across two human children. We did not approach them at first, but when we realized they were lost, we made ourselves noticeable to them. When they first saw us, they dropped to their knees in tears, happy to see another living being.

"We decided to bring them back to the village. This was when there were not as many strict rules about harboring humans as there are now, so no one had a problem with them staying," Mylinia explained. "We determined they were not from around here. They kept telling us that one second they were at home and then they just appeared in a field." Jasmine and Conrad looked at each other, aching to say something, but remembering Lestron's warning not to interrupt.

"We really did not believe them at first, but their stories were so precise. We had no reason to question what they said. Since they were unfamiliar with the customs of Felnoria, we took it upon ourselves to educate them. We also taught them how to fend for themselves if they were ever in need.

"Then, one day, they were studying in our library and an army of trolls stormed the village. They demanded that we relinquish the children to them. When we refused to do so, they lit torches and started to burn down our village. The elves were powerless in fighting the fires. The library the children were hiding in caught fire." They looked at each other again, finally realizing what Lestron was talking about, when he mentioned a fire in the library.

"Eventually most of the village was destroyed and the children were gone. At first we thought they were captured, but we later learned they escaped." High Elf Mylinia went silent, letting them ponder before continuing. "I am assuming you know why I told you this story."

"Because we were not the first two to come here?" questioned Conrad.

"But, who are these people?" interrupted Jasmine.

"No, you are not the first, but you may be surprised at who they are now."

"Who?" both asked in unison.

"They are now King Ralph and Queen Synthia of Yarlanzia, and they are twins just like you two."

Chapter 25

Conrad and Jasmine were shocked to hear two people from their world had become a king and queen in Felnoria and were also twins just like they were. They wanted to know more, so they barraged High Elf Mylinia with questions. High Elf Mylinia tried answering most of them to the best of her knowledge, but then stopped them suddenly.

"I believe you are asking the wrong person," stated High Elf Mylinia. "There are three reasons I told you this tale. First, because the trolls destroyed our village because of humans, we set new laws and cast many spells to prohibit outsiders from entering. Second, I believe what the king and queen went through is very similar to what you have experienced. Third, I wish you two to go to Yarlanzia to meet them. Since our rules do not allow humans to stay in Fos Faydian, I believe you both will be more safe and welcome in Yarlanzia. You will be among your own kind."

"Lestron mentioned earlier that we were going to Yarlanzia, but he never said anything about who the king and queen were," Jasmine said as she looked over to their elf guide.

"Yes, I informed Lestron when you first arrived that we would shelter you until you were able to be escorted to Yarlanzia. I see you are now able to walk, so I believe that you should depart tomorrow." High Elf Mylinia rose from her chair and nodded to them. "I would like to tell you more about this, but I have other important issues that require my attention. I hope you all have a safe journey. I believe Lestron will protect you well on your journey to Yarlanzia."

"Thank you for the wonderful story, High Elf Mylinia," Jasmine said courteously as she rose from the floor and bowed down. Conrad did the same. Lestron positioned himself between them and gently placed a hand onto each of their shoulders as they left the chamber. When they stepped across the threshold of the room, the warmth suddenly dissipated from their bodies.

Lestron brought them back through the maze of doors until they were finally outside again. He turned to Jasmine and said, "Please take another drink of your potion, Jasmine." She did so with a shiver as the nasty-tasting liquid went down. "I believe we should head back to your room for now," Lestron urged as he led them toward the house where they were staying.

They slowly followed him, knowing they were going to have to stay there for the rest of the night. "It is getting late and you two probably want to discuss everything you have learned today. Tomorrow we must leave the village and head to Yarlanzia, so try not to stay up too late."

Lestron stepped aside as they reluctantly entered the house. "Make sure to keep the potion by your bedside, Jasmine. Your last dose should carry you through the night, but when you wake you will need another."

"Thank you, Lestron," Jasmine replied as she watched Lestron close the door, leaving them to spend their last night in Fos Faydian in that room.

Conrad sat on the edge of the bed with a stretch and a yawn. "I can't believe there are other people in Felnoria who are just like us," Conrad said in disbelief. "What is even weirder is that they are twins."

"This all just doesn't make any sense at all," Jasmine said while shaking her head. "Twins aren't extremely rare, and yes, twins where one is male and the other is female aren't one in a million. But two sets of boy-and-girl twins transporting to some unexplained world—what's the chances of that, Conny?"

"There must be some reason for all of this, is my only explanation."

Jasmine sat on her bed and faced her brother. She reached into her pocket for her potions and placed them by her bed. She placed her cane against the wall. "I wonder if they are the only two," Jasmine thought out loud. "Do you think they came here the same way we did?"

"I'm not sure, Jas, but this is what I think. They must have lived in the same house that we were moving into before we got here. Something happened, and bam! They are here," Conrad said as he gestured to emphasize his point.

"What makes you think they came from our house?"

"Well, High Elf Mylinia said they appeared in a field." Jasmine nodded her head, agreeing with what her brother said. "Now I don't know anything about magic, but I would think that if they appeared in the same place as we did, they probably came from the same place we did."

"I guess I see what you're saying, but you have said this place is weird so logical explanations may not work."

Conrad smirked when he heard that and responded, "I guess you could be right, too. We'll have to just wait to meet the king and queen before we can learn more." Conrad watched as his sister's face suddenly turned from curiosity to despair. "What's the matter, Jas?" Conrad asked with concern.

"Conny, if the king and queen are from our world and they are still here…" Jasmine wasn't able to speak anymore as her eyes began to water.

Conrad sat beside Jasmine. He put his arm around her as she cried on his shoulder. "It'll be okay, Jas. We'll find a way home. Hey, if we can't go home, maybe the king and queen will let us be their prince and princess!" Jasmine tried to stop crying because of how ridiculous that sounded. "What do you think, Jas? You have always wanted to live in those fairy tales Mom and Dad used to read." Conrad brushed her hair from her face and looked down to see her reaction. Her eyes were closed and she was still sobbing.

He held onto her until her breathing became rhythmic and he was quite sure she had fallen asleep. Conrad gently tucked her in, making sure not to wake her. He returned to his bed and quietly lay down. Once asleep, he dreamt about his parents searching the house for him and Jasmine. After a while, the dream changed and he became the Prince of Yarlanzia, ridding the land of trolls.

There was a knock on the door at daybreak. Conrad sleepily shuffled to the door, opened it, and was blinded by the bright light. When his pupils adjusted, he saw Lestron standing with a large basket of fruit in his arms.

"I thought you two would like breakfast before we leave," Lestron smiled as he entered the room.

As Lestron entered, Jasmine was propping herself up in bed. When she spotted the fruit, she threw off her covers and quickly rolled out of bed. Her hunger made her forget about the bad leg, and as she rose to step forward, she fell to the floor with a thump.

Lestron dropped the fruit basket and ran to Jasmine to help her. "I told you to take your potion before moving around."

"I'm sorry. All I could think about was eating." Jasmine said as Lestron helped her to the bed.

He handed Jasmine a bottle of potion. A few moments elapsed after taking her medicine when Jasmine tried standing again. She made her way to the fruit unaided and selected two pears to take back to her bed. She devoured them in no time.

"When are we leaving?" Conrad asked between bites from an apple.

"As soon as you two are finished eating. We have a long journey ahead of us and I want to make it all the way to the edge of the forest by nightfall."

Their mood drastically changed once Lestron mentioned leaving, so the two ate silently. Lestron could tell they were afraid of leaving the village and going to another unfamiliar place. Lestron also didn't want to leave, but he had promised High Elf Mylinia he would protect them until they arrived in Yarlanzia.

Lestron handed Jasmine her potions and cane. Conrad slipped an apple and a pear in his pockets for a snack later on. As they were leaving the room, Jasmine stopped suddenly and asked, "Why don't we stop and say good-bye to Cleric Kareese before we leave? He did want to see us one more time before we left."

"You may see Cleric Kareese while I speak with High Elf Mylinia," replied Lestron. "She wanted me to inform her when we were leaving. We will meet at the lift in one half hour," Lestron declared as he left them, knowing they could find their way to Cleric Kareese's home.

As Jasmine and Conrad approached Kareese's house, the door swung open before they could knock.

"I am so glad you came to see me before you left," Kareese said cheerfully. "Why don't you come in for a while?"

Jasmine and Conrad accepted his gesture and walked into the house while Kareese held the door open for them.

When they walked into the house, a gust of cold air hit them. The temperature was much colder than the outside, but to them, it was quite refreshing. Many bookcases aligned the walls with many different symbols and shapes written on each of the bindings. On some bookcases stood jars with a light tan fluid and odd objects floating within them.

On a table in the middle of the room, Kareese's doctor bag was propped open with various medical supplies scattered around it. Also, many bottles just like the ones Jasmine was carrying stood on a table next to the door, making them easy to grab in a time of need. Each bottle had strange writing on it; with different colored bottles next to each other, it gave an almost rainbow look.

"Those are a lot of types of medicine you have there," Jasmine noted as she picked up one of the pink ones and looked at it.

"You are probably too young to try that one," chuckled Kareese. "It was the ninth potion I ever created and it has caused more problems than solutions."

Taking his advice, Jasmine placed it back down and stepped away from the table. Her curiosity took over again, and she started walking to the first bookcase to leaf through the books.

"This is a great place you have here," stated Conrad.

"Thank you very much. As you look around, you will see many remarkable items that I have collected over the years. I have traveled to all reaches of Felnoria to obtain these wonderful relics." Kareese walked over to the table and grabbed something before returning to Conrad.

In both hands, Kareese held an ivory-colored tooth that looked more like a tusk from an elephant. "I found this with my father nearly five hundred years ago while traveling from my hometown of Rala Varlin to Fos Faydian. This is my first possession that I placed in this house.

"Wha…what! You've been alive for five hundred years?"

"Elves live much longer than humans," explained Kareese. "We don't live forever like many think, but we do live for a long time.

"That's amazing! I wish I could live as long as elves."

"You might want to reconsider that. If you lived as long as we did, you would see a lot of people you love die in your lifetime. And that can be a big burden on someone's mind. My advice to you is, live your life to the fullest and experience as much as you can."

"I will keep that in mind," Conrad said with a nod of the head.

After a few seconds of silence, Jasmine shouted over to them. "These books are amazing. By the looks of it, many of these books are written in different languages."

Kareese placed the tooth back in its rightful place and made his way over to the bookcase that Jasmine was pulling various books from, Conrad followed closely behind.

"I have a love of many different races and cultures," explained Kareese. "It helps me create the various medicines. Also, I just love to learn new things. That's why I wish I could just sit down with the both of you and learn where you came from and everything about you two."

"If we had the time, I would love to tell you everything, but as you know, High Elf Mylinia is making us leave," Jasmine said.

"I know, I know. Maybe one day, that rule will be abolished." Kareese shook his head and clearly showed his hate for the ban of anyone but elves in Fos Faydian.

"I know you have many questions to ask," stated Conrad, "but Lestron wants us to meet him at the lift in a half hour. But we will answer whatever we can now."

"That would be great," Kareese said cheerfully.

Jasmine and Conrad answered to the best of their knowledge all the questions that Kareese asked. When their time was up, they bid their farewells to Kareese and made their way to the lift.

Chapter 26

On their way out of Fos Faydian, Conrad looked back one last time. "If we're stuck in Felnoria forever, this'll probably be the last time I ever see an elf village," said Conrad gloomily. "I wish we could have stayed longer, but rules are rules."

Hours later, when the sun was above their heads, Lestron decided it would be a good time for a break. Jasmine, wanting to rest her feet, dropped to the ground and lay on her back so she could look up at the sky and bask in the sun. Conrad, on the other hand, disappeared into the woods, reappearing a few minutes later with a large tree branch. "Would you make me another spear, Lestron, just in case something happens?"

"Why did you not grab one for your sister as well?" questioned Lestron as he took the branch from Conrad.

"She has that cane," Conrad noted. "She could beat a troll over the head with that now that she has all this newfound strength."

"I'm fine with the cane," declared Jasmine as she patted the cane that lay alongside her. "I wasn't any good with that last spear you gave me, anyway. I just got myself hurt."

"If you remember correctly, that spear saved your life. You probably would be dead right now if you had not had it," stated Lestron.

"I'm okay with the cane. I just hope none of us will need a weapon."

Lestron flexed the branch Conrad found, making sure it wouldn't break prematurely. Satisfied it could take a beating before breaking, he reached down and pulled out one of his swords. Carefully, he scraped the bark off of the branch until it was smooth, and then sharpened the tip to a point. He tapped his finger on the tip to check the sharpness and handed it to Conrad.

Conrad happily took the spear from Lestron and stepped away a safe distance before trying it out. Conrad visualized a hundred trolls charging at him through the trees. Conrad pointed his free hand to an imaginary troll that would be his first victim. The so-called fight went on for five minutes until all the trolls were slain and then Conrad doubled over to catch his breath.

When Conrad recovered, Lestron declared it was time to go. "If we do not head out now, we will never make it to the edge of the forest by nightfall." Jasmine got up from the ground, while Conrad slew one last imaginary troll that had crept up behind him.

Their trek was uneventful until they heard a commotion up ahead. Lestron placed a finger to his lips, signaling to keep quiet. All three of them slowly trod through the forest trying not to make any noise, but with every step, dead leaves and twigs cracked under the youngsters' feet. They cringed with each snap. They were amazed that Lestron was walking in the same places as they were and, somehow, was not making any sound at all. The forest became dense again, making it harder for them to navigate. The thicker the tree growth became, the louder the sounds of the commotion ahead. At one point, Lestron leaned over to the children and whispered. "That is Worling Clearing up ahead. I wanted to go through here, but I think it is best to circumvent it. But first, let us take a closer look to see what all the commotion is about."

Lestron led them to a thicket dense enough to hide the three of them. They crouched down carefully and burrowed into the tangled branches that they pushed aside to look out.

An army of chipmunks was lined up at one end of the clearing facing an army of rats congregated at the other side. A large chipmunk, with paint covering the fur upon his face, addressed the others.

"Fight us now or leave this forest forever," shouted the chipmunk.

A rat with a scar above his eye stepped forward and hollered. "We will never leave. We have families here just as you do."

"You stinky, greedy rats are eating us out of house and home. You strip all the acorns from the tree and leave nothing for us. Plus, when all the acorns are gone, there are none left to grow into new oak trees," yelled the chipmunk while pointing his paw in an accusing manner.

"We didn't know that!" shouted the rat.

"Liar!" screamed half of the chipmunks.

The painted chipmunk retorted, "You say you don't know this, so why do you ransack all the acorns where we live, but leave enough to flourish into oaks in your own territory?"

"You're out of your furry mind," snarled the rat.

"Liar," the chipmunk army chanted. From Jasmine's vantage point, she could tell the chipmunks were getting restless. The lead chipmunk noticed this as well and was trying to calm his troops when a small rock flew over his head toward the rats. It was almost as if time stopped as everyone watched the rock fly from one end of the field to the other. No one moved until it smacked one of the rats on the head, knocking him to the ground.

At first, the rats were so surprised they didn't seem like they were going to do anything about it. Suddenly, the lead rat charged toward the army of chipmunks and screamed, "Attack!"

Jasmine and Conrad watched in horror as the two armies collided with each other. The collision was followed by ear-piercing cries. Despite the carnage before them, they couldn't stop looking until a tap on their shoulders broke their trance.

"I have seen enough bloodshed in my time. I do not wish to see these animals killing each other. Let us be on our way," Lestron said.

Jasmine and Conrad obeyed and backed out of the thicket. Lestron decided upon an alternate route that skirted the clearing. Their route was out of eyesight of the battle but the trio could still hear the nerve-wracking squealing. Eventually, the battle sounds grew faint and Jasmine exclaimed, "Whew! That was awful!"

"Thank you for breaking us away from that," said Conrad.

"No one should have to witness battle," explained Lestron. "To me, watching someone fight is much worse than actually fighting. I always want to know the reason and cause when I have to fight. When watching other people fight, that understanding is missing and the battle seems senseless.

"Enough about my theories; we are almost to the edge of the forest. Let's find a safe place to set up camp."

It didn't take long for Lestron to find the perfect location for camp. He was lucky to find it so soon because the sun was quickly fading to darkness.

"Conrad, scrounge up some dead logs and branches and pile them here," Lestron ordered as he pointed in the place he had in mind for the fire. "Jasmine, pull some handfuls of dry grass to help start the fire." Conrad and Jasmine ran into the forest together, and returned a few minutes later with wood and grass.

Lestron had dug a fire pit into the ground by the time the scavengers returned. Jasmine crouched and placed the dry grass into the newly formed hole. She moved aside so Conrad could place his logs and branches in the teepee formation, as Lestron had done earlier.

"I am surprised that you did this so well, having only seen me do this once," congratulated Lestron. By the time Lestron got the fire started, it was completely dark.

Chapter 27

Kadon turned his gaze behind him as his horse galloped forward. He continued looking back as the king and his men disappeared over the horizon. The youngest man in Kadon's unit noticed his captain looking back at the king and slowed his horse in order to close in on Kadon. "I've heard stories from my father about the king and queen and how they mysteriously appeared in Felnoria one day. Do you know anything about it, Captain?"

Kadon turned to acknowledge him. "Well, I've told this story many times, but I suppose I could do it one more time for you," Kadon consented as he aligned his horse with the soldier's.

"My father and a large group of men routinely patrolled the borders of the Trilaz Woods, back when trolls essentially ruled the entirety of Felnoria. One day, around fifty years ago, they were making their rounds of the Trilaz Woods when they noticed a large cloud of smoke rising into the sky from somewhere in the center of the woods."

"My father and his men were heading into the woods to locate the source of the fire when two children, one male and the other female, came dashing out of the forest. Their faces were covered with soot and parts of their clothing were charred. The only possessions they carried were a few books.

"My father tried to get them to let go of their books so they could run faster, but they wouldn't allow it. Before he could convince the children to let go of the volumes, the boy screamed, 'Trolls!'

"When my father's men heard that, they all drew their weapons and were on alert. My father calmed his men so he could get more information from the boy. The boy explained that he and his sister had been living in an elf village called Fos Faydian when trolls entered the village parameter and demanded that the elves hand over the siblings. He said that the elves refused, so the trolls torched the village.

"The boy then told my father that three trolls had entered the library where they had been hiding. The children grabbed the books they were holding at the time of the intrusion and escaped through a window. Simultaneously, the trolls were starting the library on fire.

"Next, he described how they had barely escaped the village and ran through the forest for two days. The young fellow told my father that he was quite certain they were being pursued by the trolls who witnessed their escape.

"Hearing that, my father drew his sword and had his men shield the children. A little later, a bevy of trolls stormed out of the forest. My father and his men dispatched them quite speedily, but more and more trolls emerged with a vengeance.

"To make a long story short, all of the trolls were killed, as well as half of my father's troops. Because of his losses, the only choice Father had was to hurry to Yarlanzia. On their way, they were mercilessly ambushed by trolls on the second night. My father and the children were the only ones to survive the battle, and my father was badly injured.

"The children tended to his wounds the best they could and he probably would have died if it weren't for them. They arrived in Yarlanzia the day after the attack. I don't know if your father told you this, but Yarlanzia wasn't as magnificent then as it is now." The soldier nodded his head in understanding.

"They had only been back for a week when a troll army like none other approached Yarlanzia. The trolls completely destroyed Yarlanzia that day; every stone wall was toppled and every board burned. Almost every human was slain, except for several who managed to escape to the caves in the Soaring Cliffs to hide.

"My father was one of those few who survived. The children were not among the refugees, so my father assumed they had either been killed or captured during the fight. He later discovered differently."

"How did your father find out they were still alive?" asked the soldier.

"That is a tale best told by the king and queen," responded Kadon.

"Thank you, Captain, for sharing your story," said the soldier as he turned his horse to gallop away to the other men. He felt privileged to have heard the story and vowed to himself to remember it well.

Kadon rode alone, contemplating how he was going to locate the children. As the sun lowered beneath the horizon, he was no closer to a plan than when he began. At nightfall, he joined his men, who were encamped in a grove of trees.

Kadon chose two men to accompany him on patrol to search the surrounding area for anything suspicious. Satisfied no one was lurking in the shadows, he and the two soldiers returned to camp.

Kadon assigned shifts for keeping watch during the night and announced, "We head out when the first rays of light shine over the horizon." He lay down next to the campfire and soon fell asleep.

Kadon awoke as one of his men was shaking him. Kadon jumped up quickly and drew his sword, which lay beside him, a soldier's reflex. He assumed a battle-ready stance until he realized he was not in danger.

"I'm sorry, sir. Dawn is near and I thought you should know before I woke the others," apologized the soldier.

"It's okay. Thank you for waking me first," Kadon responded as he sheathed his sword. Relieved that no one else had seen his response, he helped the soldier wake the men.

After the soldiers ate breakfast, Kadon said loudly, "All right, men, let's head out. If we only rest once today, we should reach the forest by nightfall." The regiment mounted up and headed southwest.

The rest of the day was uneventful with only one stop for lunch at high noon. The Trilaz Woods came into view just as the stars began to appear.

"Once we reach the woods, we will find a place to camp for the night. We will initiate our search for the children in the morning," Kadon announced with confidence. He could devise a plan by daybreak.

Kadon broke trail for his men through the dense forest in search for a suitable place to camp. Kadon was just about to give up hope of finding an area large enough for all of them to rest when a faint light caught his eye.

Kadon stopped his horse and turned to his men. "Tie up the horses and come with me," he whispered. He pulled his sword from its sheath and his men followed his lead.

Chapter 28

The treacherous Soaring Cliffs towered above Felnoria. For the majority of the year, snow covered the peaks of the mountains, only melting away during the warmest of months. The mountainous region was named the "Soaring Cliffs" because of unexpected crevices in the mountains that were miles deep. If travelers weren't aware of their surroundings, they could be "soaring" down into the mountain at any time. The terrain was too dangerous to travel without experienced guides.

The rules in the mountains were different from the ones that applied to the rest of Felnoria. The most important rule was never to light a fire, even when camping out on cold nights. The creatures that lived there took fire as a sign that food was nearby. Because of the bleak living conditions, these violent creatures had to adapt and learn how to survive in this dangerous terrain. So, instead of setting up camp in the open, hunters and guides needed to seek shelter in unoccupied caves. As an extra precaution, it was best to keep guards at the cave entrances throughout the night.

The second rule applied to hunting in the Soaring Cliffs. Lone creatures sighted in the mountains were seldom alone. They most likely were decoys to lure unsuspecting hunters so they could be ambushed by the rest of the pack.

Near the summit of Soaring Cliffs, a group of hunters was thinning out a pack of wolves. Each hunter was equipped with a bow and arrows for hunting and a sword for self-protection.

A single arrow found its target; a wolf dropped dead in its tracks. One of the hunters ran over to the downed animal to retrieve the arrow.

"Great shot, Your Highness. I think that's the last of them," the hunter remarked as he yanked the arrow from the dead wolf's side.

Ralph walked closer to the wolf to check the accuracy of his shot. "Looks like I still have it at this old age," he commented with a smile of success on his face. With the last of the wolves taken care of, he proudly returned to his tethered horse and placed his bow and arrow in a quiver strung around the saddle horn. He kept his sword on his hip as a customary precaution.

"Now that we have thinned the packs, I think it is time we head to Zolar," Ralph told the hunting party as he noted the position of the sun. "We should be able to get there before dark."

Zolar was the dwarves' town that was built deep inside the Soaring Cliffs. Prior to the arrival of dwarves to Soaring Cliffs, only small, natural caves and tunnels had existed within the mountain. Out of sheer luck thousands of years earlier, the original dwarves discovered the single entrance into the wall. They envisioned a safe home inside the mountain and used their stonecutting skills to fashion large caves and tunnels. It was a haven for dwarves that few humans knew about. Ralph was one of those few.

Ralph and his men slowly made their way up the mountain, choosing their path carefully so that the horses would not lose their footing or fall into one of the crevices. There were a few instances during the climb when a horse would slip on crumbled rocks, but the riders were experienced enough to keep upright. Ralph was relieved when the ascent diminished, making travel much easier. It also signaled to him that Zolar was near.

When they reached a plateau, a huge vertical wall of rock loomed before them. The hunters dismounted to search on foot for a passageway leading to the other side. Ralph called out to them to return because he found something. They found Ralph smiling as he stared at the slab of rock, knowing he had found the entrance. With their destination found, Ralph reached into his pocket and retrieved a small round stone. He had everything he needed to enter Zolar as he approached the rock wall.

Ralph hadn't visited Zolar in many years, so he needed to run his hands across the rock until he finally found what he was looking for. A small hole about the diameter of an index finger was cut into the rock, almost invisible to the naked eye. Ralph pinched the stone between his fingers, making sure not to drop it, and carefully inserted it into the hole.

Ralph grinned as he stood patiently in front of the rock wall in anticipation of what would occur. The hunters, not having the slightest idea what was happening, looked at each other with puzzled looks. Suddenly, a loud rumbling noise seemed to surround them. The noise echoed, making it difficult for the hunters to pinpoint the source of the sound. The hunters put their hands on the hilts of their swords and frantically scanned the area until the rock wall that Ralph was facing began to shake. The façade of solid stone wall slowly moved aside, revealing a gaping entrance. The hunters were awestruck by what they witnessed.

With the door to Zolar completely open, a group of dwarves wearing full armor and carrying assorted weapons emerged. The dwarves were determined to defend their home at all costs. However, they lowered their weapons once they recognized that the one who stood before them would do no harm.

Dwarves were much smaller than humans, but their bulky features made up for their vertical loss. Their ruddy faces were obscured by enormous beards that were a source of pride. A dwarf was much stronger than any human as a result of hard labor from mining ore and metalworking weapons and armor every day of their lives. Fighting was their greatest penchant and mining was their second favorite thing to do. They lived in caves and the shafts that remained after the ore was extracted. Intricate statues and columns were carved throughout the cave system, providing a homey, civilized feeling. The rock walls also had line drawings engraved in the stone walls. At first, they appeared to be artwork but they really were maps that depicted the tunnel system.

One of the dwarves stepped forward in greeting, "It's been a long time, friend."

"So it has, Orlog," Ralph acknowledged as he approached the dwarf and patted him on the shoulder. Standing next to Ralph, Orlog's height came up to his mid-chest. A pat on the back or shoulder signified thank you, hello, or good-bye between parties that trusted each other.

"What brings you here?" asked Orlog after returning the gesture.

"I wish to speak with Lord Bontarest because I have pressing news and a favor to ask."

"I will send the message to the lord personally. Is there anything we can do for you in the meantime?"

"Yes, our horses need shelter and feed, and my men are hungry. Do you think you could arrange a stable and a place inside Zolar for us to stay while we are here?"

"That can be arranged. How long do you wish to stay?"

"Not long, as I just wish to speak with Lord Bontarest about a particular issue and, perhaps, reminisce a little about the old days."

"Whatever you wish. Once your men have boarded, I'll set them up with a guide to show them around while you wait for Lord Bontarest's summons," Orlog said as he motioned the hunters to follow him.

Once everyone was inside, the stone door closed, blocking them from the outside world. Small torches lined the walls, but even with the torchlight, the hunters and Ralph had to wait a while for their eyes to adjust. Orlog waited until everyone was able to see before leading them into the caves. They made their way through tunnels that were better suited for dwarves than humans, as evidenced by the humans needing to crouch as they proceeded. The hunters were astonished by the great detail that went into the stone statues and adornments as they wound through the tunnels. The more they paid attention to the artwork, the more they lost their sense of direction. After many twists and turns, Orlog halted in a hall that seemed identical to the previous ones.

"There are twelve rooms down this hall. Each one of you may have your own accommodations," Orlog offered as he pointed down the hall. "For you, King Ralph," Orlog snickered, as he always did when he called his friend "King" with respect to his title, "we have a special room." Ralph was intrigued by this comment but knew his friend wouldn't offer a clue.

Ralph followed Orlog through the maze of halls. Before they reached their destination, Ralph stopped suddenly when he realized where his friend was leading him. "You are not taking me to where I think you are?" questioned Ralph.

"As a matter of fact, I am," responded a smiling Orlog. Orlog stopped in front of a door very familiar to Ralph. The door had been carved from oak nearly a hundred years earlier. The primary distinguishable feature was a large gash that ran up from the bottom almost two feet. When Ralph first moved into that room nearly fifty years earlier, he had been carrying an axe that was too heavy for his strength. He remembered losing his footing on a loose stone while carrying that axe. He came close to cutting off his right arm. "So long ago," he breathed. "I can't believe you have kept this room for me," said Ralph as he looked down to see his mistake from ages ago.

"Well, Lord Bontarest said that if you or your sister ever returned, your rooms should be ready at all times."

"So you're telling me that Synthia's room is reserved for her as well?" Ralph questioned.

"It's the least we could do."

Ralph sat in front of the door, recalling the fun he had inside Zolar. Many stories that he had told his men originated in that room. "Ah, the great times we had here," recalled Ralph as he faced Orlog.

The stone room was completely bare except for a bed and nightstand. Despite its starkness, the feeling of home still resonated within Ralph. Even though all his belongings were gone, it still had its familiar smell.

"Yes, we had many good memories here, but also bad ones," responded Orlog with a frown on his face.

"I know, my friend, and I still apologize to this day for some of the things that happened to Zolar and your race because of me."

"Dwarves are a stubborn lot and we certainly hold grudges, but that doesn't mean we don't still like you," Orlog reassured Ralph as he patted him on the shoulder. "Enough about the past. I will leave you in your old room while I go inform Lord Bontarest that you wish to see him. Enjoy yourself and I will return shortly." He then left the room and closed the door behind him.

Ralph stood, staring blankly, until he suddenly snapped out of his reverie and decided to lie down. As he plopped onto his old bed, a puff of dust rose in the air. He didn't mind; he was in a familiar place where memories abounded.

Chapter 29

Ralph must have fallen asleep while he was stretched out on his bed. He jolted when someone knocked on his door. A little disoriented, he opened the door to Orlog who was just about to knock again.

Orlog observed Ralph's grogginess. "Did you enjoy your rest? I hope you will look more alert when you see Lord Bontarest." Orlog snorted as he laughed.

"Enough laughing at me," chuckled Ralph. "I'm assuming you came here because Lord Bontarest is ready to see me."

"Correct," Orlog said with a trace of a grin remaining on his square dwarf face. Orlog turned and led Ralph to Lord Bontarest's chamber.

When they reached the enormous wooden door leading to Lord Bontarest's chamber, Orlog patted Ralph on the shoulder. "I will see you around, friend," Orlog smiled warmly before leaving Ralph alone.

Ralph watched Orlog until he disappeared around a bend in the tunnel. Ralph entered the room and immediately noticed some changes since his last visit. The ceiling was still about forty feet high, but the walls were different. The walls used to be quite plain. They were now adorned with sculptures depicting former dwarven lords. Their names were engraved at the base of each sculpture. Bontarest sat on his throne in the middle of the room with an empty chair beside him. Behind Lord Bontarest, there was a map of Felnoria engraved in the stone that took up half the wall. Pleased by the changes, Ralph closed the door and approached Lord Bontarest with a smile on his face.

Lord Bontarest stepped down from his chair to greet him. Ralph extended his arm to pat Lord Bontarest's shoulder, and before Ralph could reach him, Bontarest drew near and embraced his friend.

"It's been a long time, friend!" Bontarest bellowed as he stepped back from the hug.

"It has, Lord Bontarest. I see you have been doing some remodeling. The chamber looks remarkable."

Upon hearing the word "Lord," Bontarest shook his head. "There is no need to call me lord. You know as well as I how uncomfortable it is to hear one's friends address you with a title. Do you want me calling you 'King Ralph' while you are here?"

"Of course not, Bontarest," Ralph chuckled.

"Take this seat next to me and tell me what has happened since we last saw each other." Bontarest's throne was carved from granite and covered with sheepskin for comfort. On its left was an old high-backed wooden chair that had seen better days. Ralph and Bontarest sat down and started to converse right away.

After a few minutes of reminiscing, Bontarest asked, "So what brings you here? I doubt you came here just to tell me stories."

"I have been getting reports lately that the wolves are coming down from the Soaring Cliffs and killing the livestock on my land. I recall our agreement that you would keep the wolves controlled," Ralph said, hating himself for being so direct about it.

"Aye, we still do have a deal. There are just more wolves than we can deal with at the moment," explained Bontarest. "The foxes and coyotes that normally compete with the wolves for food were driven out. As a result, the wolves have been multiplying so fast we can't keep up with them. Also, I am wary about overkill. Wolves may be a nuisance, but you don't want them to go extinct. They have a place in the world just like you and I."

"Would you like me to send a few hunters up here every so often to help?" asked Ralph, hoping it wouldn't offend his friend, but also hoping the offer would be enough to solve the problem.

"Ordinarily, that would be a good idea, but you know I don't like humans knowing the location of Zolar."

"How about the five men I brought along with me today?" Ralph proposed. "They already know the location and I can vouch for each and every one of them."

Bontarest stroked his long white beard before saying, "That would be acceptable. I will arrange for an entering stone to be issued to each of them before you leave." Bontarest stared at Ralph, curious about the real reason his old friend was visiting him. "I doubt the wolves were the only reason you came here."

"You're right. There is one other thing. I have a very big favor to ask of you. You already know the story about how my sister and I got here in the first place. Well, it's happening again." When Bontarest heard that, a terrified look shot across his face and his fingers wrapped tightly around the arm of his throne. Ralph noticed his friend's stress, so he quickly added, "Don't worry, I'll make sure the same result doesn't happen twice. That is why I'm asking you to help us if the trolls come to Felnoria again." Bontarest shook his head, not pleased with what he had just heard. Suddenly Bontarest was lost in thought, just like Ralph had been when he saw his old room. Bontarest snapped out of his contemplation and looked directly into Ralph's eyes.

"I remember that day when I first met you and your sister. Orlog and I had just climbed over a rocky slope when we saw you two being chased by trolls. Your sister tripped and fell to the ground. By the time you lifted her, you were overrun by those good for nothin' trolls. It's because of the stinking trolls that we now live in the Soaring Cliffs. But that is a story for another time.

"We tried to come to your rescue, but we knew there was no way we could reach you in time. I still laugh to this day when I think about how you and your sister drew your swords. The trolls didn't take you seriously at first. But after you dispatched half of the trolls before they had their wits about them, their attitude changed mighty fast.

"By the time we got to you, the rest of the trolls were dead. I've never seen humans fight as fiercely as you and your sister, and I still haven't to this day.

"We were taught by elves, Bontarest. You know they are the best fighters in the land," Ralph explained hesitantly, knowing he had just brought up a delicate subject by mentioning elves to a dwarf.

"Those stick-figured berry-eaters," Bontarest moaned. "Our weakest dwarf could take out their best any day. If they weren't the good guys, I'd show them a thing or two with my axe." Ralph knew Bontarest exaggerated, but he allowed his old friend to defend his race with dignity.

Not wanting to discuss the puny elves any longer, Bontarest continued his story. "When we got you back to Zolar, the dwarves were enraged that we were offering humans refuge, but we really didn't have much choice. The only possessions you had were the clothes on your back, the swords on your hips, and the packs with those stone-blasted books. One day before I die—or you die, whichever comes first—you must tell me what is written in those books."

"One day, my friend, one day," was the only response Ralph gave. That was the only information he offered anyone when asked about the books.

Bontarest then admitted, "I'm sorry, friend, but if I had known the trolls were going to attack us because of two humans, I never would have allowed you to stay here. That is the only time in Zolar history when war was fought in our town. Many of my men were killed that day and I would have been included in that number if you hadn't saved my life."

"I am still so sorry we led the trolls to Zolar. When my sister and I were escaping to the Soaring Cliffs, we had no idea this was dwarven land. Yarlanzia was destroyed and we were just running for our lives and had no idea we were being followed. I'm happy we stumbled upon you, but we never had any intention of putting you in danger," apologized Ralph.

"With all the trouble you brought, I still don't know how you ever convinced me to build you that beautiful castle and all of those houses around it," pondered Bontarest.

"It's not my fault that you dwarves hold life debts so seriously." Ralph smiled as he patted Bontarest's back.

"If I would have known this life debt would be such a nuisance, I would have just pushed you away and let that troll kill me," replied Bontarest with a smirk on his face.

"You don't mean that," said Ralph complacently. "It's not like I have pushed the life debt on you at all since you built me Yarlanzia."

"Yes, but that was one big building we constructed for you," argued Bontarest. "Give me time to think this over and I'll let you know soon enough. How about I show you around Zolar? A lot of things have changed since the last time you were here," offered Bontarest.

"I'd like that." In a joking tone of voice, he added, "as long as you don't push me off a cliff for complicating your life!"

Ralph and Bontarest left the chamber patting each other. It was unfortunate their reunion was a result of potential trouble, but they were determined to make the best of it.

Chapter 30

Quilzar stood silently inside Uzgal's sleeping chamber as he waited for his master to return. Quilzar became restless and began pacing around the room, examining various objects to keep himself occupied. The room was lined with tall shelves with dozens of skulls arranged randomly. Under each skull was a notation of the species the skull belonged to and the year Uzgal had killed it. Because the shelves took up all of the wall space, Uzgal's bed sat directly in the middle of the floor.

Quilzar was staring at a plaque that read "Dragon," which had no accompanying skull in front of it, when the door behind him opened. Uzgal noticed Quilzar was examining his collection and said, "The dragon is the only species in all of Felnoria I haven't yet been able to kill. I am hoping someday that space will be filled with the largest dragon skull in existence," Uzgal said as he stared at the empty spot. "I have heard there is a cave northeast of here where I just might find such a beast."

"That will be one mighty battle, sir."

"Indeed, and when that dragon lies in a dead heap at my feet, my collection will be complete."

More curious about why he had been summoned than about the skull collection, Quilzar turned to Uzgal. "You sent for me, Master?" Uzgal wasn't pleased by the sudden change of subject cutting off his gloating, but he knew there were more pressing issues at the moment.

"Yes, I just finished speaking with Sage Morlok. He has had another premonition," explained Uzgal. "He claimed the children were still in the Trilaz Woods in an elf village. I'm guessing they are in Fos Faydian."

"But I thought Fos Faydian was impossible to find. I have been through those woods many times and never found it."

"That is true, but I also know that the elves do not allow other races to stay in their villages and the children will probably be evicted soon enough. I want to send twenty additional trolls with you in the event you encounter elves on the way." Quilzar wanted to protest that those twenty extra trolls would be better suited for taking over Yiorling, but decided not to second-guess his master. He had made that mistake once in his life and he still had the scars on his back to prove it. "When you get to the Trilaz Woods, split your men into two parties and patrol the outskirts of the forest."

"I will do that, Master," Quilzar replied.

"I also want you and your men to head out right away. We will meet you in Yiorling." When Uzgal said nothing more, Quilzar took the silence as a cue to leave. Quilzar left Uzgal staring at his empty dragon shelf. Knowing exactly where to find twenty additional trolls, Quilzar walked through the tunnels until he entered the trolls' training room at the end of a maze of tunnels.

The training room was the largest cave inside Thundering Mountains. It was spacious enough to comfortably hold a thousand trolls. There were always at least a few hundred trolls sparring with one another, training for battle. They took their practice seriously, as evidenced by the many occurrences of injuries and deaths during training sessions. Clashing and clanging of swords and shouts from warriors reverberated in the stone room. Each warrior was clothed only in a loincloth. They believed that not wearing armor during practice helped them hone their defense skills. The cave smelled like damp rock and perspiration.

Quilzar observed several sparring matches before raising an arm to get attention. The sweaty trolls ceased sparring immediately. Quilzar shouted, "I'm looking for twenty men to follow me to the Trilaz Woods."

"Ah, to kill elves?" one asked.

"No, Uzgal needs us to retrieve two humans," Quilzar replied. Quilzar was their commanding officer, but they quickly lost interest once they learned no killing was involved. Most of the trolls resumed their sparring, ignoring Quilzar's request. Quilzar, furious by their response, eyed the trolls and spotted a sizable group resting in an alcove. He stormed over to the hapless victims and threatened, "You have two choices. You either can fight me," Quilzar announced as he reached for his sword, "or you can live and follow me to the woods."

They didn't have much of a choice. They knew there was no possibility of beating Quilzar, so they all consented. Quilzar pulled his hand off his sword's hilt, turned to exit, and said, "We leave now."

He led the reluctant twenty to join his original twenty in the armory where weapons were hung on the wall for selection. Each troll, except Quilzar, chose a wooden club as his weapon during the hunt for the humans. A troll club is like a baseball bat but much more bulky at the large end. Instead of being smooth and polished like a baseball bat, the clubs had wooden spikes sticking out to inflict more pain. To cover their bodies, all of the trolls, except Quilzar, placed dented steel armor over their chests, keeping their legs and arms free of armor for better mobility.

After all the trolls were armed, Quilzar led his forty-strong through the tunnels. They exited at the northern foot of the Thundering Mountains and Quilzar addressed his troops. "We are to go to the Trilaz Woods to bring back two humans for Master Uzgal. Neither of them is to be killed under any circumstances. Once we have captured the humans, we are to meet Uzgal in Yiorling. If we accomplish our mission quickly enough, we might get there before Uzgal has all the pitiful humans there killed."

The trolls beat their feet on the ground and chanted with enthusiasm about a potential fight. They shouted, "Death to all humans!" Quilzar basked in the excitement of the trolls, until the battle cry subsided. With his soldiers' mood heightened as he intended, he turned in the direction of the Trilaz Woods. "Let's not waste time!" shouted Quilzar. "We will make haste until we reach Trilaz Woods." Quilzar began to run, pacing himself, because the run would take three long days.

They ran throughout the day and rested for only a few hours the first night. Trolls were accustomed to running tirelessly for days, but Quilzar didn't want to push them. He didn't know if they would encounter elves once they reached the Trilaz Woods.

Early the next morning, Quilzar spotted a group of humans with a herd of animals. He motioned to his men to halt before the humans got closer. "We are in luck. There is a group of humans ahead." There was a murmur among the men. Quilzar whispered, "By the looks of it, they are herding cattle. We will rush them and kill the whole bunch before they know what hit them. After we finish off the humans, we will feast on beef!" The trolls were elated.

Quilzar split his party in two. One group was to attack from the west and the other from the east. He motioned to the men to run in opposite directions, crouched low and out of sight.

When the men were in position, Quilzar let out what sounded like a crow's caw, which was the signal to attack. This side-to-side tactic, which was known as a "pincer attack," was one of the troll's favorites. They would close in on their opponent from both sides, with one group reaching the center first. This would usually cause their opponent to run in fear in the opposite direction where the other group of trolls would be waiting for them. It was a tactic that had never failed them in the past.

The plan worked perfectly once again as Quilzar's men on the east side reached the humans first and caused them to scramble in the opposite direction. All the humans were dispatched quickly, leaving the cattle for the taking. "Let's feast!" Quilzar shouted as he executed a cow with one swing of his enormous sword. While they ate, one of the trolls asked, "Why are these humans so important?"

Quilzar was not in a particular habit of explaining his motives to his men. This day was different because he was in a good mood from the successful raid. Quilzar started the story.

"About fifty years ago, two humans came to this land from another world. Uzgal's father tracked these humans from Trilaz Woods to Yarlanzia, devastating both regions in his path. It wasn't until later he found them hiding in Zolar."

"He sent an army to Zolar to infiltrate its borders, but they turned back when Uzgal's father was killed. Do you know who these two humans are?" The troll who asked the reason for the mission shook his head. "They are King Ralph and Queen Synthia," Quilzar revealed.

The troll was shocked by the revelation. "Uzgal believes that these two new humans may follow in the king and queen's footsteps," Quilzar explained. "That is why we must get them before the humans do. Does that answer your question?"

"It gives me more reason to find them," the troll responded.

"Gather the trolls. We're getting out of here. My goal is to reach the Trilaz Woods after nightfall tomorrow. The humans will not be able to see us coming in the dark," Quilzar ordered.

The forty trolls faced Quilzar as he said, "If we keep up this pace, we should reach the Trilaz Woods by tomorrow night." He got into a run at a slower pace than the day before. This time his stomach was full from the meat. His regiment followed with the same full feeling.

They traveled that day and the next with no incidents. They reached the Trilaz Woods as it was getting dark, just as Quilzar had planned. "Before we enter the woods, let's split our party in two; that way, we can cover more ground. One will search the northern woods while the other will take the southern. We can use the same two groups that we used to hunt the humans the other day."

Quilzar waited until everyone was in place before continuing. "My group will head south, and if anyone from the northern party finds the two children wandering in the forest, report to me before doing a thing. Plus, if any elves are sighted, do not let them see you. Killing elves is not a priority. Is that understood?" shouted Quilzar as he scanned the northern party, making sure they got the point. Everyone nodded even though they all would have preferred being able to kill an elf or two for fun.

The northern party progressed slowly through the forest, trying to make the least possible amount of noise. They continued their search until one of the trolls noticed a faint light ahead. He stopped the rest of the party, and whispered, "There is a light ahead. I will check it out before we report it to Quilzar." With that said, he slowly crept forward, leaving the rest behind. When the troll neared the light, he saw two humans and an elf sitting around a campfire. Not believing his luck, he thought of how glad Quilzar would be when he told him that he found the humans. He wasted no time returning to his group.

The scout informed the rest that he had found the humans. They were anxious to capture them, but knew they had to wait until Quilzar was notified. "I'll tell Quilzar," the scout announced as he took off to the south. He returned later with Quilzar and his party following closely behind.

"We are going to charge in, kill the elf, and take the humans," Quilzar explained quietly. "The children must stay alive at all costs." The trolls from the initial party were happy to hear about a possible elf kill and were ready to go.

Quilzar lead his men forward and was shocked when he spotted a group of human soldiers at the campsite. He was too close to stop his troops now. He slowed down a bit to let a few of his trolls pass him so they would arrive first. Quilzar initially wanted to kill the elf, but now he would let his trolls have fun even if it meant they might die in the process.

Chapter 31

"How long does it take to get to Yarlanzia from here?" asked Conrad as he carefully placed his feet close to the fire to warm them. Jasmine sat next to her brother trying to warm herself as well.

"It will take us nearly a week on foot," answered Lestron.

"Couldn't the elves provide us with horses?" asked Jasmine, not looking forward to walking that far.

"You are lucky they even let you stay there for a while. They would never share precious horses with humans. I would have asked—" Lestron stopped suddenly and drew one of his swords as he leapt from the ground.

"What's the matter?" Jasmine started to ask, but Lestron placed his finger to his mouth to signal her to be silent. He motioned for them to stay near the fire as he disappeared into the trees. Jasmine was immediately frightened for her life and crawled alongside Conrad and put her arms tightly around his waist.

Lestron slowly crept through the woods in complete silence, as only an elf could do, until he found the source of the noise he had heard while talking to Jasmine and Conrad. In the distance, a group of soldiers was making its way through the trees. He realized they were creeping toward the campfire, so he wasn't sure if they were friend or foe. "What are you doing in the Trilaz Woods?" Lestron interrogated, disguising his voice to make it sound like it had come from somewhere else.

The soldiers halted and looked around in an attempt to find the source of the voice. No matter how hard they looked, they couldn't find the person. Kadon stepped forward from his men and announced, "We are seeking two human children."

Lestron was surprised that there were humans searching for the children but kept calm. "And what is your business with these humans?" Lestron questioned, still throwing his voice.

"We have been sent by the king and queen of Yarlanzia to escort them there."

"How can I trust that you are what you say you are?"

"I will have my men sheath their weapons and I will approach you on my own. We can speak about this." Kadon turned toward his men and motioned to put their weapons away as he sheathed his own weapon. "Where would you like me to go?" Kadon asked as he stepped away from his men. Lestron contemplated the proposal until he decided there was no harm in talking.

With all the weapons sheathed, Lestron shouted, in a normal voice, "Come to the campfire, seeing you were headed that way." Lestron ran back to warn Jasmine and Conrad about the intruders.

"What's out there?" a nervous Jasmine asked while clutching her brother's waist.

"It seems they are a group of humans from Yarlanzia," said Lestron. "You will learn more in due time, but for now, I want you to hide in the hollow behind those trees," explained Lestron as he pointed to where he had in mind. "Hide there until I tell you to come out. I want to make sure they are who they say they are first." Obeying his command, they left the fire and ran behind the trees, making sure they could still see the campfire. As Jasmine and Conrad watched, someone emerged from the darkness and stopped a safe distance away from Lestron.

Kadon took a quick glance of the area. A clearing stood in front of him that could easily fit all of his men and many others. In the far western section of the clearing, a well-lit fire burned. Shadows from the trees made it impossible to see more than a few feet into the forest. From his standpoint in the clearing, an elf stood by the fire, glaring at Kadon as he looked around. He was disappointed the children weren't in sight.

"Drop your weapon onto the ground," demanded Lestron. Kadon slowly reached to his side, pulled his sword from its sheath and tossed it on the ground next to Lestron's feet. "Do you mind if I check you for any concealed weapons?" Lestron asked.

"If you must, go ahead." Kadon raised his arms and Lestron walked over to Kadon. Lestron patted down Kadon until he was satisfied that the soldier wasn't hiding anything. To be on the safe side, Lestron walked backward to his previous location, keeping an eye on Kadon at all times. Once he was a safe distance away, Lestron turned toward the twins and waved his hand, signaling them to come out since the newcomer seemed to pose no harm. "Stay close to me. He may be unarmed, but he still might be dangerous," Lestron told them as they walked out from behind a tree and stood beside Lestron.

Kadon was surprised and happy at the same time to see them. It was beyond his best hopes to find the children so easily. He assumed he would be searching the woods for days and then returning home empty-handed, probably forced out of the woods by the elves. "Are you the two who appeared in the forest about a week ago?" Kadon asked as he examined the children to make sure they were the correct ones.

"Yes we are, and who are you?" questioned Conrad.

"My name is Kadon, and I'm the captain of the king and queen of Yarlanzia's army."

"So you know them personally?" asked Jasmine.

"Yes I do, Young Lady, and if you don't mind me asking, what are your names?"

"My name is Jasmine, and this is my brother, Conrad," Jasmine introduced herself and held her arm out toward Conrad. "And this is…"

"Lestron of Fos Faydian," finished Lestron with the same bow he had given to Jasmine and Conrad when they had asked his name.

"It is my pleasure to meet you all," replied Kadon.

"Now, you said you know the king and queen," said Conrad.

"Yes, I do, Conrad," Kadon responded once they were comfortably seated next to the fire again.

"So… are they like my sister and me? I mean, did they just appear here one day like we did?" Conrad inquired.

"From what they have told me, that would be correct."

"Does that mean there is no way of going back?" asked Jasmine with a dreadful look on her face. She started losing all hope of ever returning home.

"Now that is a question I cannot answer. When we get to Yarlanzia, you can ask them personally," Kadon suggested. He could tell that being in Felnoria scared her, but he didn't feel like it was his position to ask anything about it.

"Does that mean you are leaving us, Lestron?" asked Jasmine as she turned toward Lestron with fear still on her face.

"No, I said I would get you safely to Yarlanzia and I will stay with you both until you get there," Lestron said consolingly. Lestron then faced Kadon and apologized, "I'm sorry if that's a problem, but that is what I must do."

"You are more than welcome to stay with us on our journey back to Yarlanzia, but I only brought two spare horses with us."

"If you don't mind taking the horses a little slower than usual, I can run alongside," offered Lestron.

"I am fine with that," returned Kadon. "With our introductions completed, do you mind if I get my men?"

"I do not have a problem with that. There is not much room here, but you are welcome to stay the night with us."

Having found the children, Kadon had hoped to ride through the night to deliver them as soon as possible. However, a good night's sleep before the long ride would be good for his men.

"We will just find a clearing nearby and build ourselves a fire, if you don't mind. But first I would like to introduce my men to the three of you." Not wanting to leave without his sword, Kadon walked over to Lestron to pick up his weapon from the ground. Before he reached it though, Lestron bent down, flipped it with his hand, and presented the hilt end to Kadon. Kadon accepted it with a nod before sheathing it and turned toward the trees.

When Kadon disappeared into the forest, Conrad stood up and approached Lestron and whispered, "Do you really think we can trust him?"

"I have been to Yarlanzia many times and I have met him before, but it seems he does not remember me," responded Lestron. Not pleased with being left out of the conversation, Jasmine walked over to find out what they were discussing.

"What are you two whispering about?" asked Jasmine.

"Lestron knows Kadon so we can trust him."

"He seems like a nice enough man. I could have told you we could trust him from the start," Jasmine said huffily as Conrad and Lestron shook their heads at how trusting she was.

"Since we are going to have company, I am going to look for more wood for the fire. Wait here to greet our guest if I don't make it back in time." Lestron wanted to return before the soldiers arrived, so he walked quickly into the woods. They stood in silence watching where Kadon had gone, until a sound like clanking metal could be heard in the distance.

Chapter 32

The clanking metal sound grew louder and louder until Kadon and his men could be seen in the firelight. Conrad and Jasmine were shocked that so many soldiers had been sent just to accompany a couple of children. When everyone was in the camp, they counted eleven soldiers in front of them. Kadon approached them and asked while looking around, "Where did Lestron go?"

"He just went to get more logs for the fire," Conrad responded as he turned and was relieved to see Lestron reappearing from the forest with an armload of wood.

When Lestron appeared from the woods, there was a stir among the soldiers. Most of Kadon's men were startled by the appearance of Lestron, since most had never seen an elf before. Lestron noticed the soldiers' reaction and took it in stride since it wasn't the first time he had seen that reaction. He placed the logs next to the campfire and then moved toward Jasmine and Conrad in a protective manner.

"With everyone here, let me start with the introductions," Kadon began. As Kadon was in the middle of his introductions, Jasmine swore she heard noises coming from the forest. She shot a quick glance in the direction she thought it came from, but it was too dark to see anything. She looked over to everyone else and they were all caught up in the introductions and gave no indication they heard anything strange. She dismissed it since no one else seemed concerned.

But when Kadon reached the end of his introductions, the sound returned, much louder this time. Jasmine heard it, and a few of the others, including Lestron, heard it as well.

"You don't have any more men out there patrolling, do you, Kadon?"

asked Lestron, with concern in his voice. Kadon shot around quickly taking a head count of his men just in case he had missed someone during the introductions. Counting ten, not including himself, he lowered his arm to his waist and drew his weapon. Taking Kadon's lead, his men also drew their weapons and assumed a battle stance.

Conrad did not have his new weapon near to defend himself with. He remembered placing it alongside the fire pit. He ran over to retrieve the spear and noticed Jasmine's cane lying right next to it. He grabbed both of the weapons and quickly ran back to his sister's side. As he tossed the cane to Jasmine, a large group of trolls stormed out of the woods screaming a battle cry.

With little time to prepare, Kadon positioned himself so he was directly in front of Jasmine and Conrad with Lestron standing next to him, in order to shield them together. "Form a wedge formation," Kadon yelled to his men, trying to give them the most protection possible. The soldiers quickly followed their captain's orders as immediately as they could, with Jasmine, Conrad, Kadon, and Lestron in the center of them.

The last of the men were in position when the trolls charged the wedge, causing the trolls to split into two separate groups. Steel and wood collided with each other as half the trolls fought the left side of the wedge and the other the right. The sound was like an axe chopping a tree, the only difference being the swords couldn't penetrate the hard, rocklike wood of the clubs. The soldiers were skilled with their weapons and easily defended the trolls' attacks, despite being outnumbered. But as the trolls continued attacking, it became obvious the soldiers wouldn't be able to keep them at bay much longer.

As each soldier held his own, an unseen club hit the last soldier on the left flank of the wedge, dropping him dead. Lestron looked over and saw the gap in the wedge. Having no choice, he left Kadon to protect Jasmine and Conrad so he could fill in for the lost soldier.

Lestron jumped into position just in time as another club swung at the next soldier in line. Lestron slashed his left sword, and knocked the club, and the troll who held it, to the ground. Lestron stepped forward and plunged his sword into the fallen troll's belly.

Taking in everything at once, Kadon noticed several trolls circling around the wedge from the right to get to them. He shouted to his men to move toward Jasmine and Conrad, but they were too occupied fighting. Having no choice, he left their side to halt the trolls' progress. He caught the trolls by surprise and managed to kill one, but the other two attacked him at once. He was put on the defensive as he dodged their weapons and was not able to make any type of offensive move.

With Lestron and Kadon not protecting them anymore, Conrad and Jasmine were left on their own. Being in the center of the battle overwhelmed them as weapons clashed all around them and the thunderous sounds were deafening. Conrad made an attempt to help by thrusting his spear at any troll who came near. He hoped every direct hit he made helped the soldiers who fought to defend their lives and his.

Jasmine wanted to scream because everything was just too much for her, but instead, she stood stiffly watching trolls and humans fighting to their death. Then, out of the blue, an enormous sword appeared above the heads of the soldiers in front of her. It lingered in the air for only a second before disappearing from sight. Suddenly, three soldiers in front of her collapsed to the ground, revealing a troll with a sword almost as long as he was tall. Jasmine screamed in sheer terror at the sight of the enormous troll and what he had done.

Lestron came to the aid of a soldier being attacked by two trolls. He brandished both swords at once and impaled both trolls with ease.

While Lestron was taking care of the duo, a different troll sneaked around a tree and reappeared on Lestron's left side, catching him off guard. As Lestron was withdrawing his swords from the trolls, a club swung at his head. In the nick of time, he dropped to the ground and avoided a crushed skull. The guard next to him wasn't as fortunate, however.

Kadon also fought two trolls at once and was finally able to get a swing in as the two trolls began to tire. Kadon was lucky because his swing hit its mark perfectly, leaving him with only one troll in front of him. Kadon yanked his sword back up just in time to block the oncoming club from the other troll. As the two fought, Kadon noticed the three men at the front of the wedge drop to the ground at the same time. In the split second he took his eyes off the fight, the troll took advantage of the situation.

Instead of swinging his club at Kadon, the troll decided to hurl his body at him. The force of the impact caused Kadon to drop his sword and fly backward. He landed on his back right next to the campfire, with the air knocked out of him.

The center of the wedge was nonexistent because of the troll with the enormous sword. A troll took advantage of the gaping hole in the hu-man's defense and charged through in hopes of capturing the twins. He made his way to the center and grabbed Jasmine's arm. When Conrad saw the troll pulling his sister, he thrust his spear in a desperate attempt to thwart the troll, but his spear was knocked away by the troll's free arm.

Jasmine dropped her cane and grabbed onto the troll's right arm that was clutching her, in hopes of freeing herself. Remembering her new-found strength, she squeezed the troll's arm so hard that it snapped. The troll screamed, let go of her, and supported his broken limb with his left hand. Seeing both of the troll's hands were occupied, Conrad thrust his spear into the troll's chest and shoved him to the ground.

Lestron sprung from the ground and raised his swords just in time to block the next club swing from behind. Lestron could tell right away that this troll was much more skilled than the ones he had fought thus far. Each time he lashed his swords, they were knocked aside and he had to dodge another swing of the club. They continued fighting in this manner, but Lestron knew time wasn't on his side and he needed to try a new tac-tic. The next time the club was swung toward his head, Lestron fell back-ward instead of ducking. Once his body hit the ground, he thrust out his legs and kicked the troll's knees.

The sudden rush of pain caused the troll to double up and fall to the ground. As the troll fell, Lestron planted his hands behind himself and flipped to his feet. He lifted his sword above his head with both hands and thrust downward into the vulnerable troll. Lestron took a split second to regroup and turned to take on another foe.

When Kadon recovered from being winded, he rolled over and pulled a log from the campfire. One end of it was still aflame. He slowly made his way back to his feet, his body aching from the blow. Once back on his feet, he spotted the troll that had knocked him down killing another of his men. He also caught a glimpse of his sword lying on the ground right near the troll's feet. Kadon focused on that sword and charged at the troll while brandishing the log to force the troll to move. As he charged toward the troll in his furious state, the troll stepped back and exposed the sword within arm's reach. As Kadon stretched to retrieve his weapon, while still holding the burning log, he saw an object hurtling across the battlefield. He heard someone scream his name but, before he had time to react, a sudden burst of pain rushed into his head and everything went black.

Jasmine watched as the rock soared through the air. Before it reached its destination, she screamed, "Kadon," in hopes he would move, but she was too late. Upon impact, the fiery log flew from his hands, and set the grass ablaze as soon as it reached the ground. The fire raced across the clearing and cut off the trolls from the humans. Two unfortunate soldiers were caught on the wrong side of the fire and were taken down by the trolls before they had time to defend themselves.

The fire roared between Conrad and Jasmine. Conrad was the unfortunate one, being on the side with the trolls. Jasmine screamed his name as the flames licked the air. The last two remaining soldiers heard her scream and ran through the blaze to rescue Conrad. However, the second they made it through, Quilzar's sword was waiting for them. With one swing of the sword, the last two soldiers dropped. With no one else to fight, Quilzar approached Conrad.

The battlefield was ablaze and the plumes of smoke made it impossible to see ahead more than a few feet. Lestron faintly detected a troll lifting a large rock off the ground. The troll hoisted it over his head and aimed it in Jasmine's direction. Lestron was closer to Jasmine than the troll so he dashed to her as the rock was hurtling thought the air toward Jasmine. Having no choice, he dove into Jasmine at full force, and knocked her to the ground as the stone passed inches over their heads.

From where Quilzar stood, it looked like the rock hit Jasmine, but he couldn't be sure because the smoke was getting so thick. He was disappointed that one of the human children might be dead and was more determined to nab the boy who stood a few feet ahead of him. He wanted to make sure the human was in his grasp before any more of his soldiers disobeyed the only rule he gave them.

Conrad thrust his spear at Quilzar, but the troll quickly dodged to the side and the spear missed its target. Before Conrad could pull it back, Quilzar grabbed onto the spear and the two were tugging back and forth. Quilzar ripped the spear from Conrad's grasp and threw it into the fire so the human couldn't get to it. Conrad turned to run but was blocked by the rising flames. As he was turning around to find a different route, Quilzar grabbed him and threw him over his shoulder. With one of the prizes secure and the other most likely dead, Quilzar screamed, "Retreat!" It wasn't because they were losing, but because their foes were dead and the fire was growing dangerously. Besides, he wanted to get the human to Uzgal as soon as possible.

Chapter 33

When the last of the trolls disappeared into the trees, Lestron slowly lifted himself off the ground. He looked down at Jasmine and was relieved to see that she was unharmed by the rock. "Are you okay, Jasmine?" Lestron asked in a concerned tone as he reached down to help Jasmine to her feet.

"I'll be okay," Jasmine groaned as she was being lifted to a standing position. "What happened?"

"My guess is that the trolls found out about Conrad and you, just like the king and queen of Yarlanzia did." Still in shock, Jasmine didn't even realize that her brother was missing. Before she could ask more questions, she rubbed her eyes that were stinging from the smoke. When she pulled her hands away, she noticed they were covered in soot and so was her entire body. She wiped her hands on her dress and felt something damp. The pocket that once held all of her precious potion to help her walk was now drenched with the nasty smelling liquid.

She reached into her pocket to see how many of the bottles broke when she cut her finger on a shard of glass. She peeked in the pocket and saw nothing but jagged pieces of glass. "What am I going to do?" Jasmine moaned as she realized all of the bottles had broken when she fell.

"Forget that for now. The fire is spreading and your brother is gone. We need to see if any of the soldiers survived and get out of here," Lestron snapped.

Jasmine began to panic when she realized her brother wasn't with her. "What do you mean, Conrad is gone?" she shouted as she spun around in circles, seeing only flames and smoke.

"I will look for him and survivors. You stay put," yelled Lestron as he dashed out of sight. Jasmine was left alone, screaming her brother's name until she was hoarse.

While Lestron ran from soldier to soldier, the fire crept closer to Jasmine, forcing her to move a few yards away. Through the dense smoke she noticed the outline of a body lying on the ground where the campfire had been. Jasmine bent down and was horrified to see it was Kadon. A wall of flame was inching toward him so Jasmine frantically fell to her knees and began to shake him.

She detected a faint moaning noise. Happy that he was alive, she shook him harder, but he didn't come to. She continued shaking until she realized she wouldn't be able to wake him up. She screamed, "Lestron! Lestron, help!" in hopes that Lestron would hear her above the roar of the fire, which had spread to the trees.

Lestron was still checking bodies when he heard Jasmine's shouts. He ran back to where he thought he left her, but flames surrounded that area. He heard her shout again and finally found her kneeling by Kadon. He thought Kadon was dead until he saw a twitch in Kadon's right hand.

A huge gash ran across the side of Kadon's face, but no other signs of injury were visible. "We have to get him away from the fire," Lestron hollered as he flung Kadon over his shoulder. Even with the weight of Kadon on his shoulder, Lestron stood up easily. As he stepped away from the fire, a huge clap of thunder shook the ground and was followed by zigzags of lightning that split the sky. An instant later, the rain came.

Jasmine followed closely behind Lestron when Kadon suddenly raised his head and looked at her. "He's awake!" exclaimed Jasmine. Relieved, Lestron searched for a dry place to lay him down to check the wound. Lestron was in luck because a small grove of maple trees was just ahead. The branches formed a canopy ideal to shelter them from the downpour. Once they were under the trees, Lestron slowly fell to his knees and slid Kadon gently onto the still-dry ground.

"What happened?" Kadon asked in confusion.

"Now is not the time to talk about that," said Lestron. "You have a large gash across your head that needs tending," Lestron explained as he examined the cut. "Hmm, Jasmine, do you remember those herbs that we picked for your brother when he was hurt?"

"Yes, the balsap herbs," Jasmine replied.

"I need you to find some again."

"But what about Conrad?"

"He wasn't with the dead so the trolls must have taken him."

"What are we going to do?" Jasmine cried, frightened by the realization that her brother had been abducted.

"Once Kadon is stable and we figure out what to do about your potion problem, we will go after the trolls."

It was too dark to search for the herbs, so she ran back toward the fire and found a burning stick to use as a torch. With a light source in hand, she ran into the smoldering forest in search of the balsap herb.

Even with the torch, she was having a hard time seeing anything. Jasmine lowered her body and torch so she could see the forest floor better. She continued crouching as she searched until she saw a white hoof.

Startled by the hoof, she jumped back and screamed. She turned to run before seeing what the hoof belonged to. "I will not harm you, little one," a voice said calmly. Jasmine realized the voice was speaking to her telepathically and immediately knew who was there. She turned back, relieved to see a white unicorn standing patiently as he stared at her. She recalled the etiquette for introductions from the first time she met the unicorn. She bent down on one knee to greet the unicorn properly. She extended both of her hands, one still holding onto the torch, and stared into its eyes without blinking.

"It has been a while, little one," came the voice in her head. "Why are you in these woods by yourself?"

With so much to say and so little time, she quickly recapped what had happened to her and her brother since she had first met the unicorn. She quickly added that she was searching for balsap herbs, in hopes that she would be as fortunate with her luck at finding them, like the last time.

"You have been through so much since we last parted. The story about the encounter with the spiders is amazing. Not many live to tell about it."

"I may have survived the spider's sting, but I suffer from loss of strength in my leg as a result of it," Jasmine said in her mind, as she reached down to pat her bad leg. "Now that my potions are gone, I have no idea how I will be able to keep up with Lestron to search for Conrad," she lamented.

"Because you have been so generous in telling me your tale, I wish to give you something." Before Jasmine could ask what it was, the unicorn's horn began to glow a beautiful blue color. Jasmine was fascinated by the glowing horn and curious about how it could help her. The unicorn stood face-to-face with Jasmine and bent its head down until the tip of its glowing horn touched her bad leg. A warm sensation spread from her leg to the rest of her body. She experienced a wonderful feeling that everything would be better and she would be safe from harm.

The sensation disappeared as fast as it had come. She fell to the damp ground, taxed by what the unicorn had done. The torch fell to the ground and was quickly extinguished on the wet grass. When she sensed she was capable of standing, she haltingly rose herself from the ground. The voice came to her again. "You will never have a problem with your legs again, little one."

"What did you do to me?" Jasmine mistakenly said out loud, then repeated again in her mind.

"You have been through much and have much more to do. I would hate to see you separated from your brother for a long time. As for the herbs you seek, just look behind you." Jasmine turned around and saw what she had been looking for all this time. She turned to thank the unicorn, but it was gone. She shouted a thank you in her mind and bent down to collect the herbs. She quickly picked all she needed and stuffed them in the pocket that wasn't saturated with potion.

Returning to Lestron and Kadon was difficult without the torch. When Lestron finally came into view, she ran to him in case he was worried about her being gone so long. She reached into her pocket and pulled out the balsap herbs.

"Go back to the fire and see if there are any live embers," Lestron ordered as he took the herbs from Jasmine. "We need them to start a new campfire." Jasmine was crestfallen that she wasn't being complimented for finding the herbs, but she knew Lestron was probably too worried about Kadon. She also wanted to tell him about the unicorn, but decided to wait until she returned. She just nodded her head and ran off again.

Most of the wildfires were out when she reached the area where the campfire had been. A few embers smoldered there. She found some large wet leaves and made a "plate" to carry the hot coals. She was proud of her cleverness when she presented Lestron with the embers. After she helped Lestron start a new fire, he showed her the balsap herbs he smashed to make into an ointment for Kadon.

Jasmine sat next to Lestron on a fallen log and watched him make the ointment. "I met the unicorn again," Jasmine said softly. Surprised at what she said, Lestron stopped what he was doing and looked at her.

"What did the unicorn say?" inquired Lestron.

"The unicorn was curious why I was wandering the forest alone. I told the unicorn why, and then he wanted to know what has happened since we last met."

"And I bet you asked the unicorn where you could find the balsap herbs again."

"Yes, but then the unicorn did something to me."

"What?" Lestron asked quickly.

"Well, his horn glowed a magnificent blue color and then the unicorn lowered its head until the horn touched my bad leg."

"The unicorn bestowed upon you the greatest gift it could give," Lestron said in amazement. Not once had he ever met someone who had been given such a great gift.

"He said I wouldn't have trouble with my leg anymore."

"You surprise me yet again," Lestron said, shaking his head as he returned to the ointment project. Jasmine, not having anything else to say about the unicorn, slid off the log and leaned her back against it. She watched Lestron make his concoction until her eyelids began to feel heavy. She tried staying awake, but failed.

Chapter 34

Ralph sat on his bed thinking about everything that had happened in the last few days. "Hopefully, Kadon has found the children by now," he said to himself. "I really need to get back to ready the troops by the time they return. If the trolls attacked when Synthia and I first came to Felnoria, they will probably do it again."

Believing he had stayed in Zolar long enough and needing to protect his people, Ralph got up and walked to his bedroom door. As he peeked out, he startled a dwarf walking down the tunnel. The dwarf was wary until he realized it was Ralph at the door. "I need to speak with Lord Bontarest as soon as possible," Ralph informed the dwarf. "Would you be so kind to relay that message to either Lord Bontarest or Orlog?"

"Oh, I just saw Orlog a few minutes ago. I will bring him to you," the dwarf offered as he turned in the direction from which he came. Ralph shut the door and paced around the room until he plotted a perfect way to convince Bontarest to help him. The knock he was waiting for finally came. "You may enter," Ralph said anxiously. The door opened and Orlog stepped in.

"I heard you need to see Lord Bontarest," Orlog stated.

"I do, and I need to see him soon."

"What do you need Lord Bontarest for so urgently?" asked Orlog.

"I know I haven't given him much time to make the decision, but I really must get back to Yarlanzia. I was hoping to get an answer to my request of him before I leave."

"I cannot guarantee that he will see you right away, but your friendship might help expedite an audience." Orlog turned and said, "Follow me."

As they walked through the maze of halls, Ralph explained to Orlog why he had come to Zolar. He knew telling Orlog without Lord Bontarest's permission was against dwarf policies, but since Orlog and Lord Bontarest were good friends, he might help convince Bontarest what needed to be done.

Ralph had just finished explaining everything when Lord Bontarest's chambers came into view. Orlog halted and turned toward Ralph. "I will go in there and see if I can help your situation," explained Orlog. "Just wait here and I'll come back for you when I'm done talking with him." Ralph was pleased his plan was working thus far.

Ralph waited impatiently outside the entry. He placed his ear to the door in an attempt to hear the conversation, but the words were muffled through the thick wooden slab. The moment Ralph heard footsteps coming his way, he pulled back. The door creaked open and Orlog stepped out.

"I did the best I could. There's a chance he'll help you out," he stated with an uncertain look on his face.

"What did you say?" questioned Ralph.

"I may have mentioned the life debt he owes you and a few other things," explained Orlog, with a large grin.

"Hey, that was what I was going to use against him, but I think it was much better that you said it." Ralph returned the smile and patted Orlog on the back.

"Enough chitchat. Lord Bontarest wishes to see you," Orlog nodded as he returned the pat on the back.

"Thanks for everything, Orlog."

"Good luck," Orlog said encouragingly as he stepped away from the door so Ralph could get in.

Ralph took a deep breath and entered the room. He was pleasantly surprised. Lord Bontarest sat in his chair with his arms crossed and a large smile on his face.

"That was a manipulative thing to do, sending our friend in here to deal with me. Most of all, using the life debt to get what you need," Lord Bontarest chuckled while he uncrossed his arms and motioned for Ralph to sit.

Ralph walked up to Lord Bontarest and took his seat beside him. "Actually, I only mentioned to Orlog that I wanted you to help us with the trolls. The rest was his idea." Ralph said this, but deep down he was pleased that his plan had worked perfectly.

"Well, whoever's plan it was, it worked."

When Ralph heard that, he was at the verge of jumping out of his chair and giving Bontarest a bear hug.

"So, you will help us then?"

"Did you really think I was going to deny you? We both know if those children get to Yarlanzia, trolls will be close on their tails. Since I built that village down there, I have no desire to rebuild it. Life debt or not!"

"Thank you, friend."

"So, what is your plan, Ralph?"

"Since the five men who arrived with me have entering stones, I will send them when the time comes. But please be ready at all times, since Kadon, hopefully, is on his way back with the children as we speak. Before it's too late, I need to head back to Yarlanzia to prepare."

"Be safe, friend, and when the wind blows from the west, think of us."

"I will," Ralph responded as he headed to the door. As he opened it, Orlog almost fell into him. "Were you eavesdropping?" asked Ralph.

"Maybe," was the only response Orlog gave as he stepped back to let Ralph through the doorway.

"Well, if you didn't hear, Lord Bontarest said he would help," explained Ralph as he scurried down the tunnel in a rush to get back home. "With everything in place, I need to get to my men and head back to Yarlanzia."

They stopped at Ralph's room to get his gear and then gathered his men in the entrance hall. "I hope to see you soon," Orlog said, patting Ralph's back as they waited for the exit door to open.

"Yes, and when I see you next, I hope it to be a very victorious day."

When the door was completely open, the five hunters and Ralph exited the cave with anticipation.

Chapter 35

When Quilzar screamed "Retreat!" the trolls stormed into the woods in the direction from which they had come. At first, they had a hard time finding their way because of the smoke that filtered into the forest. Occasionally, they caught a glimpse of Quilzar running ahead with the human boy over his shoulder.

Once Quilzar was out of the woods, he turned around to wait for his men to appear. As the first of his men exited the woods, lightning lit the sky like daylight and thunder boomed. The thunderclap caused the captive Conrad to jolt, even though he was securely in the troll's arms. The sudden shake caused his body to slip down the troll's shoulders. Quilzar felt the human slipping and repositioned him, holding with an even tighter grip.

When he figured all of his surviving trolls made it out of the woods, he did a quick head count to see how many were left. There were thirty-three, not counting himself; seven trolls had been killed. "We did well today. We got ourselves a prize for Master Uzgal and only lost seven comrades," Quilzar declared as he shook Conrad. "We didn't get them both, but we got one and the other is dead."

The trolls cheered and Quilzar interrupted their exuberant response. "Now, which one of you took down the elf and that girl with the rock?" A troll from the back of the group hesitantly approached Quilzar.

"I am, sir," the nervous troll admitted.

"I want to reward you for your performance."

The troll was stunned because trolls were never praised for doing their duty. "Thank you, sir." Quilzar reached back with the hand not clutching Conrad, and drew his sword. The troll was confused by Quilzar's sword pulling and stood motionless.

"Killing an elf is a remarkable accomplishment that few trolls can claim." When the troll heard this, he thought Quilzar would bestow him with a higher rank or make him a commander of his own men. His dreams were shattered when Quilzar's slashing sword decapitated the troll. "But killing the human girl was not smart. Uzgal wanted both of them alive," Quilzar scowled and sheathed his bloody sword. "I thought I made that clear when we left."

Conrad was devastated when he heard his sister had been killed. Between the fighting and the fire, he never saw the rock that had hit his sister. Conrad had assumed Lestron had protected Jasmine after the troll had taken him. A grief-stricken Conrad began flailing and beating his fists on Quilzar's back while crying for his sister.

Irritated by Conrad's reaction, Quilzar decided to horrify the child a bit more by turning so Conrad could see the troll's head on the ground. Conrad stopped beating on Quilzar long enough to look down, not expecting to see what he saw. He closed his eyes and gritted his teeth. He'd seen too much death already.

Quilzar turned to his men, "Thirty-two is still a good number," he said to himself. "Does anyone have a problem with what I did?" Quilzar asked while he placed his hand on the hilt of his sword. When no one responded, Quilzar shouted, "Let's head out!"

While the trolls ran on through the night, the rain drenched Quilzar and made him slippery. Conrad squirmed a little every so often to test the troll's hold on him. When he thought the grip loosened, he started rolling his body and crying in hopes the troll would think he was just acting out his grief again. The more he twisted, the more his body felt like it was slipping. Then, like a cork flying out of a bottle, he shot out of Uzgal's arms. Conrad slid face first down Uzgal's back until his hands hit the ground and he tucked his head in and did a summersault.

Safely on the ground, he jumped to his feet and ran through a small opening between a pair of trolls. The grass was wet and he had trouble keeping his footing. He didn't get far before a sharp pain in his calf caused him to lunge forward and fall to the ground. Conrad looked down and was shocked to see his pant leg torn and a bloodstain quickly forming. He looked back and saw Quilzar pointing his sword at him. Conrad wanted to scream in excruciating pain but he knew enough to keep quiet.

"Master Uzgal only said the human child was to be taken alive. He said nothing about *how* alive!" shouted Quilzar. All the trolls burst into laughter.

Conrad tried to get to his feet so he could run again, but pain shot up his leg and he collapsed on the ground. He got onto all fours and started crawling through the wet grass, but he gave up when the trolls walked alongside him, laughing wildly.

"Bandage the human's leg. I don't want him bleeding to death on the trip," Quilzar ordered one of his trolls. The troll approached Conrad with a disgusted look on his face. He grabbed Conrad's leg forcefully and ripped a strip off Conrad's pant leg. He tied the makeshift bandage around Conrad's leg, pulling so tightly the blood flow was almost cut off. The troll gave the bandaged leg a hard tap just to see Conrad wince.

Quilzar threw Conrad over his shoulder and snarled, "If you try that again, you will have more than a scratch to worry about. Maybe you won't have a leg to scratch!"

Hearing that, Conrad started to cry, giving up all hope of living through this ordeal. He closed his eyes and thought of his mother and father. He regretted the way he had teased Jasmine and wished he had been a nicer brother. His heart ached when he thought of the family sitting in a circle as his mother read to them.

"Uzgal should have already taken Yiorling by the time we get there," explained Quilzar. "If he hasn't reached Yiorling by the time we get there, we will find a place to hide until he arrives." All the trolls cheered again upon hearing Yiorling being taken from the humans. Quilzar shouted again, "Let's head out."

They ran the rest of the night. Conrad was lost in his dream world until they stopped the next morning to catch their breath. While the trolls rested, Quilzar placed Conrad on the ground next to him.

"So, pitiful human, are you sad that your sister is dead?" Conrad looked at him, surprised that this horrible being knew anything about feelings. "Well, you better not have had hopes to be like the king because you are not going to live long enough to see him," Quilzar taunted in an attempt to dash any hopes the boy had left. "The only king you might see is Master Uzgal sitting on the throne in Yarlanzia. That is, if he lets you live long enough."

Conrad couldn't stand hearing any more from the monster. He rolled to his side and turned his back to the troll. He closed his eyes and drifted into memories of his family in a circle, safe, listening to stories.

Chapter 36

Morlok lay in his bed, relieved to be out of the dungeons. He was also pleased that his cough had finally gone away after drinking two more potions throughout the day. Every time he sat quietly, he hoped another premonition would come to him. He knew as long as he was having them he would not be destined to live the last of his life in the cell he was just released from. Morlok thought about making up premonitions, but if Uzgal ever found out he lied, the dungeons would be the least of his worries.

He tried to return to sleep. His mind was just shutting down when he was startled by the door to his room bursting open. Uzgal charged in and grabbed Morlok's arm.

Morlok was terrified. He figured Uzgal's enraged state could only mean his master's plans had changed and he would be sentenced to that dark, wet cell. Uzgal yanked him out of the bed and shouted, "We are leaving for Yiorling."

"Y-Y-Yes, Master," Morlok stuttered, still shaken.

Uzgal stormed out, with Morlok tagging close behind. He followed Uzgal through a maze of tunnels until sunlight was seen in the distance.

Morlok was astounded by what he saw when he reached the outside of the caves. Nearly five thousand trolls and about the same number of goblins stood before him. The legion spread across the Thundering Mountains as far as the eye could see.

Uzgal climbed to the top of a rocky cliff that overlooked his vast army, and Morlok stayed below. The troops silenced and looked up at Uzgal as he shouted, "By this time two days from now, we will have destroyed another helpless human village." The army roared with satisfaction. "We will march day and night until we reach Yiorling. Once there, we pillage and plunger and leave no human alive." The crowd was in a killing frenzy and was anxious to head out.

"Once we take Yiorling, it will not stop there. We then move on to Yarlanzia." The crowd quieted to a distant mumble. Most of the soldiers knew battling Yarlanzia's humans at the castle meant high casualties. Then again, they also knew they would die from Uzgal's hand if they didn't.

Uzgal finished his speech and descended the cliff. He strode over to Morlok who looked dumbfounded. "How was that, Sage Morlok?"

"Very good, Master, but are you certain about Yarlanzia?"

"Are you questioning me, Morlok?"

"No. No, Master. I was just wondering why the rush to seize Yarlanzia, when we could easily take all the surrounding towns and then attack Yarlanzia."

"When we take Yiorling, the news of our victory will travel fast," explained Uzgal. "The more time we give the humans of Yarlanzia, the more time they will have to ready their army."

"That is very wise, Master, but if you don't mind my asking, why are you bringing me along?"

"I have brought you along for two reasons. The first is in the event you have more premonitions, I will be nearby for you to tell me. Second, when Quilzar brings the children from the Trilaz Woods, you are to guard them."

"But why me, Master?" Morlok was confused why he was the one chosen to watch the humans.

"Because you are kind of mentally attached to these children. If you are near them at all times, you might be more apt to catch glimpses of their future."

"Why do you say that, Master? I've only had premonitions about things just about to happen. I have never once predicted the far future."

In order to clarify himself, Uzgal explained something about his father's past. "Before you had the premonition nearly fifty years ago, my father had another sage just like you. This sage saw many things in his dreams and faithfully relayed them to my father. One of his premonitions involved two elves hiding inside our caves. He told my father about this and the two elves hiding in the caves were captured.

"The sage was assigned watch over the elves one day when he visualized them killing my father. He was shocked by what he saw and told my father of the vision. Due to my father's arrogance, he brushed it off because he was skeptical of the captured elves breaking free and killing him.

"Then one day, the sage was talking with my father and a horrible feeling swelled inside him. It was much like déjà vu. Everything seemed familiar, even though it was just happening. Then, all of a sudden, the sage realized that what he was feeling and seeing was the same as his vision about the elves.

"The sage dove at my father just as two speeding arrows, intended for his master pierced the sage's back. The sage was dead immediately and the elves were restrained and executed. That is why, when you had that premonition nearly fifty years ago, my father so willingly bestowed the title of Sage on you. He believed if it happened once, it could happen again."

"Thank you, Master, for having faith in me. I will not let you down."

Uzgal didn't wish to talk any more about his father. He stepped away from Morlok and announced, "It's time to march and take back the land that once was ours." The trolls cheered as they marched to Yiorling.

Chapter 37

Quilzar and his army marched throughout the day, stopping only when the sun was directly above them. The trolls could not tolerate the high noon heat. They were accustomed to living in dingy caves. Noontime on a march was when a troll was lucky enough to get some rest time.

Quilzar wanted to take a break so he slid Conrad off his shoulder. Conrad fell onto his back in a soft patch of grass. "So, human, are you ready to talk?" Quilzar snarled. Conrad just stared at him, not wanting to say a word.

"If you don't want to speak, then you must not have any use for that tongue of yours." Quilzar reached for a dagger sheathed at the waist of a troll that happened to pass at that moment.

"What do you want from me?" demanded Conrad.

"Me? Nothing. It is my master who wants you," Quilzar responded as he threw the dagger, implanting itself in a nearby tree trunk.

"Why did you kill my sister?"

"It was a most unfortunate mistake, and, as you saw, the troll responsible for it was punished."

"Will I die as well?" Conrad asked as he looked down at his blood-soaked bandage.

"Eventually, but not any time soon."

"Why am I wanted?" Conrad implored as he unwrapped his bandage, noticing the wound was almost completely healed. He was baffled by his quick recovery. He didn't want the troll to notice that his leg was better, so he quickly rewrapped it. It occurred to him it might be to his advantage later.

"You can ask my master why when you meet him."

The trolls rested until the sun slowly descended, and then they continued their march. Almost an hour later, a large group of humans could be seen in the distance. Most looked like women and children with a few older men trailing behind. Their clothes were tattered and torn with black soot covering them. The humans seemed to be always looking back, never keeping their eyes on the road ahead.

"Looks like we get to have a little fun," Quilzar shouted. "After them, men! Kill 'em all." Quilzar would have loved joining a good slaughter but he didn't dare leave Conrad. He thought of sticking someone else with the task but recalled the botched job with the sister and decided to stay.

The humans didn't notice the trolls charging in their direction until it was too late. They tried to turn and run, but Quilzar's blood-thirsty trolls were too fast for them. Quilzar watched from a distance as the humans were felled one by one at the hands of his soldiers. "By the state those humans were in, Uzgal must be in Yiorling," Quilzar said to himself.

When his killing team returned, he pushed his army to run even faster. The closer they got to Yiorling, the more humans they crossed. Each time Quilzar spied humans, he let his soldiers run ahead to have some bloody fun.

Quilzar knew he was right about Uzgal being in Yiorling when smoke could be seen rising over the horizon. Initially, he was happy to see the sight, but then he realized if there was smoke visible from this distance, the town must have already been taken. "If that is the case, we missed out on a good chance to fight humans," Quilzar said to himself. When the town was in full view, flames and smoke clearly convinced Quilzar there wouldn't be anything for him to slay.

A large stone wall blocked them from entering the town. The town was planned with only one opening in the center of the eastern rampart for entrance and exit. It was a good idea because soldiers only needed to be stationed in one section to keep the residents safe. Because the trolls approached the town from the west, they had to circle around the massive wall that surrounded Yiorling.

While Quilzar's trolls moved clockwise around the wall, three humans were running counterclockwise. One of the humans collided with Quilzar, while the other two stopped short. Quilzar was not angry about the collision. In fact, he was ecstatic because there were a few human stragglers he would have the pleasure to kill. Shifting Conrad slightly higher on his shoulder, he reached for his sword and in a flash dropped all three in their tracks before they could defend themselves.

"I guess I got a little fun after all," Quilzar said happily as he sheathed his weapon. His men laughed in response, but not for long. They were anxious to search for any other humans who needed killing.

When they finally reached the wall entrance, Quilzar turned to his men. "Split up. Find Master Uzgal and bring him here. I will keep watch on the entrance while you search. Only kill the humans that cross your path. Finding Master Uzgal is more important right now than hunting humans."

The trolls split and ran immediately as commanded. But, as Quilzar expected, it didn't take long for some of his men to disobey his orders. Two humans appeared from the side of a house and four of his trolls took off to chase them. "Always out for blood, never for duty," Quilzar muttered to himself.

Quilzar lifted Conrad off his shoulders and placed him on his feet directly in front of him. "Take a look. This is how weak you humans are. Half of them fled from their homes without even putting up a fight. Trolls would never surrender or run from a battle."

"But why?" Conrad asked, shocked by the destruction and mayhem that he witnessed.

"You humans have made our lives miserable. It's time you pay. If you want to blame anyone for this, blame the king and queen. They have had their men hunting us for ages and now it's our turn. Before they arrived, all this land was ours to begin with. They slowly pushed us back to the Thundering Mountains, which we took from the dwarves ages ago. " Before Quilzar could explain any more, Uzgal emerged from around the corner of a burning house.

Chapter 38

Lestron's ointment concoction was finally ready to use after a night of preparation. Lestron carried the salve on a green leaf that he set on the ground near Kadon.

"What will that do?" asked Kadon curiously as he pointed to the ointment.

"It will heal your wound," explained Lestron as he cleaned the cut on Kadon's head the best he could with a few more green leaves and rainwater. Kadon cringed during the procedure and was relieved when Lestron finally finished. Lestron smeared the ointment onto his fingertips and gently swabbed the gash.

"Your wound should disappear in moments."

"Thank you. Are we still planning to track the trolls?" asked Kadon as he slowly stood with a twinge of dizziness.

"Indeed, but if you prefer to go back to Yarlanzia, you may. I will keep my promise to High Elf Mylinia to deliver both children to Yarlanzia, not only one."

"I made the same promise to King Ralph and Queen Synthia, which I plan to keep, also."

"With that many trolls out there, it should not be too difficult to track them," stated Lestron.

"When do we leave?"

"We will head out after we eat. Please wake Jasmine and have her get ready to go." Lestron took a quick glance at the sleeping girl before walking away.

Kadon stepped toward Jasmine and became nauseous. He hesitated until the queasy feeling passed. He knelt down and tapped her gently.

Jasmine opened her eyes and smiled when she saw Kadon, happy to see that he was getting better. She looked around, and asked, "Where's Lestron?"

"He went off to get us some food. He'll be back soon," explained Kadon as he helped Jasmine get up from the ground.

"After breakfast we're going to go get your brother." Jasmine brightened with the thought of finding Conrad, but she continued to worry about him being with those dreadful trolls.

Lestron appeared from within the forest with berries, nuts, and apples. "We're heading out to find my brother?" Jasmine asked as she sat next to the fire. Lestron nodded and handed her the meager breakfast.

"Finding the trolls should be simple; rescuing Conrad is a different matter. More than likely they are heading to the Thundering Mountains."

"What are the Thundering Mountains?" Jasmine asked.

"It is a land of towering rock formations south of here. The trolls live there, so it is likely that is where they will take your brother. It would be best if we could overtake them before they reach the safety of the Thundering Mountains."

"Why is that?"

"The Thundering Mountains are riddled with caves and tunnels that would take years to search. If the trolls get there first, there will be no way to find your brother."

"Then we need to get going," demanded Jasmine as she tossed an apple core into the fire.

Lestron stood up and said, "Let us head out then."

They plodded carefully through the smoldering clearing and the smoky forest. Fortunately, rain had stopped the fire from spreading farther. Lestron, living in the forest his whole life, was devastated by the carnage that was left from the fire. He wished he could do more but knew that this was not the time to mull over that matter.

Disgusted by the sight, Lestron turned to Kadon saying, "Let us go find two of the horses you brought last night." Not wanting to be in the area any longer, he veered into the direction that Kadon had come from the night before.

Lestron and Kadon each rounded up one of the soot covered horses. The horses had made it through the Trilaz Woods to a great plain that stretched as far as the eye could see. They began their search for what few troll tracks might have remained after the downpour.

Shortly after they split up to track, Jasmine shouted, "I found some."

Kadon checked the tracks in the mud that Jasmine found. "Sure, the one who never tracked in her life is the first to find troll prints." Kadon said as he and Lestron shook their heads. The trolls had a lead so Lestron gave Jasmine a boost onto the horse and hoisted himself so he could ride behind her. Kadon mounted his horse and they began searching for more footprints. They found evidence of a group of trolls but their tracks confused Lestron.

"These prints are moving east, and the Thundering Mountains are to the south."

"Where did they head to then?" Jasmine inquired.

"The closest place I know in that direction is Yiorling," responded Lestron. "Do you know of anyplace else in that direction, Kadon?"

"Not that I'm aware of, but why would they go to Yiorling?" Kadon sounded perplexed.

"I guess there is only one way to find out," said Lestron as he poked his heels in the horse's side to break into a gallop. If it weren't for Lestron sitting behind her, Jasmine would have fallen backward from the jolting start.

They continued riding at full speed until shadowy lumps could be seen on the ground up ahead. Lestron and Kadon realized what they were, but Jasmine didn't.

"Jasmine, wait here with Lestron and I will be right back," Kadon ordered as he rode in the direction of the objects.

"Where is he going?" asked Jasmine.

"Just stay with me, Jasmine," commanded Lestron as he pulled on the reins to stop the horse.

Jasmine watched Kadon jump off his horse and run from one object to the next. He rode halfway back and yelled, "Lestron, come here. Alone."

"Stay right here with the horse," Lestron told her as he dismounted. He approached Kadon on foot.

Kadon whispered, "None are alive." Lestron nodded, accepting the information before turning and staring at Jasmine.

"Why are there so many dead bodies in the middle of nowhere?"

"I have no idea, but now is not the time to figure it out. It is more important now than ever to find Conrad before he ends up like one of those." Lestron, getting the point, stopped the conversation and the two walked back to a confused Jasmine.

"What are those things up there?" Jasmine asked excitedly.

"You do not need to know," responded Lestron. Kadon nodded his head in agreement.

"What are they?" Jasmine pressed angrily.

"They are people," Lestron said hesitantly.

"Conny," Jasmine wailed in realization of what was out there.

"No, Conrad wasn't one of them," explained Kadon.

"Let's go," Lestron said as he mounted up. He led his horse in a wide swath around the bodies so Jasmine could not see them.

The farther east they traveled, the more evident it was that the trolls were heading toward Yiorling. They found more and more bodies as they got closer to Yiorling, and Lestron zigzagged the horse to protect Jasmine from the sight. At sunset, they spotted smoke.

Chapter 39

Uzgal emerged from behind a burning house. He looked at Conrad and then asked Quilzar, "Where is the other?"

"She was killed during a terrible fight, Master," explained Quilzar.

"I told you to bring back both of them alive."

"Yes, Master, but there was more than just the elf to contend with."

"More elves came to help the humans?" questioned Uzgal with a baffled look on his face.

"No, Master. The children were surrounded by what looked to be a group of Yarlanzian soldiers. We attacked and killed the soldiers and the elf, but the female was killed during the skirmish. One of our men aimed a rock at the elf and accidentally hit the female, too."

"Are you sure she was dead?"

"I saw the stone hit her with my own two eyes. I didn't check, but there is no way anyone could have survived a hit to the head like that," explained Quilzar. He omitted it was smoky and almost impossible to see and that the rock was aimed at the female not the elf. He most importantly left out that he wasn't entirely sure she died. Too much detail would only complicate things, Quilzar thought.

"This changes my plans, but one is better than none."

"What are your plans, Master?"

"Not in front of the human. I don't want him more upset than he already is," Uzgal said with a smirk in Conrad's direction.

"What should we do with the human for the time being?" Quilzar questioned.

"I brought Sage Morlok to watch over him."

"I'm just wondering, Master, why did you choose Morlok?"

"I'm hoping he can do for me what my father's sage did for him," explained Uzgal. "We'll talk about it later. Right now we need to take this pitiful human to Morlok," Uzgal noted as he turned from Quilzar and walked away. Quilzar tossed Conrad back on his shoulder and followed closely behind Uzgal. As they made their way to Morlok, Conrad watched as trolls ran around looking for prey. Dead bodies lay everywhere, which made Conrad's stomach churn. Every house they came across was set ablaze, with faint cries coming from some.

Uzgal led them to the northwestern end of town, where three houses were still intact. Uzgal headed to the entrance of the middle house, which seemed to have best survived the chaos.

Once in the house, Quilzar looked around to find a place to put the boy. He found a room with a smoky smelling bed in it. Quilzar dropped Conrad onto the bed with no regard for his comfort. There was a window by the bed and on the other side there were two doors. One led to the entrance to the house and the other led to an identical bedroom.

Morlok appeared from the adjoining bedroom and looked at Conrad. "Where is the other?"

"The other one was killed when we fought to get them," explained Quilzar. "He's your responsibility now. I missed out on a lot of good killing because I was stuck with the boy. I am not missing anymore."

"Morlok, do not let this human out of your sight. If he escapes, you had better hope he kills you, because if not, I will kill you personally," threatened Uzgal.

Uzgal and Quilzar turned and left Conrad alone with Morlok. Morlok walked to the bedroom door and watched Quilzar and Uzgal talking. They eventually left the house, slamming the door behind them.

Conrad gazed at Morlok watching the trolls in the next room. Taking advantage of the opportunity, he quietly crawled out of the bed and double-checked to see if the troll was still looking away. Satisfied, Conrad crept to the window and was just about to open it when Morlok screamed, "What are you doing?"

Conrad frantically tried to unlatch the lock when Morlok grabbed the boy's outstretched arm. Conrad tried to break free, but a sudden yank on his arm sent him crashing to the floor.

"Don't ever think about escaping," Morlok screamed as he let go of Conrad's arm. Conrad crawled as fast as he could and hid under the bed.

"Get back here," Morlok shouted as he bent down and grabbed one of Conrad's legs and pulled him out. Conrad screamed while trying to find something to grab on the bed frame but nothing was within reach. Morlok didn't care too much about the screaming; all he wanted was to make sure the human wouldn't try to run away again.

"Scream all you want, but you're not going anywhere," Morlok declared as he grabbed Conrad by the shirt. Morlok lifted him off the ground and threw him onto the bed. Morlok stormed into the other bedroom and quickly returned with rope. Conrad had no time to react before Morlok held him down by placing his foot on Conrad's chest. He bound Conrad's legs and arms together and said with a laugh, "Try running away now, human."

Morlok inspected his slipknots and decided more bondage was needed. While Morlok was in the other room looking for more rope, Conrad struggled with the ropes in hopes of escaping. The ropes tore into his arms and legs the more he tried, but he kept squirming anyway, until he heard the troll coming back. Not wanting to get caught, he stopped and acted like he hadn't been doing anything. He added a few fake tears to be convincing.

"Having just your arms and legs tied up isn't enough," Morlok snarled as he revealed another rope. He pulled Conrad to the head of the bed and tied his bound wrists to the bedpost. Conrad shed real tears as the ropes cut into his flesh.

"There. Now you'll stay put," said Morlok, gloating over his ability to control the boy.

Morlok started pacing the room thinking about the premonitions Uzgal wanted. "With the brat tied up, I should try relaxing to see if I have any premonitions," Morlok said to himself.

He thought of the consequences if he was found resting, but how else did Uzgal expect him to have these visions? He looked at Conrad and then at the floor next to the bed. "There's no way he can escape," he mumbled to himself. Morlok stretched out on the floor and closed his eyes.

Chapter 40

The western outskirts of town lay in front of them and it was quite evident that the settlement was burning within the large wall surrounding it. Because there was no sound of battle, they assumed the trolls must have already laid siege. There was no urgency to rush to help the people in need, so they found a clump of trees to tie the horses and decided what to do next. "This town is built inside a walled enclosure," explained Kadon as he checked for any patrolling trolls. "The center of the eastern wall is the only entrance and exit."

"So, how do we plan on getting Conny back?" Jasmine asked nervously.

"I think whatever we decide, you should probably stay with the horses," Lestron explained.

"But I want to help!"

"You will be helping by making sure the horses don't run away. We may have to fight while we are in town, and Lestron and I can't be watching you as well."

Jasmine wanted to argue, but she knew it was a lost cause. Instead, she stood there silently while Kadon and Lestron surveyed the town.

"Will we be able to climb that wall?" Lestron asked Kadon.

"No, it's a sheer wall top to bottom, with no handholds. The wall was built that way on purpose."

"Now that it is dark, we might be able to stay in the shadows until we reach the entrance." Kadon nodded in agreement.

"Without seeing the layout of the eastern wall, I cannot decide what to do until we get there," said Lestron.

"You're right; without seeing the entrance, there isn't much we can do," responded Kadon. "There could be thousands of trolls blocking the entrance or it could be deserted. The only way of finding out is by being there."

With a strategy in mind, they led Jasmine back to the horses. Lestron instructed Jasmine, "If we do not return by the time the sun peeks over the horizon, take one of the horses and ride to the north." Lestron pointed in the direction of north for her. "You will eventually get to Yarlanzia if you stay on course."

"But—," Jasmine started to say.

Before Jasmine could complain, Kadon jumped in, "Please, just do this. Someone needs to get to Yarlanzia to tell the king and queen what has happened. If we are not back by then, it is not likely we will be coming back." She was scared witless at the possibility of them never returning and of having to ride so far alone. Deciding there was no way for her to change their minds, she walked to one of the horses and petted its mane, turning her back to the two so they would not see her fear.

Kadon and Lestron left Jasmine and crept to the edge of the trees. They looked both ways to make sure no one was coming before they ran as fast as they could until they were sure they were safely under the shadows of the wall.

They safely made it past the western and northern walls without incident. Before they turned to follow the eastern wall, Lestron peeked around the corner. He quickly scanned the area, trying to memorize the landscape before pulling his head back to Kadon. "Kadon, there is an overturned cart that we can hide behind and then a little farther up is the entrance," whispered Lestron. "From what I saw, there's only one guard at the entrance. We should be able to take him easily."

"Let's go for it." Kadon whispered as he drew his sword.

Lestron peeked back around the wall, waiting for the guard to march in the opposite direction. When that time came, he motioned Kadon to follow him. They sped just short of the cart, diving to the ground the last ten feet. Making sure they were out of sight, they propped their backs against the overturned cart as Lestron unsheathed his swords. He lowered one of his swords and softly tapped it against the cart. Lestron took a quick peek and spotted the troll coming in their direction. He turned back with a smile on his face, glad his plan was working.

Lestron and Kadon kept their bodies flat against the cart so the troll wouldn't notice them until it was too late. As soon as a foot came into view, Lestron jumped up and stabbed the troll. Kadon and Lestron each grabbed a leg and pulled him out of sight, concealing the body in the deep grass alongside the cart. They waited a few minutes to make sure the troll wouldn't be missed before moving on. When they felt it was safe, they left the cart and slowly crept along the wall until they reached the entrance to Yiorling. The iron gate that once protected the village now lay in pieces. Lestron carefully stepped over fallen rocks that had once held the gate in place and peeked around the corner.

Lestron turned back to Kadon with a grin on his face. "It is crawling with trolls."

"What's so funny about that?" Kadon almost said loudly.

"Except for a few keeping guard, they are all sleeping."

"How many are there?" questioned Kadon.

"My guess would be thousands." Kadon was shocked by the enormous number and was even more shocked that they were asleep.

"Well, let's take advantage of this while we can."

They slipped around the entrance wall, keeping their backs against the wall at all times. When inside the entrance, they quietly sneaked along the inside wall. "With this many houses destroyed, it shouldn't take us too long to find Conrad," Lestron remarked, disgusted by the sight before him.

"I can't believe what they—" is all Kadon said when they heard two voices. They both sprawled on the ground to make themselves look like just another pair of dead bodies as the two trolls approached.

"Humans are spineless," one of the trolls said.

"With humans so easy to kill, I wonder why it took Master Uzgal so long to attack," the other said with a belly laugh.

"We could have done this without those putrid goblins."

"I'm just happy they are sleeping outside because they stink worse than my feet," chuckled the troll.

The rest of the conversation was lost as the trolls slowly walked out of sight. Kadon and Lestron were both shocked at the notion that goblins were around as well, and even more shocked that they had gone around three sides of the town and had never run into a single goblin. The two rescuers stood up and started their search for Conrad. They followed the wall until the northern wall came into view. When they reached the northeast corner of town, the first two houses that weren't totally burned down came into view.

"Let us peek in the windows to see if there are trolls inside," Lestron whispered to Kadon. Kadon nodded and looked around before crouching down and dashing to the first house. They went from window to window making sure to stay in the shadows at all times. From each window they could see trolls sleeping on any flat surface they could find. When they came to the conclusion that Conrad wasn't there, they made their way to the second house.

As Kadon peeked in the first window, Lestron figured that something was suspicious when he saw the expression on Kadon's face. Kadon kneeled at the window with his hands gripping the windowsill so hard his knuckles turned white. Lestron took a look and saw two trolls talking. The first was the troll with the enormous sword who had captured Conrad, and the other one also looked familiar to him. It was Uzgal, the ruler of all the trolls.

Lestron knew that if he killed Uzgal, the trolls might leave without leadership. But if they failed, Conrad would definitely die. Plus, Lestron knew the troll with the huge sword was a formidable opponent. Lestron backed away from the window, grabbing onto the back of Kadon's chest armor to pull him away as well. "We need to avenge my men for their honor, Lestron," Kadon whispered once they were backed far enough away from the window.

"I know you want to kill them right here, but now is not the time," explained Lestron. "If something goes wrong, Jasmine will be alone and Conrad could be killed if he has not been already."

"But I can do this, it's only two trolls."

"Yes, but you saw how skilled the one with the sword is and you know the other one is Uzgal, right?"

"Yes, I know. All the more reason to slay them now."

"No. We came here for Conrad and that is what we are going to do. When we get him back, we can race to Yarlanzia and inform the king and queen. Then we seek revenge."

"Fine, but if we ever meet the one with the sword ever again, he is mine."

"Let us check the other windows to see if Conrad is in here," Lestron suggested as he moved to the next window. When they had looked in all the windows, they met back at the wall. "I didn't see him," Kadon reported.

"Neither did I. Let us keep searching before we lose the darkness. If we do not get back before light, Jasmine will think we were killed."

They crept to three surviving houses in the northwestern section of town. They searched the first house with no luck, but when they reached the second house, their hopes were raised. Kadon peered through a window and saw Conrad tied to a bed, asleep. A troll was sleeping on the floor beside him.

Chapter 41

Once Kadon saw Conrad, he backed away and motioned to Lestron. Lestron approached him and Kadon pointed to the window and whispered, "Take a look." Lestron peeked in and saw what Kadon had seen. He took the opportunity to study the layout of the room to decide how to reach Conrad. With his plan in mind, he backed away.

"I know how we are going to get him out, but first let us check the other windows to see if there are any other trolls," whispered Lestron. "If that is the only troll, this will be a cinch." They split up to search all of the windows and then returned to the window nearest to Conrad.

"I didn't see any other trolls," Kadon reported.

"Neither did I," whispered Lestron. "First, let us get Conrad's attention and then we will sneak in from the window over there." Lestron pointed to the window that led to the other bedroom. "That way, if the troll awakes while we are sneaking in, Conrad can try to keep him occupied," explained Lestron.

"That seems logical enough." They both approached the window that overlooked Conrad. Lestron raised his hand and gently tapped his finger against the window. He watched Conrad, but the boy didn't stir. The troll didn't arouse, either. Lestron tapped at the window a little harder this time and was relieved that Conrad's body shifted within his bindings. He lowered his eyes to the troll and made sure it still was asleep. Braver this time, Lestron tapped the window again. This time, Conrad turned to find out where the noise was coming from.

Conrad almost cried out in happiness at seeing his two friends staring at him, but remained silent so he wouldn't wake the horrible creature beside him. Conrad saw Lestron put his finger to his mouth, signaling for him to be quiet. Lestron then pointed to the left. Conrad didn't understand the second gesture but took it as a plan. Lestron and Kadon suddenly disappeared from the window. Conrad was afraid for a second that something bad had happened outside but was relieved when he heard a clicking noise from the adjoining room. He finally realized what the pointed finger meant.

Conrad quietly shifted his body and struggled with the ropes until he could get a view of the troll from the side of his bed. He wanted to make sure the troll didn't awaken from the sounds next door. The troll lay sound asleep and even snored a little. Conrad smiled when Lestron and Kadon tip-toed toward him, making an effort to be as quiet as possible.

Lestron circled around the bed, keeping an eye on the troll as Kadon approached Conrad. In Kadon's hand he held one of Lestron's swords; his was too large for this job. When Lestron gave Kadon the signal to proceed, he cut the ropes, careful not to nick Conrad. Once free, Conrad reached to his back and scratched an itch that had been bugging him all night, relieved the annoyance was finally gone. He rubbed his wrists where the rope had practically cut off his circulation.

Conrad carefully slipped off the bed, cringing when the floor creaked as he stepped down. He looked at Lestron with a sorry look on his face. Lestron gestured for Conrad to continue, so he took a few more steps, this time with no extra sounds from the floor boards.

"Follow us," Lestron mouthed as he backed away from the troll.

"What about the troll?" asked Kadon, as he handed Lestron's sword back to him.

"There is no reason for senseless violence," Lestron explained as he walked back into the adjoining room. Kadon and Conrad followed Lestron to the open window. Lestron quietly helped Conrad though the window before climbing out himself. Once Kadon was through, Lestron went back to the other window to make sure the troll was still sleeping. He then joined the other two.

"Stay right between us and make sure to stop when we stop and move when we move," Lestron commanded Conrad. Lestron took the lead and Conrad followed right behind him. They slowly crept along the walls, safely making it without incident until they were half way along the eastern wall. The same two trolls that had been patrolling earlier began walking in their direction. Lestron and Kadon dove down to the ground instantly, but it took a second for Conrad to react.

As they lay there, Lestron slowly lowered his hands next to his swords just in case the trolls noticed Conrad's delayed reaction. The tension mounted as the trolls walked closer and closer but, thankfully, the trolls passed by and were soon out of sight. The three stood up and Lestron looked around, making sure there were no more trolls patrolling before slipping out of Yiorling.

Once they were outside the protective wall, they slowly crept through the shadows until they were across the field from the patch of trees. Lestron stopped them and said, "You two stay here for a second. I will be right back." Before anyone could ask what he was doing, Lestron ran off toward the southern wall.

Lestron ran to the end of the western wall and peeked around the wall like he had done previously. What he saw confirmed what the trolls were talking about. Camps were everywhere, with legions of goblins sleeping on the ground. Not taking any chances, he turned around and ran to Conrad and Kadon.

When he reached them, Lestron explained, "The trolls were right, Kadon, there are thousands of goblins camped out on the southern part of town. We are lucky we took the path we did. Let us get Jasmine and head to Yarlanzia before they know what happened."

Conrad's mouth dropped open and a wave of relief passed over him when he heard his sister was alive. All the sorrow he had felt the last few days finally washed away and was replaced by sheer joy. He wanted to ask how she survived the rock hit and everything else that had happened the past few days, but decided now wasn't the appropriate time. They ran across the clearing, only stopping when they were in the safety of trees again. Lestron turned around and took a quick look to see if they had been followed. All was clear.

When Jasmine was in sight, Lestron and Kadon stopped walking so that the two children could reunite privately. Wanting to surprise her, Conrad slowly crept behind Jasmine who was preoccupied with the horses. When he reached her, he raised his hand and gently poked her in the back.

The poke startled Jasmine and she whirled around to see what it was. The last thing she expected was Conrad standing in front of her with an ear-to-ear smile on his face. No words could escape her mouth. The only thing she could do was stand there in shock and thankfulness that her brother was still alive.

Conrad was so moved by his sister's reaction he reached out and embraced her with tears in his eyes. Jasmine's attempt to hug back was thwarted as Conrad lifted her off the ground. They held onto each other crying until Conrad couldn't hold her up any longer.

"I thought you were dead," Conrad cried as he pulled himself away from his sister. "When the trolls took me, they said you were crushed by a rock. The troll with that large sword even killed the one that supposedly killed you."

"No, Lestron saved me at the last second. But I thought you were dead, too," Jasmine responded as she dried her eyes. "While we rode here, there were dead bodies everywhere. Lestron and Kadon always rode ahead and checked the people. I was afraid one of them would return and tell me bad news, but thankfully they never did. By the time we got here, I had hoped that you might be alive."

"The trolls that brought me here slew most of those people," explained Conrad.

Knowing that he should give the two children more time together, but also knowing it was dangerous to remain there, Lestron approached the children. "I know you two have not seen each other for awhile, but you will have plenty of time to talk when we get to Yarlanzia. There are thousands of war-ready trolls and goblins back there and Yarlanzia needs to be warned. Also, when they find out you are gone, they will be searching for you."

"One thing before we leave," Conrad requested as he bent down and pointed to his leg. "I tried escaping two days ago and was cut on this leg. Somehow, it's healed over already."

"Remember when we placed the ointment made of balsap herbs on your head injury when we were washed down the river?"

"Yeah."

"Well, the ointment runs throughout your blood for many weeks before the effects wear off. Any cuts you receive within weeks will heal quickly."

"That's amazing," Conrad replied as he reached down and removed the blood-covered bandage with no need to fool the trolls any longer. He then rubbed his leg before standing back up.

Jasmine went to untie the horses and Conrad joined her to assist. They each held the reins while Lestron and Kadon prepared to help them mount up.

Lestron grabbed onto Jasmine's waist and helped her onto the horse. Kadon bent down onto one knee and cupped his hands together to give Conrad a boost onto the other horse. With both children on the horses, Lestron and Kadon led the horses out of the trees before mounting the horses themselves.

They pushed their horses for a whole day before coming across a small village as the sun was slowly disappearing over the horizon. They commanded the villagers to abandon their small town and make way to Yarlanzia. Before leaving, they exchanged their worn horses for new ones. They felt bad about it, but they need to get to Yarlanzia as quick as possible to warn the king and queen.

Not resting at night, they continued to push their new horses. Each took turns sleeping as the horses galloped on their way. When Jasmine and Conrad woke up, the other two would stop the horse only long enough to switch places to let Jasmine and Conrad lead the horses while they slept.

The only other time they stopped was early in the morning on the second day. From a distance, the group noticed a large line of animals scurrying across the plains heading to the East. When they were close enough, they realized the animals were rats. It was really odd that they had what appeared to be all their possessions strapped to their backs. Each one of them looked frantic and many looked injured as well. Jasmine wanted to ask why they were marching to the east, but she knew the reason. The chipmunks must have won the battle in the Trilaz Woods.

Chapter 42

Uzgal stood patiently, listening to Quilzar's report of what had happened the past few days. Quilzar went into detail about the fight with the humans, how he captured the human child and watched the other one die, how they journeyed to Yiorling, and about all the humans they found on their way. Uzgal looked pleased during that part of the report, since some of the humans that could report to the king and queen would never reach their destination. Quilzar ended the report recapping when he and Uzgal left the human boy in Morlok's safekeeping earlier that day.

"I'm not pleased that the female human died, but we still have one left. We certainly did well taking over Yiorling with minimal losses. Now we need to march to Yarlanzia as soon as possible," explained Uzgal. "It's not going to take long for the humans that got away to reach Yarlanzia and call on the elves and dwarves for help. Tomorrow we will prepare and the next day we will march to Yarlanzia. Hopefully, by that time, Morlok will have had a vision for me."

"What are you planning to do with the boy, Master?" questioned Quilzar.

"I actually have two things I want to do with him. One you already know, which is using Sage Morlok to predict the future. Second, I plan on taking the boy to Yarlanzia and spilling his blood on the castle's steps in my father's memory once we capture the town. Since the last two humans that came to Felnoria destroyed my father's empire, I just feel it would be appropriate to destroy this male child in the king and queen's town," Uzgal explained with a heartfelt desire to avenge his father's death.

"Do you really think Sage Morlok will predict anything?" asked Quilzar.

"I can hope. He did predict that humans would come to Felnoria for a second time, and he was correct. Hopefully, tonight he will have some type of vision. We'll check on him first thing in the morning. For right now, I need to get some rest." Quilzar took leave of Uzgal and left him alone in the house.

Early the next morning, Morlok awoke angry at himself for not having any visions of the future. As he lay there staring at the ceiling, thinking about what Master Uzgal would say when he didn't have any visions, he tossed around the idea of making up something. Then he thought against it.

"As long as I stay near the human at all times, I am bound to see something," Morlok said to himself. "The last sage was able to predict the future, so I should be able to as well." He lay there a bit longer, not really wanting to start the boring day of sitting around watching the human as everyone else pillaged outside. However, the longer he lay there, the more he felt like something was wrong. It was extremely quiet inside the room.

Morlok shot up and saw his worst nightmare come true. Only a pile of ropes lay where the human had been. Morlok moaned in anguish at the thought of losing the child. Not knowing what to do, he frantically searched every nook and cranny in the house. When he entered the bedroom next to the one he slept in, he noticed the window was open. "How could this be?" Morlok asked himself as he slammed his fist against the wall. "If Uzgal hears about this, I'm dead. I need to get out of here before Uzgal comes back."

Morlok ran to the front door of the house. He opened the door just enough to stick his head out and looked in every direction to see if Uzgal was near. He was in luck because Uzgal was nowhere in sight.

Morlok pushed the door open and headed for the entrance to the town, trying to be as inconspicuous as possible. When he finally reached the outside of town, he started running in no particular direction and never looked back.

When Uzgal woke, his first thought was to see Morlok. If Morlok had any visions, maybe he'd know if the next battle would be won. Before doing anything else for the day, he decided he would check on Morlok. As Uzgal was leaving the house, Quilzar was approaching from the east.

"Master, Master, I have some distressing news for you," Quilzar said breathlessly as he bowed to Uzgal.

"Walk with me to Morlok's house and we can talk along the way." As they walked to the house, Quilzar reported that a dead troll had been found hidden outside of town. He usually wouldn't report something like this because many trolls had been killed the day before, but it seemed odd that the body had been concealed. Uzgal pondered it and decided that it was just an escaping human who tried hiding the body to cover his tracks out of town.

When the house came into view, they noticed the door was open. "I wonder why Morlok left the door open?"

"Maybe the stupid troll left the boy alone," responded Quilzar.

"He better not have left that human unattended," Uzgal snarled as he sped up his pace to the house. When they entered the house, they noticed many disturbing things in the entrance room. Without examining the situation, they walked directly into the room where they had left Morlok and the boy the night before.

"Where are they?" demanded Uzgal, furious that the human was not where he left him.

"By the looks of this," Quilzar observed as he approached the bed and lifted the ropes, "the human must have escaped. Morlok must have slackened his watch thinking he had securely tied up the human. The human must have escaped sometime last night while Morlok slept." Quilzar then examined the ropes with a puzzled look on his face, and growled, "They look like they have been cut!" He threw the rope to Uzgal so he could take a look himself.

Uzgal caught the rope and quickly examined it. Outraged, Uzgal threw the rope to the floor and asked, "Where is Morlok?" He didn't feel it appropriate to call him Sage anymore.

"If I remember correctly from last night, you told Morlok you would kill him if the human escaped. So, my guess would be that he either ran off to find the human, or he didn't feel like sticking around to endure your wrath."

"That is nonsense," Uzgal denied as he approached the bed, bending down and lifting the bed. He then shoved it with all his strength until the bed crashed against the wall and broke to pieces.

"Let's check the rest of the house," shouted Uzgal.

Uzgal started in the bedroom next to the one they had been in where he noticed the window was open. Taking it as a clue, he stuck his head out of the window and saw footprints in the damp ground. Uzgal grabbed the open window and slammed it shut, shattering the glass to smithereens.

As Uzgal stormed out of the room, he snarled at Quilzar, "Follow me."

They circled around the house until Uzgal stopped in front of the window that overlooked the shattered bed. Uzgal bent over and examined two sets of prints that were underneath the window. Remaining crouched down, he followed them to the now-shattered window. He could tell that when the footprints entered the house, there were two sets, but when they left, three.

Uzgal spun around and turned to Quilzar, "You said they were all dead," shouted Uzgal. "If I didn't need you now, I'd kill you. Organize the trolls to depart for Yarlanzia this instant. There is no way we can catch them before they reach Yarlanzia, but we can ruin their celebration."

Chapter 43

By sunset, the weary travelers were finally coming to the end of their exhausting journey. Their bodies ached from riding horses for two days and they were tired, dirty, and hungry. As the horses were cantering over a hill, the first signs of Yarlanzia were coming into view.

Lestron was the first to notice the top of the castle, but because of sleep deprivation, he first thought it was just his eyes playing tricks on him. Kadon noticed the castle as well and sighed in relief at finally being home.

Lestron tapped Jasmine's back, waking her up from sleep. Jasmine woke up but didn't open her eyes at first. "Is it my turn already?" Jasmine moaned as if she was talking in her sleep.

"No, Jasmine. Yarlanzia is just ahead," Lestron explained as he tapped her once again.

Jasmine opened her eyes. Once focused, she exclaimed, "Finally! I don't think I'm ever going to ride another horse for the rest of my life."

When Kadon tapped Conrad's shoulder, Conrad raised his hand and knocked Kadon's off his shoulder. "Wake up, Conrad, we're here," Kadon stated as he poked Conrad harder this time.

"We're here?" Conrad asked as his head shot up and looked forward, almost smacking Kadon in the chin. "That place is huge."

"Yes, Yarlanzia is the largest castle in Felnoria," explained Kadon.

"And what are those black things over there?" Conrad asked as he pointed toward the field between them and the castle. When Conrad said that, everyone saw a large black line that looked like ants from the distance.

"Those would be soldiers patrolling from Yarlanzia," explained Kadon. As the army of "ants" came closer, Conrad noticed they were actually men on horseback. When the soldiers noticed two horses coming toward Yarlanzia, they sent a small party ahead to see who it was. The soldiers were relieved when they recognized Kadon.

"Captain Kadon, we have been waiting for you," one of the soldiers stated. "You were expected back days ago."

"Yes," a tired Kadon said. "We ran into some problems and we need to speak with the king and queen immediately."

"Are these the children?" the soldier asked.

"Yes, these are the ones the king and queen seek."

"And the elf?" the soldier inquired as he put a hand to his sword.

"He is a friend. He means no harm. But we don't have time for introductions. Send one of your men to inform the king and queen of our arrival. Have the rest of your men continue patrolling."

"Yes, sir." Once the soldier had chosen his man to inform the king and queen he sent everyone on their way. "I would be honored to escort you, Captain."

"That will be fine, and when we reach the king and queen I want you to stay with us because I believe the king will have something for you to do once he hears what I have to say."

They rode slowly to the castle, hoping to cool the horses on the way. Jasmine and Conrad watched as the scenery changed from flat grass plains to farmland and houses. When they reached Yarlanzia, it wasn't like it had been when Kadon had left. There wasn't a parade of people waiting to celebrate his triumphant return. Instead, the streets were abandoned with only a few stragglers here and there. There was an eerie feeling like everyone already knew the trolls were coming. The king and queen stood patiently at the top of the steps to the castle. Kadon and Lestron dismounted first, then turned to help the twins get off the horses. The four of them wearily climbed the stairs in the company of the soldier.

Lestron and Kadon greeted the king and queen. The royal couple recognized Lestron right away. Synthia said, "Lestron, are you the elf who helped the children escape the trolls?" Kadon was surprised that Synthia knew who Lestron was, but kept silent.

"I am, Your Highness," Lestron responded, once he had risen from his bow.

"We are greatly in your debt for all you have done."

"Thank you, Your Highness," Lestron responded as he stepped aside so the children could be acknowledged. They bowed before the king and queen, then stood up as straight as their aching backs would allow.

"And what are your names, children?" Synthia asked.

"My name is Jasmine, and this is my brother, Conrad," Jasmine said as she made a weak curtsy.

"I know you have many questions for us, and we have many for you, but I can tell that you are tired and we can talk more when you are well rested." Jasmine and Conrad were relieved that they could finally rest and that they didn't have to talk. They nodded in acceptance and stepped beside Lestron.

"Now tell me, Kadon, why did it take so long for you to bring the children?" asked Ralph.

"The trolls reached the children the same time my men and I found them," explained Kadon.

"Where are your men now?"

"None of them survived, Your Highness. I wouldn't have survived either if it weren't for Lestron and Jasmine."

Ralph looked quite confused because Kadon left out Conrad's name. "What about Conrad?" questioned Ralph.

"He was taken during the fight. That is why it took us so long to get here. We had to track his captors all the way to Yiorling before we were able to get him back."

"Yiorling," Ralph said in confusion, "Why would trolls take him there?"

"I am sorry to tell you this, Your Highness, but the trolls have taken Yiorling," Kadon explained with a grim look on his face. Synthia gasped and grabbed onto Ralph's hand.

"Did anyone survive?" asked Synthia as she gripped harder onto her brother's hand.

"I am sorry, but Lestron and I sneaked into the town to find Conrad and there were no humans left alive. We didn't search much, but there was no way anyone could have survived. Even as we rode to town, bodies were scattered all over. They probably slaughtered everyone so there would be no one left to contact you."

"How could this be? We were just there last month and they seemed well fortified," explained Synthia.

"There were thousands of trolls and goblins encamped around the town while we were there. We believe they will be coming here shortly."

"I feared that would happen, since it happened when my sister and I first arrived. How long do you think we have?" asked Ralph.

"We were able to rescue Conrad almost three days ago and we rode straight here without resting. My best guess would be in two days, maximum."

"That doesn't give us much time for preparation," exclaimed Ralph. As Kadon, the king, and the queen spoke, Lestron thought of a plan. Feeling that his presence wasn't crucial, he finally decided to interrupt.

"I am sorry, Your Highness, I do not wish to interrupt, but I could ride to Fos Faydian to see if my people will come to your aid in this fight," offered Lestron. Even though he was exhausted from the trip, he wanting to give as much support as possible.

"Thank you for your help, Lestron. I will have someone supply you with a fresh horse right away." Lestron bowed and ran down the stairs.

Once Lestron was out of sight, Ralph spoke up, "Let's move to the throne room where this conversation would be better suited, and we can get Conrad and Jasmine a place to sleep."

Chapter 44

With the children finally resting, the adults convened in the throne room. Synthia sat on her throne as her brother paced around the room impatiently. Kadon and the soldier stood in silence. Finally, Ralph stopped pacing and everyone looked in his direction. "There are many preparations that must be done in the next two days," explained Ralph. "I must first find the five hunters who went with me to Zolar."

The soldier stepped forward and volunteered, "I will find them and send them here, Your Highness."

"Very well. I don't care if they are sleeping or not, just get them here now."

"Right away, sir," the soldier nodded before he turned to run out of the room. Ralph began pacing again, trying to think of everything else that needed to be done. Flustered at watching her brother, Synthia stepped from her throne and approached him.

"You need to sit down and relax. You are not as young as you used to be," Synthia reminded him as she grabbed onto her brother's arm and led him to his throne.

Once Ralph was seated, he continued. "Kadon, I want you to get every family that is not protected by these castle walls to the caves in the Soaring Cliffs. Make sure every woman and child is brought there, and have every able man brought to the armory to be suited for weapons and armor. You may send your wife and children to the caves or to the castle. That is for you to choose."

"I will do that, sir," Kadon obliged as his mind wandered for a second to his family. "Is there anything else you need of me?"

"Once you have all the men separated from the women and children, get a rough head count of how many men we will have for this battle and add that to the number of soldiers we have stationed here and report to me."

"I will, Your Highness," Kadon stated as he turned to leave.

"One last thing, Kadon," mentioned Synthia as Kadon paused and turned. "You did a good job out there."

"Thank you," Kadon responded as he bowed low in gratitude for the compliment. He then turned again and walked from the room.

Once alone, Ralph and Synthia began to discuss all of the measures that needed to be taken. In their fifty-year reign, they had never had an invasion of Yarlanzia. They had small villages pillaged and plundered by small armies but nothing to the scale of what Kadon described. This would take all the wisdom they had acquired over the past fifty years and every alliance they had ever formed to defeat those trolls.

They were discussing Lestron and the elves of Fos Faydian when the soldier who was sent out to find the five hunters returned. Ralph was surprised at how fast they arrived but was pleased at the same time. They stopped talking and watched the men approach. Ralph stood up from his throne.

"You five men were given a precious gift by the dwarves. I wish for you five to go back up the Soaring Cliffs and speak with Lord Bontarest for me. Tell him that the time has come and that they are needed immediately."

"Yes, Your Highness," the five hunters responded in unison.

"I wish for you to leave immediately. There should be five horses ready at the stable for you. Take only enough supplies to get to Zolar and make sure to take the entering stones. The lighter your load, the faster you will reach Zolar."

"Yes, Your Highness," the soldiers responded before they marched out of the room.

The lone soldier faced the king and asked, "Is there anything else you wish of me, Your Highness?"

"You lead the soldiers that patrol the outskirts of Yarlanzia?" questioned Ralph.

"That is correct."

"I wish for you to form two additional units and have them patrol the area with you. I know it's late, but I would like you to collect those men now and send them out immediately. If any ask why they are being sent out, tell them it's for training. I don't want to cause any sudden panic until we have everything organized."

"I will, Your Highness," the soldier said as he turned to leave the room.

The king and queen felt the plans were in place and it was time they got some rest. They went to their separate rooms, and both of them lay sleepless in their beds as they dwelt upon what was going to happen soon to their peaceful town.

Chapter 45

The next morning, Ralph made sure to wake before the children. He went to his sister's chamber and discussed what they should do about them. They always hoped a day would come when someone like them would come here from their world, but they never believed it would be this late in their lifetime before another arrival. They had many discussions over the years, but as they grew older, their hopes faded. As the sun was rising, they decided what needed to be done and went into the throne room to wait for the children.

They sat patiently on their thrones until Jasmine and Conrad entered, escorted by one of Synthia's chambermaids. Both Ralph and Synthia were pleased that the children looked well rested, since what they planned for them would take much energy. For many decades, they wanted to pass down their knowledge to someone from their world, and today was finally that day.

Before the children reached Ralph and Synthia, they stopped to enjoy the beautifully decorated room. They were still absorbing the room when the chambermaid tapped their backs to cue them to approach the king and queen. They greeted the king and queen formally as the chambermaid quietly exited.

"High Elf Mylinia told us that you two came to this world the same way we did," said Conrad.

"That is correct," responded Synthia. "My brother and I arrived here nearly fifty years ago."

"She told us you were twins."

"That is also correct."

"Do you think it's weird that you two are twins and we are twins?"

questioned Conrad as he stepped closer to his sister to accentuate the resemblance. They could tell that Ralph and Synthia were surprised to hear that they were also twins.

Synthia decided to explain how she felt when she came to Felnoria. "When I arrived here fifty years ago, I believed everything here was strange. Many things from our world weren't the same here in Felnoria. And, as you have noticed, there are many different races that live here. But, as time passed by, I grew accustomed to Felnoria and all of its oddities," Synthia smiled as she spoke.

"But didn't you ever try to get back home?" asked Jasmine in hopes that they would say they had found a way back but just decided they liked it better here.

"At first we thought about it, but as time passed, we believed we came to Felnoria for a reason, and that reason was to help these people survive," explained Synthia as she placed her hand gently on top of her brother's. Ralph looked over to his sister and smiled.

"Do you think we came here for that reason as well?" asked Conrad.

"That is for you and your sister to decide. But I don't take coincidences lightly. When my brother and I arrived here, this land was in turmoil, as it is now. So, if you wish to stay here and help the realm, we support you. If you wish to leave, you will have all of our men at your disposal to help you. But first, we must deal with these trolls before we can address your needs."

"Jas and I haven't talked it over yet if we want to stay or not. But I understand that if we want to leave it's going to have to be after all this is done and over." Conrad glanced at his sister and asked, "Is there anything we could do to help?"

With the words Ralph had hoped so dearly to hear from them, he stood up from his throne and walked to a single bookcase that stood at the back of the room. The bookcase was filled with hundreds of books, but it only took Ralph seconds to find what he was looking for. He pulled out five books before turning around and walking to a wooden table that was against one of the walls. Synthia left her throne and motioned for the children to follow her to the table.

Ralph carefully placed the books on the table, making sure the children couldn't read the titles. "These are our prized possessions. These books mean more to us than the castle we now live in," explained Ralph as he selected the first one. "When we were in Fos Faydian and the trolls attacked, these are the only objects we escaped with. They are the same ones we took to Yarlanzia, before this castle was built. The trolls destroyed Yarlanzia and we escaped with only our weapons and these books. Nobody but the elves and my sister and I know what is written in these books. The elves believe they were lost in the fire when Fos Faydian burned, so we are the only ones other than you two who know they still exist."

"What's inside of them?" asked Conrad curiously. As he tried to peek at the cover of one face up on the table, Ralph pushed the book farther away.

Ralph placed the book he had in his hand in front of them and it read, *Weapon Training for Beginners*. Then he reached for the next and read from the cover, *Advanced Weapon Training*. Third was *The Many Defense Stances and When to Use Them*. The forth read, *How to Live Off of the Land and Survive*. When Ralph got to the fifth book, he held the book up and then held it against his body almost like he was hugging a newborn baby. "This one you are not ready for. When the time comes, I will present this one to you," Ralph explained as he turned to his sister and they both smiled.

"So they are books on how to fight and defend yourself?" questioned Conrad as he reached over to grab one of the books, but stopped suddenly to look over to Ralph for permission. With the nod of consent he desired, he picked up one and handed it to his sister, then he reached for one for himself.

"That is correct, but these are different from any other books in the world," responded Ralph.

"How is that?" questioned Jasmine as she leafed through the book, noticing many pictures and diagrams on every page.

"The difference is that once you have read what is inside these books, you will know how to do what they instruct instantly."

"Are you saying that if we read these books, we will be able to fight like Lestron and Kadon?" asked Jasmine as she stopped leafing through the book and closed it suddenly.

"That is not possible," stated Conrad.

"But it is. This is how Synthia and I learned how to fight and defend ourselves against the trolls. You will not be experts in a day, but you will learn in weeks what takes most people a lifetime."

"Do you plan on us fighting when the trolls come?" asked Jasmine.

"No, but if the worst happens and our soldiers can't hold off the trolls, it would be best if you knew how to defend yourselves. So, please take those four books with you to your sleeping quarters and read every word. I will have one of my men send practice swords to your room so you can try out your skills as you learn them." Ralph then pointed to *Weapon Training for Beginners* that was in Jasmine's hand and to *The Many Defense Stances and When to Use Them* book that still lay on the table. "It would be best to study those two first," he recommended.

"I will escort you to your rooms now, so you can start your training," said Synthia. Jasmine and Conrad just couldn't believe that reading a book would enable them to do such things. They did, however, accept that Felnoria was a strange place.

Anxious to begin, Jasmine said, "We'll do it," as she took one of the other books off the table and let Conrad take the other one. Conrad grabbed *Advanced Weapon Training* too, just in case there was time to study it. Synthia walked with the children to their room to make sure they started studying right away. There was so little time for them to learn everything they needed.

Chapter 46

Jasmine and Conrad lay on their beds, carefully reading each page of the books. Every page of *The Many Defense Stances and When to Use Them* had extremely detailed pictures of various fighting techniques and stances. Under each picture were written descriptions on the proper times to use them and what techniques worked best in certain situations. *Weapon Training for Beginners* was organized into chapters, with each chapter describing a certain weapon and the proper way to use it.

Jasmine and Conrad took turns reading those two books. That way, they would learn everything simultaneously.

Neither of them talked to each other as they read. Both were too absorbed in their studies to chat. As they were just about to swap books for the fourth time, a knock at the door disturbed their concentration.

Conrad set down his book and rolled off his bed. He opened the door and saw a soldier with an array of wooden weapons in his arms.

"Why did you bring so many?" Conrad asked as he noticed the guard struggling with the fake weapons and grabbed a few from the soldier to help him out.

"I wasn't sure what type of weapons you wished to practice with, so I brought as many as I could carry," the soldier explained as he walked up to Conrad's bed and dropped his load of weapons. Conrad followed closely behind and placed his on the bed once the soldier stepped away.

"Thank you for bringing them," Jasmine exclaimed as she slipped out of bed and picked up a wooden sword.

"Is there anything else you need?" asked the soldier. When neither of the children responded, he saw himself out of the room.

"There are a lot of weapons here," Conrad said in amazement as he searched through the pile until he found what he was looking for. Jasmine already decided right away what she wanted to wield and it didn't take her long to have her two weapons selected. With each armed, they eyed the other's choices.

Jasmine had two identical wooden swords in her hands. She wanted to imitate the way Lestron fought. Conrad grabbed one large sword because he admired Kadon's fighting style in the troll battle. They placed their ideal weapons on Jasmine's bed, not wanting to mix them with all the weapons on Conrad's bed. They moved all the furniture to the walls, leaving a nice-sized practice area in the middle of the room.

They took their weapons off Jasmine's bed and stood in the center of the room facing each other. Jasmine swung her weapons around in the air trying to get a feel for them and Conrad did the same. Conrad stepped forward and swung his sword in his sister's direction, holding back his full strength, since he didn't know if these books really worked. He soon discovered the books were for real when Jasmine parried his move and nearly knocked his weapon to the floor.

Jasmine was shocked by her response to the sword swing and how easily she knocked it away. But since Conrad attacked her, it was only appropriate to return the gesture. Jasmine swung one of her swords, not both, because she did not feel ambidextrous enough to swing both together at her brother. Surprisingly, her sword was easily blocked, as well. Both were excited as they realized the possibilities.

They continued attacking and defending and increasingly took risks with their sparring until Conrad was smacked in the arm. The impact from the wooden blade caused his arm to go numb for a second. Furious that Jasmine beat him, he walked over to his bed and swept all the unused weapons onto the floor. He snatched Jasmine's book and then jumped onto his bed to continue studying, to ensure a win next time. Jasmine, taking the win as it was and not gloating about it, grabbed Conrad's book and made her way through the clutter of weapons.

They continued studying until one of the chambermaids brought food to their room. They ate in silence until they were stuffed and resumed reading. A bit later, Conrad decided that it was time to spar again since he believed he was prepared to beat his sister. They met in the center of the room and attacked with more intensity and more faith in their capabilities. This time, it was Jasmine who was smacked, and Conrad shouted in triumph. Jasmine, admitting her defeat, dove back to the books.

The cycle repeated itself until they were exhausted and it was time to call it a night. They both went to bed, but once Conrad knew his sister was sleeping, he sneaked over to the table and grabbed *Advanced Weapon Training* and brought it back to his bed. He opened it up and studied some of the harder maneuvers until his eyes would not stay open any longer.

While the twins studied in their room, Kadon had finally reached the last of the houses and informed the residents about the emergency and where they had to go. With all the females and children heading to the caves, Kadon stopped in the armory for a rough head count of the male civilians and soldiers ready for battle. Kadon wasn't pleased with the number, but there wasn't anything he could do about it except hope the dwarves and elves would come to their aid in time. He went to the king and queen's chambers to report his progress.

Ralph and Synthia were battle-planning when Kadon walked into the throne room. Kadon greeted them properly before stating his business. "We have only about three thousand men to defend the town, Your Highnesses."

"And you estimate around ten thousand coming our way?" Ralph inquired in dismay.

"That is correct, Your Highness," Kadon was saying as a soldier stormed into the throne room. The soldier positioned himself next to Kadon and quickly bowed before stating his business.

"The two parties that you sent out nearly a week ago have returned, Your Highnesses," the soldier said excitedly.

"Do you know how many men they were able to find?" Ralph asked.

"I would say roughly five hundred each."

"Could you make sure they are all sent directly to the armory to be outfitted with weapons and armor? They are going to be needed soon enough."

"Yes, Your Highness," the soldier responded as he turned and left.

"Well, that brings our count to four thousand, but still not enough to defend the castle," Ralph stated as he glanced at Synthia. Ralph knew it was going to take a miracle to defend themselves against that many trolls and goblins. Looking at his sister, he could tell she was thinking the same thing. "Let us hope that the dwarves and elves reach us in time."

"If they don't, we'll be doomed." stated Kadon.

"I just wish we had more time," Synthia exclaimed. "Kadon, go down to the armory and post the soldiers at the perimeters of Yarlanzia in anticipation of the trolls' arrival. Have them out there by sunset."

"I will, Your Highness," Kadon said. "Is that all?"

"No. Once finished at the armory, spend some time with your wife and children. I understand you sent them to the castle instead of the caves. But when the sun sets, make sure you are out on the battlefield."

"Thank you, Your Highness!"

Kadon left the throne room. The only thing he could think about was finishing up at the armory as quickly as possible so he could spend some time with his loving family.

With Kadon off to the armory and the children studying, Ralph and Synthia took a moment to reminisce about the past.

"Well, sister, it looks like all the joy we have had in the last fifty years may come to an end," Ralph said sadly as he held on to his sister's hand.

"There is still time," Synthia responded as she placed her other hand over his to comfort him. "There is a chance the elves and dwarves may get here to help."

"Yes, but the trolls could get here sooner than Kadon expects. I have a feeling we will not be getting much sleep again tonight."

"But we must, because we are too old to fight like we did when we were young," Synthia explained. "We need as much rest as possible to lead those who can."

"Well spoken. For now, we should get our weapons and armor ready for the battle tomorrow and then rest."

They both left the throne room and went to their sleeping quarters, preparing themselves for the next day. Before Synthia went to bed, she opened one of her closets. It was the one in which an old chest was stored. The chest had not been opened for decades but she believed it was time to open it again.

Chapter 47

The dew drops on the grass glistened at sunrise the next morning as the three patrolling parties made their rounds on the outskirts of town. The unit that patrolled the southern section of Yarlanzia spotted black specks in the field in the distance. At first there were not many, but in a matter of minutes, the horizon quickly filled with the black dots. The patrollers sensed trouble and turned back north to warn Yarlanzia.

They didn't have to ride all the way back, because an army of their own waited for them on the outskirts of Yarlanzia. Kadon stepped forward when he saw the soldiers racing their horses to the maximum. The soldiers veered their horses in his direction. Kadon shouted, "Have you seen anything?"

"A large army is headed this way," one of the soldiers explained. "I dispatched two men to bring back the other patrol, Captain."

"Very well, and how long do we have?"

"I would say only an hour, two at the most, sir."

"Good job, soldier. I will inform the king and queen. Everyone make yourselves ready."

"Aye," all the men shouted.

Kadon rode full gallop toward the castle. As he rode past his troops, Kadon yelled over and over, "The trolls are coming. Prepare yourselves!" Kadon pushed his horse harder than he had ever before, until he reached the steps leading to the castle. He jumped off his horse before it came to a complete stop and ran up the stairs, skipping many steps on the way.

He burst through the throne room door and approached the king and queen, without formalities. "Trolls have been sighted, Your Highnesses," Kadon reported once he was able to catch his breath.

"How long do we have?" asked Ralph as he shot up from his throne.

"They will be arriving within an hour or two," Kadon explained.

"Thank you, Kadon. Return to your men and prepare for battle. We will be there shortly."

After Kadon left, Ralph and Synthia stood motionless. Not a single dwarf or elf had shown up to help and they were an hour from combat.

"I will get the children while you get outfitted," said Synthia. "Let's meet outside in fifteen minutes to prepare to ride out." Ralph nodded and quietly left the throne room.

Synthia hurried out of the room and cornered one of the soldiers stationed in the hallway and commanded him to follow her. They first stopped at her room where she donned her armor and chose her weapons. She then ordered the soldier to carry the chest that she had pulled out of her closet the night before.

Conrad and Jasmine were in the middle of an extremely advanced fighting stance where they worked together when Synthia and the soldier entered the room. They noticed the soldier carrying a large wooden chest that looked extremely heavy. Synthia announced, "The trolls are going to be here soon. I have brought you some gifts that should help you today." Without explaining any further, they carried the chest to Jasmine's bed and set it down carefully.

As Synthia opened the chest, a flood of memories flashed through her mind. She recalled when she and her brother had received the contents of this chest. Now, they were going to be passed on to people just like them. Synthia stood aside so Jasmine and Conrad could take a look. "These are the weapons and armor that Ralph and I wore when we fought the trolls in Zolar. I wish to give them to you now."

"Wow!" they exclaimed together. Knowing there wasn't much time, Conrad dove in, snatching up armor pieces and placing them on Jasmine's bed. Because of the books they read, Conrad itemized all the pieces as he removed them from the chest.

Conrad realized that there were two sets of armor, so he placed their components in two separate piles. With all the armor removed, only the weapons remained at the bottom.

Jasmine pulled out a sword that was the same size as the one Conrad had been practicing with. As she handed it to Conrad, Synthia added, "That sword was created by a dwarf lord by the name of Bontarest. It is rare for a dwarf to fashion a weapon for non-dwarves, so this is an honor." Conrad carefully examined the sword and was awestruck by the miniscule carvings on the hilt.

Jasmine reached in and retrieved two identically crafted swords that were much smaller than Conrad's. "These swords were crafted by an elf, Lendal, and they are also extraordinary treasures for a human to possess," Synthia explained.

Jasmine walked to the center of the room and swung the swords to get a feel for them. She was surprised at how light they felt in her hands. The soldier walked to the bed covered with armor and started outfitting Conrad with the armor designated for him, while Synthia helped Jasmine strap on her armor.

With the twins suited up, they moved around the room to see how it felt. They were surprised by how light the armor felt. "Why is it so light?" asked Jasmine.

"Bontarest created this armor especially for Ralph and me when we first came to Zolar. We were your age when we arrived and also needed to battle the trolls. Bontarest wouldn't let us battle without armor so he crafted this magical armor that wouldn't weigh us down like regular armor would," explained Synthia as she double-checked Jasmine's fittings.

Synthia and the children met Ralph, who was waiting at the bottom of the castle steps with the horses. Ralph was stunned when he saw them equipped in the armor from his past. Ralph inspected their gear before helping them onto their horses. As they rode to the rallying point of the soldiers, they didn't spot a single troll. The closer they rode, the more afraid Conrad and Jasmine became. They had read about battles like this in fairy tales but never imagined they would fight in one.

They rode to where Kadon stood and exchanged greetings. Kadon looked dismayed as he asked, "How can you possibly let these children fight? They don't know the first thing about warfare."

"They will stay with Ralph and me," replied Synthia. "They will only fight if they need—"

"But, Kadon, we've learned to fight," interrupted Conrad.

"There is no way anyone could learn to fight in one day," Kadon said disbelievingly as he shook his head.

"But we have," exclaimed Jasmine. Kadon gave no response because he had more pressing issues to deal with. He turned his horse around and rode through the soldiers as they stepped aside for passage.

"The time is drawing near, and there is still no sign of dwarf or elf troops," said Ralph.

"They will come," was the only response Synthia would give.

"Lestron will not let us down," said Jasmine encouragingly. "Just wait and see."

Chapter 48

Uzgal and his men were exhausted by their travels, but that wasn't going to stop them from engaging in the battle of a lifetime. As they reached the top of a grassy hill, they spotted an army of soldiers on foot and horseback near the castle. The ranks of trolls marched up the hill behind him. They halted and waited for Uzgal's orders to attack.

Uzgal laughed to himself when he saw the pitiful army in the distance. "We have more worthless goblins than their whole army," Uzgal pointed out to Quilzar.

"When would you like us to attack, Master?" Quilzar asked.

"Go out there and see if they want to surrender," Uzgal commanded. Uzgal had no intentions of letting any humans live, but he thought it would be fun to make them believe he would. Quilzar, obeying his master, ran to the center of the battlefield.

Kadon noticed the troll he despised running to the battlefield. Kadon felt he should be the one to discuss the terms of battle, so he mounted his horse and rode out. Kadon stopped his horse within a sword's reach of the troll. Quilzar placed his hand on the hilt of his sword in anticipation.

"Surrender now and I give my word we will spare you humans," Quilzar growled.

"Your word is worthless," Kadon responded, "You'd slaughter everyone whether or not they surrender."

"I take it you are not surrendering then?" Quilzar inquired as he inched his hand to his sword.

"Never—not even if I'm the last one standing—will I surrender to scum like you."

"Then you will die," shouted Quilzar as he turned from Kadon and ran back to Uzgal to report what the human had said.

Uzgal wasn't surprised. He turned toward his army and commanded, "I wish for all the goblins to come forward." He watched as the mixture of trolls and goblins shuffled around. Once a line of goblins stretched out in every direction, he turned toward the human army.

Kadon noticed the movement at the foot of the hill, but didn't see any advancement. He kept his men at bay, not wanting to make the first move. The air was thick with tension.

Uzgal raised his arm above his head. A hush fell over the throng of soldiers who were frenzied to fight. Uzgal thrust his arm down and screamed, "Goblins, attack. Leave no human alive."

Waves of goblins charged past him with only one goal on their minds: bloodshed in Yarlanzia. Uzgal thought, "With all these pathetic goblins killing the humans, I can send the trolls in once every human is close to dead. That way, I will have almost no casualties." For Uzgal, goblins were nothing but fodder.

When Kadon noticed the goblins charging his army, he raised his sword and screamed, "Attack!"

He charged ahead, leading his troops, who yelled as they advanced with swords held high. Most of Kadon's troops rode on horses. Kadon considered that to be a great advantage when fighting mere goblins that were on foot.

Conrad and Jasmine were overwhelmed by the clanking and shouting. They moved aside to get a better view and saw Ralph and Synthia standing on a mound of grass watching their men charge. The two young people quickly ran to the mound and stood alongside the king and queen, just as the two armies were about to collide.

Conrad and Jasmine stood in shock as the two armies became one. From where they stood, it almost looked like their army had a winning chance because the horses were running over the goblins with the soldiers riding on top just directing the horses where to run. But it didn't take long before the horses lost momentum and the soldiers had to rely on their weapons to take care of the goblins.

An unseen goblin yanked Kadon from his horse when the steed faltered. His back hit the ground but he was able to roll and jump up in time to stab the attacker. He lost his vantage point from atop his horse and it was impossible to see how his men were faring. He swung his sword at anything green that moved. With every swing of his sword, he fought for his life and his family. The more he fought, the more he realized they were losing ground. Instead of moving forward with every swing, he was moving backward toward Yarlanzia.

Uzgal watched as the goblins started pushing the humans back toward Yarlanzia. For every human killed, two or three goblins died. Uzgal wasn't upset by this, but pleased that the goblins were doing any killing. "If this continues, you and I are not going to have many humans to exterminate, ourselves," Quilzar complained to Uzgal, disappointed that he wasn't out there killing the humans. He had lost out on the last battle and he definitely wasn't going to miss this one.

"We will have fewer losses this way," explained Uzgal.

"Let's go out there and finish the job right now," suggested Quilzar.

"Give the goblins a little more time and then we can finish off the king and queen," replied Uzgal with a grin. Not wishing to push his master, Quilzar watched as the goblins had all the fun, but if the humans started dropping faster, he had no intentions of obeying his master.

Ralph watched from atop the grassy mound as his soldiers were slowly drawing nearer to him. He was pleased that his men were killing so many goblins, but there were still thousands of trolls that hadn't even entered the battlefield, yet. Ralph knew there was no way they were going to survive this day, but something had to be done to boost his men's morale.

Ralph turned toward his sister. "Should we call them back?" he asked displeasingly.

"It seems the time to do it," Synthia responded as she looked to her side to see if their backup plan was in position. Lying concealed in the thick grass were hundreds of archers with arrows pointing upward, ready to be launched at any second.

Ralph was not happy that he would have to rely on the hidden archers so early in the battle. With a sigh, he mounted a horse and rode out to his army and called for a full retreat.

Uzgal was ecstatic to see the humans retreating from the battle. With the humans' backs toward them, Uzgal raised his arm once again. "Attack!" Uzgal shouted as the rest of his army charged past him. This time, he followed them. This victory was going to be much easier to achieve than he had expected.

The soldiers who were still on horseback safely made it back to the king and queen; but those on foot, including Kadon, had a rougher time. Many died during their retreat. When the remaining soldiers on foot returned, Ralph turned to his right and Synthia turned to her left. In unison they screamed, "Fire!"

At that instant every archer jumped out of hiding, and released a cloud of arrows. The twang noises of hundreds of bows proceeded, filling the sky with the killing darts. It almost looked like locusts swarming to devour anything in their paths.

Conrad and Jasmine watched in awe as the arrows rained down on the goblins who were entirely unaware. The arrows stopped many in their path, but there were still hundreds lucky enough to dodge the shower of arrows. The goblins were dropping fast and Ralph and Synthia's hopes were renewed. Then they gasped as they saw the sea of trolls advancing on the battlefield. With humans, goblins, and soon-to-be trolls crammed together, the archers threw down their bows and unsheathed their swords. Fear was setting in.

With the charging trolls coming their way, and no other tricks up their sleeves, Ralph turned toward Conrad and Jasmine. "I never wished for you to begin your life in Felnoria like my sister and I did," Ralph told them with watering eyes. "All I ask of you is to fight valiantly and take down as many as you can." Without saying anything else, Ralph looked at his sister with a look of despair and ran out to join his troops.

Conrad and Jasmine stood there watching the king disappear and turned to each other. "Let's stay together and fight side by side," said Conrad, his hand trembling from the realization of what was happening. "We'll use the techniques we learned yesterday and hope that knowledge will keep us alive."

Jasmine held out her two swords, both shaking uncontrollably, as she readied herself for battle. "Don't leave my side, Conny," Jasmine pleaded as her face turned pale.

"Let's go out there and show Kadon we know what we're doing." He grasped his sister's arm and ran with her into the chaos. Synthia remained on the knoll, not sure if her aging body could endure battle.

Conrad and Jasmine were at the back of the army; the soldiers were shoulder-to-shoulder and the children were jostled around as they tried to get into the fight. They wedged their way through a pack of soldiers and came out face-to-face with two goblins. Their intuition kicked in and they dispatched the goblins before the goblins could even raise their weapons. The twins were shocked by how quickly they reacted and were happy that their first fight was already finished. They fought better with each kill.

The second before the trolls entered the battle, the soldiers braced themselves for the impact. When the trolls hit the first line of men, the soldiers toppled backward onto the line of soldiers behind them. Ralph noticed this domino effect and realized that they didn't have a chance of surviving the battle. But he continued anyway.

The disheartened king was fending off enemies when a large gust of wind blew from the west. At first he ignored it, but when another gust arose, he recalled, "Be safe, friend, and when the wind blows from the west, think of us." He remembered Bontarest saying that before he left Zolar. Ralph took a quick glance to the west.

Ralph's mood changed that instant as he saw a large group of dwarves running toward him. To bolster his men's morale, he yelled, "The dwarves have come to save us." He pointed to the west. The men who were not immediately engaged in combat turned and looked. Word spread throughout the remaining troops, and the soldiers started swinging their swords harder than ever.

Chapter 49

As Uzgal watched from the back of his army, his trolls were annihilating the humans. However, the humans seemed to be fighting harder, as if they all had a spike of hope or something. He noticed many of the humans looked to the west and back, so he looked over to the west. A huge army of dwarves charged in his direction.

Uzgal, having to think fast, screamed, "Dwarf attack, due west." He continued shouting commands until half of his army had turned from the humans and started charging toward the oncoming dwarves. Uzgal was pleased that he had enough troops to split and fight both fronts. He was also pleased that both of his battalions were larger than that of either of the enemies, which meant he could still easily defeat them.

Conrad and Jasmine noticed many of the trolls running away from them. They had to focus on defending themselves and had no opportunity to see what caused the movement. As they finished off a group of trolls, a fresh set was circling around them when Conrad screamed, "Balarosk," which was a back-to-back fighting routine they had practiced the day before. Jasmine heard his directive and pivoted her body to place her back against his. With back sides protected, they were prepared for all directions. Five trolls charged at them at the same time. Jasmine swung first, knocking a troll away and then she sensed pressure on the left side of her back. Conrad was signaling her to step to the right. As she did, Conrad stepped to his left at the same time, blocking a sword whose destination was Jasmine. They continued circling around, blocking and slashing any aggressive trolls until they were the last two standing in that part of the battlefield.

Kadon noticed Conrad and Jasmine fighting. His mouth dropped completely open in shock at how skilled they were and how well they worked together. As he continued watching, he believed they were good enough to defeat him if they fought him together. He wanted to keep watching but heard a troll ambushing from behind. Kadon turned around just in time to put his sword up to block a spear that the troll was thrusting. When the troll was down, he turned back to see how the twins were faring, but they were lost within the clatter of humans and trolls swinging weapons.

Bontarest and Orlog led their dwarves to battle. They charged on foot toward the oncoming trolls that had separated from the humans. They noticed their numbers were smaller than the thousands the trolls had, but that didn't scare them. They knew they were much more skilled than the rotten trolls. The second before his dwarves intertwined with the trolls, Bontarest thought to himself, "Many of my men will die today, but at least they will die in battle." Bontarest held his axe high in the air, with a smile on his face, and swung it down when the first troll approached.

Bontarest realized right after the first blow that he was a little rusty, but he easily got into the swing of things. Orlog looked like he was having fun slaying. When Bontarest had a second, he turned to Orlog, and said, "We have to push these trolls back to the humans. Unless we fight side-by-side with the humans, they will not survive." Orlog nodded his head in acceptance and started swinging his axe even harder. He then had a brilliant idea.

Orlog turned to Bontarest and gave him a grin. "What are you thinking?" Bontarest asked between swings of his axe.

"This should help," Orlog shouted over the clatter and began singing. Bontarest noticed right away that Orlog was singing an old dwarf battle song. Thinking that was a great idea, he began to sing as well. The louder they sang, the more dwarves followed their lead, until every dwarf bellowed. The singing was accompanied by swings of axes. Orlog's plan was working because with every troll they took down, they stepped closer and closer to the humans.

Ralph, having realized early on that he wasn't as young as he used to be, went back to his sister at the top of the mound. He and Synthia watched the singing dwarves slowly push the trolls backwards. They continued watching as the first of the dwarves mixed into the humans' lines. It became clear to Ralph that there were still more trolls than humans and dwarves. He scanned the area to see if the children were still alive but could not see them in the crowd. He was upset that the children's lives were going to end so early for something he felt was his fault.

Conrad and Jasmine continued fighting alongside each other until they could barely breathe. They realized that they knew how to fight and defend themselves, but they didn't have the stamina. "Let's try to make our way back to the mound where we stood before the battle," Jasmine said between gasps of air. "I need to rest." Conrad felt the same way, so he nodded his head and turned with his sister, but they were halted when a new set of trolls stood blocking their path. Even in their tired state, they readied themselves artfully as the trolls charged toward them.

The first swing was for Conrad's head, so he dove sideways to the ground to defend himself. With Conrad diving in one direction, Jasmine had to dive in the opposite so the sword wouldn't hit her next. Taking the advantage, a troll attacked Conrad when he was down. Before the club could find its target, Conrad swung his foot around, and tripped the troll. The enemy fell and his club flew from his grasp. Conrad jumped up and quickly finished off the troll. With the troll dispatched, he looked around and noticed his sister wasn't there.

Once Jasmine hit the ground, she quickly rolled and popped up with both swords readied. One troll came from her right while another came from her left. She ducked as both clubs passed over her head, which resulted in the clubs smacking the trolls on the opposite side. She could tell from the sound of the impact that neither of them would rise again. When she stood up, she noticed her brother wasn't anywhere near.

"Conrad," she screamed, but the clashing of metal on metal and wood was too great for her voice to reach beyond a few feet. She took a quick glance around in every direction before a new set of trolls charged toward her.

As Ralph and Synthia stuck to the back of the battle, a few trolls were starting to break through the line. They defended themselves, and killed every troll that reached them, but their bodies ached with every swing. They both knew they wouldn't last much longer in this state.

Uzgal continued to stay behind his army, watching his men fight. He participated only when a human was stupid enough to attack him. Unlike most trolls, he used a sword much like Quilzar's, but much smaller. The sword was his father's and his only plan was to use it to finish off the children and the one who killed his father, the king. Quilzar stayed close to Uzgal, but didn't wish to stand around like his master did. Whenever he saw a group of humans or dwarves, he ran up to them, swinging his sword. With the power of a giant behind each swing, Quilzar easily took down any human or dwarf in his path. Sometimes he took two or three at a time, thinking, "There is no one in Felnoria who can take me down." Quilzar continued killing until he heard a strange sound rise over the clashing of weapons. His first assumption was that it was the dwarves so he ignored it until he realized it was coming from the south. Quilzar looked back and was shocked to see an army of elves on white horses charging in his direction.

"Elves!" Quilzar shouted in warning to Uzgal and the other trolls.

Ralph heard the noise as well, but much more clearly than Quilzar did. A deep trumpeting sound bellowed from somewhere unknown. Ralph knew he had heard that sound before, but he couldn't put a finger on where. But, when he looked to the south and saw Lestron and Mylinia leading thousands of elves in his direction, it all came back to him. It was a horn the elves blew to signify battle. It reminded him of the only the time he heard it in Fos Faydian. But back then, the battle horn was much closer and the loud bass the horn made had vibrated throughout his body.

"The elves have come to help," Ralph cheered hoping to boost his men's morale again. Ralph wanted to watch as the elves clashed with the trolls but he didn't have time. Another group of trolls broke through the line and attacked Synthia and him.

When Bontarest heard Ralph scream something about elves, he stopped his singing long enough to tell Orlog the news. They both grumbled at the thought of elves, even if they were there to help. "We can handle this ourselves," Bontarest said as he felt sick to his stomach with the thought of fighting side by side with puny elves.

"Maybe if we kill these last few thousand trolls in the next few minutes, we will not have to deal with them," Orlog stated with a smile on his face.

Chapter 50

Uzgal was forced to make his way into the center of the battle so he wouldn't be killed by the elves approaching from the south. The trolls knew they were in trouble when the elves joined the battle. They were now sandwiched between humans and dwarves on one side and elves on the other.

Uzgal had to defend himself and attack at the same time. He fought humans and dwarves with little difficulty until he glimpsed the male child. Having nothing else on his mind but to kill the child, he plowed through soldiers and bodies to reach the boy. Uzgal was in luck, the boy's back was to him, and he was oblivious that he was going to die soon.

Once the elves entered the battle, Lestron jumped off his horse, because he fought much better on the ground than on horseback. High Elf Mylinia jumped off her horse at the same time as Lestron. They both flew from their mounts and, simultaneously, they quickly unsheathed their weapons as they landed. As soon as their feet were on the ground, they were already fighting their first round of adversaries. Lestron fought alongside Mylinia until he saw Kadon having trouble.

"I must help him," Lestron stated as he left Mylinia's side and ran in Kadon's direction. Lestron wanted to stay to protect Mylinia, but he knew she could defend herself. He didn't want to see his new friend killed that day.

Lestron reached Kadon as he was knocked to the ground. Trolls closed in on Kadon, but their progress was halted when Lestron jumped in front of Kadon. He fought the trolls alone until Kadon was able to get up. Kadon slowly circled around the trolls while slashing his sword. By the time he stood directly across from Lestron, the last of the trolls were killed. Their victory was short-lived, though. A large sword rose above them. "He's mine," Kadon shouted as he charged in the direction of the sword.

"Let us do it together," Lestron yelled, knowing there was no way Kadon would be able to kill the troll on his own.

Uzgal aimed his mighty sword straight ahead and ran forward with all intentions of plunging it into the human boy's back. Uzgal's father's sword was inches away when two swords appeared from nowhere and foiled his attack. Hearing the clash of metal right behind him, Conrad turned around and was shocked to see the enormous troll right behind him. He was more shocked that Jasmine had the troll's sword pinned to the ground. Jasmine's arm quivered as she strained to hold down the sword, but Uzgal raised his arms and sent her flying backwards.

Bontarest looked over to Ralph and Synthia and noticed a group of trolls sneaking around the mound of grass where they stood. Without saying anything, he left Orlog's side and sped to stop the stalking trolls from reaching his friends. He screamed out to them, but they were too preoccupied by the trolls in front of them to hear anything.

Kadon was the first to attack Quilzar. Incited by the loss of so many of his soldiers, he swung his sword as hard as he could at the troll leader. Quilzar easily knocked it aside with his sword and pushed him back a few feet in the process. Lestron jumped in to take his turn at Quilzar. Trying to knock the large troll off his feet, he swung his swords at his legs, hoping the impact would be enough to drop him to the ground. But Lestron's swords were parried at the last second, causing him to spin out of position to attack again.

"We must do this together," Lestron shouted once he got his balance.

Kadon moved across from Lestron with Quilzar standing between them. They attacked him simultaneously, but every slash they made at Quilzar was either dodged or blocked. The pair realized Quilzar was too much for them. Quilzar continued moving and blocking each lunge until there was a momentary break. Quilzar swung his sword at Kadon as hard as he could. Kadon held out his sword with both hands and braced for the impact. When the two swords hit, he flew backwards and his hands went numb.

Lestron saw Kadon's fall and knew trying to block a move by that huge troll was useless. Lestron stepped forward to prevent Quilzar from finishing off Kadon. The troll slashed his sword and Lestron ducked, tucked, and rolled. The troll repeated the move and Lestron reacted the same way. But, Lestron underestimated Quilzar's arm reach and was slashed in the arm by the tip of the enormous sword the next time he dove out of the way. He writhed on the ground as pain ran through his limb and he hurt too much to retrieve his sword that lay next to him.

Quilzar victoriously approached Lestron and raised his sword to impale the fallen opponent. Lestron watched in disbelief as the troll hovered over him, knowing there was nothing he could do. But before Quilzar thrust down, his back arched and he screamed out in agony.

Kadon stood behind Quilzar with his sword protruding from the troll's back. Kadon thought he had finished off the foe until Quilzar failed to fall down. He obviously wasn't dead because he raised his sword at Kadon. As Kadon tried to reach around the troll to grab his sword hilt, Lestron leapt up and plunged his last sword into Quilzar's heart. Lestron stepped aside as the oversized troll fell lifeless to the ground.

When Bontarest rushed up to Ralph and Synthia, they were still unaware of the danger behind them. Bontarest dove forward and knocked Ralph to his side, Ralph fell at his sister's feet. As Ralph fell, a sword passed exactly where Ralph had been standing only a second earlier. Bontarest swung at the troll, who missed his target. The troll was dead instantly. Synthia and Bontarest annihilated the last of the trolls before Ralph got to his feet.

Bontarest approached Ralph. "We're even now. No two people should have life debts for each other." Bontarest smiled. Before Ralph could respond, Bontarest was already running back to join Orlog.

High Elf Mylinia and her comrades fought valiantly and it was evident there was not a single troll who could match the swordsmanship of elves. The elves' tradition of intense training contributed to Mylinia's ability to fight three or four trolls at one time without getting tired. She and the other elves were brave and skillful on the battlefield.

Meanwhile, Conrad was trying to protect Jasmine, who had just stood after having been knocked to the ground by Uzgal. Conrad circled around Uzgal and stood alongside his sister. "Sorlina," Conrad shouted, which was a side-to-side technique. Uzgal swung his sword at the children, with the intention of knocking both of them down with one swing, but it was knocked aside by Conrad. Conrad and Jasmine took their turn and swung three separate weapons at Uzgal, but somehow, every one of their attempts was blocked.

They continued attacking and defending, but the two knew they were too tired to last much longer. Conrad frantically tried to recall other advanced techniques he had learned the night before. At just the right moment, he remembered the perfect technique. He dove to the ground, and slid between Uzgal's legs with his sword to his side. As he passed through the troll's legs, the sword cut Uzgal's calf and he buckled to one knee.

As Uzgal dropped, Jasmine swung both her swords in tandem and slashed the troll across the chest. The two cuts were mere scratches to Uzgal, and they only enraged him. Uzgal slashed at Jasmine while still down on one knee.

Conrad returned to standing position as his sister slashed Uzgal, and he saw Uzgal swing at Jasmine. Conrad slashed his fancy weapon across Uzgal's sword hand at the last second and the sudden surge of pain caused Uzgal to drop his blade. With the troll defenseless, Jasmine swung her swords one more time and ended him for good.

When Uzgal dropped to the ground, his surviving troops cried out in horror. Those who didn't witness the kill quickly heard about it. With their leader and their second in command dead, the trolls' morale plummeted and they began to flee. The exhausted humans cheered as the trolls ran away, but the dwarves and elves had no intention of letting any of the trolls escape that easily. The dwarves chased them on foot while the elves chased them on horseback.

Chapter 51

The following night, a grand celebration party was being held in the great hall in the castle of Yarlanzia. Everyone physically able to attend sat at large tables that extended the length of the enormous room. They were enjoying a feast that had been prepared the morning after the battle. As everyone dined and drank mead, they traded war stories.

At the head of the ballroom, at the table reserved for only the king and queen, now sat two others. Conrad and Jasmine sat by Ralph and Synthia, enjoying their meals and talking of magical swords. Jasmine was dressed in a white silk gown that looked much like the one Synthia was wearing. Conrad was dressed in a purple shirt with a red cape tied loosely around his neck. While seated, the cape hung over the back of his chair, similarly to the cape Ralph was wearing.

Once everyone was finished eating and the tables were cleared, except for the mead, Ralph and Synthia stood up to speak to the guests. A hush fell over the room as the people awaited a speech.

"There are many thanks that must go around today," Ralph announced. "Everyone fought valiantly, but there are a few here that went beyond expectations. I would first like to acknowledge our friends and allies from Zolar. Lord Bontarest, would you please approach us?"

Bontarest rose from one of the tables that had a mixture of humans and dwarves and approached Ralph and Synthia. "Thank you for sending your dwarves in our time of need," shouted Ralph so the whole room of guests could hear.

When Bontarest responded, he made sure the king and queen were the only ones who could hear him. "I told you earlier, King Ralph, I didn't want to see this castle destroyed since we dwarves were the ones to build it," Bontarest said with a smile. "Like I said on the battlefield, now that I saved your life, our debts are cleared."

"Even though I'm not in debt, if you ever need help, you just come here and I will help whatever way I can," whispered Ralph. In a loud voice, Ralph said, "A toast to Lord Bontarest and his warriors!" Bontarest bowed respectfully and walked back to his table amidst cheers and applause.

Synthia continued with the acknowledgments. "Would Lestron and High Elf Mylinia approach the table?" Synthia watched as the two elegantly strode to the head table. Lestron's arm was in a sling and Mylinia's face was bruised. Synthia resumed, "I regret my brother and I caused you so much grief years ago, and we are eternally grateful for the role you played in this victory," said Synthia.

"We are still recovering from that day, but we are slowly returning to our former life," explained Mylinia. "I am now trying to convince the elves to allow humans into Fos Faydian, but it will take time. Hopefully, one day you will be able to visit us again."

"If there is ever a way for us to pay our debts to you, just ask," Synthia told her. Mylinia nodded her head in acceptance, pleased by the offer.

"As for you, Lestron, if you hadn't left the children's side and raced back to Fos Faydian, we would not be sitting here today." A few of the dwarves started grumbling at hearing that the elves were such heroes because they clearly believed they didn't need the elves' help to win.

"I only did what I thought was necessary," responded Lestron.

"Is there anything we can do for you, Lestron?"

"No, the only thing I wish for at this moment is to be back in Fos Faydian. I have been gone for much too long." With that said, they stepped away from Ralph and Synthia to return to their table.

As they approached their seats, Ralph stood and shouted, "A toast for Lestron and High Elf Mylinia!" The crowd cheered and gulped more mead.

"Next, I would like to acknowledge Kadon for leading our men to victory," Ralph shouted. Kadon turned to his wife and children and kissed them before he approaching Ralph and Synthia. "Kadon, you brought these precious children back here safely at great risk to your own life. These children did not deserve to die young, and because of you, they will live to tell the story of their journey. Ralph glanced over and looked at the twins sitting beside him.

"I only did my duty," stated Kadon.

"Yes, but you went beyond your duties these last few days. For that, I commend you, and propose a toast to Kadon."

"Thank you, Your Highness." Kadon replied, then stepped away and walked back to his family as the guests shouted and clanked tankards of mead.

"Last, but not least, I would like to give a special thanks to two people who arrived here just over a week ago," Synthia said this as she looked past her brother to Jasmine and Conrad sitting next to him. Cheers from everyone erupted throughout the ballroom. Even the elves were cheering, and they never congratulated anyone. Conrad and Jasmine, not knowing what to do, stood up and stared at the smiling faces in disbelief.

Once the cheers died down, Synthia continued, "I knew when you two arrived that good things would happen. But I never believed that you would kill the infamous Uzgal. He has ruled the trolls since his father was killed in Zolar, and he has been our arch enemy."

"We only defended ourselves," stated Conrad humbly.

"You may say that, but I believe it was fate. You both have rid Felnoria of the curse of the trolls. There is not one gift that we could give you two that would express our gratitude. I do have one question for you both, if you are ready to answer it." They had an inkling of what the question would be.

"Do you wish to stay with us or find a way back home?" Synthia asked as the crowd sat silent.

"Jas and I have thought about this and, even though the trolls are gone, there is a lot of stuff that needs to be done in Felnoria. So, for now, we'd love to stick around and help out." Everyone started cheering and gave a standing ovation. They all raised their tankards and toasted the brave newcomers to Felnoria.

When the toast was completed, Conrad turned to the king and queen. "We miss our mother and father greatly. The only thing we ask is that you help us try to find a way to contact them. We want to let them now that we are alive and safe."

"We will do everything possible to help fulfill that request," responded Synthia.

The celebration continued through the night. The conversations ranged from the battle the previous day to a peaceful future without the threat of trolls ravaging their land. The children were talking with Kadon when Lestron approached Jasmine. "You surprise me yet again, young lady," Lestron stated as he reached out his good arm and wrapped it around her. Jasmine smiled and respectfully returned the hug. Lestron pulled away and looked directly into her eyes. "Since both of you have decided to stay here, please feel free to call upon Fos Faydian if you ever need loyal allies. You will always be welcome in our land."

"We will remember your kind offer," Jasmine responded as tears trickled down her cheek. Lestron dabbed them away before turning around, allowing Jasmine to finish her conversation with Kadon.

By the end of the night, there were only a few stragglers in the celebration hall. When those stragglers finally left, only Ralph, Synthia, Conrad, and Jasmine remained. Conrad and Jasmine were talking between themselves when Ralph asked for their attention.

"I am very happy that you chose to stay with us," Ralph said happily as he turned around and lifted something off the table. When he held it up, the children noticed immediately that it was the black book that Ralph had refused to show them before. Running down the center of the blank cover, a crack ran from end to end.

"Synthia and I have decided that it is time for you to have this book." Ralph turned it over, revealing the title. Written in golden print across the top of the cover were the words *The Proper Ways to Rule a Kingdom.*

Acknowledgments

First, I want to thank Erin. If it weren't for her battling through the very first draft, it never would be where it is today. Also, I want to thank Joe, Connie, and Bonnie for everything they did. I also want to thank Steve and Alma Conway, who paid me to work even when I was just sitting around writing this book. Thanks for all the downtime our job provides. I would also like to thank my editor, Amie McCracken; I expected the worst and I'm happy I was completely wrong. Last, I want to thank Jeannie Milakovich. She showed me that you can cover a creative writing paper in red ink and still get an A. She probably doesn't know it, but she has been a very big inspiration to my writing.

About the Author

Christopher Pertile was born in Ironwood, Michigan. He has a degree in computer-aided design and automated manufacturing and design. After using his CAD degree for a while, he realized that wasn't what he loved. He currently lives in Woodruff, Wisconsin, where he has worked as a theatre manager for the past eleven years, which gives him the love of a job and the time to read and write.